THE VOX POPULI STREET STORIES

BY THE SAME AUTHOR:

Skyblue the Badass, Doubleday (Paris Review Editions), 1969
The Transparent Eye-Ball & Other Stories, Burning Deck, 1982
The Kansas Poems, Cincinnati Poetry Review Press, 1987
Going to the Mountain, Burning Deck, 1988
Skyblue's Essays, Burning Deck, 1995
Our Asian Journey, MLR Editions Canada, 1997

DALLAS WIEBE

THE VOX POPULI STREET STORIES

Burning Deck, Providence, 2003

Some of these stories were first published in *First Intensity* ("Vibini in Labor" and "Vibini on the E-Mail") and *North American Review* ("Vibini and the Virgin Tongue"). *Prolegomena to the Study of Apocalyptic Hermeneutic*s (2001) and *Vibini in the Underworld* (2003) are chapbooks from Obscure Publication.

Thanks to all those who contributed to these stories: Jeff Hillard, Heather Hall, Martina Lauer, Tony York, John Battistone, Harry Gotoff, Archie Christopherson, Annie Finch, Arthur Conan Doyle, Richard Thomas, Bernard Hoepffner, Jon C. Hughes, Rosmarie and Keith Waldrop, Tom Kindle, John B. Wolgamot, Thomas Idinopulos, Lee Chapman, Wilkie Collins, Joannes Chrysostomus Wolfgangus Theophilus Mozart, Marc Baskind, Robley Wilson.

Special thanks to the Ohio Arts Council for an Individual Artist Fellowship that made this book possible.

Cover by Keith Waldrop

Burning Deck/Anyart
71 Elmgrove Ave.
Providence, RI 02906
Burning Deck is the literature program of Anyart: Contemporary Arts Center, a tax-exempt (501c3), non-profit organization.

© 2003 by Dallas Wiebe
ISBN 1-866224-64-1, paperback
ISBN 1-886224-65-x, paperback, 50 numbered & signed copies

THE VOX POPULI STREET STORIES

CONTENTS

Vibini at the Bat 9
The Hong Kong Umbrella 19
Vibini in Labor 31
Hemingway's Valise 40
The Thrall Street Conundrum 52
Vibini and the Spectre Father-In-Law of the Bride 62
Vibini on the E-Mail 75
Vibini and the Indian in the Woodpile 88
Vibini and the Virgin Tongue 101
La Folle Journée ou le Nozze di Vibini 129
Amazing Grace 155
Vibini in the Underworld 170
Prolegomena to the Study of Apocalyptic Hermeneutics 222
In Excelsis Deo 267

VIBINI AT THE BAT

I HAVE DISCOVERED that life begins with retirement.I was a medical doctor for thirty-eight years and when I retired on January 3, 1995, at the age of sixty-five, I felt as if my life had begun all over again. I felt unburdened because I was no longer on call twenty-four hours a day. I no longer had to adjust my life to the schedules of the sick and dying. My family was gone, my wife having committed suicide in 1980 in Wuppertal, Germany, and my four children all committed for life in St. Dympna's in Gheel, Belgium. I could finally and lazily indulge my interest in Italian military history. Because I was retired, I could loaf. I could go out and take walks at my leisure. That's how I met Dallasandro Vibini and discovered the beginning of my career as a writer.

I first met Vibini when I was walking down Clifton Avenue. I was out for a stroll. It was Easter morning, April 16, 1995, a beautiful, wonderful spring day. I was trying to lose some of my 300 pounds by walking it off. I've gained weight since retiring and that weight is an embarrassment because I'm only five feet eight inches tall. I enjoyed my walk that day. The jonquils and daffodils were out. The cars whipped by. The mourning doves called from the telephone wires. I was amazed that God would send his blessings so abundantly on the condemned.

Just as I was passing Our Lady of the Denunciation Church a man came running out of the front door. He was yelling and gesturing. I heard him yell, "Father Schlag, I will not kiss your aspergillum. No way. I don't care whether you like it or not. Anathema or no anathema. Excommunication or no excommunication." He was a thin man, about six feet tall and weighing about 150 pounds. His graying hair stuck out from under his green beret. He was wearing a red cape, black penny loafers and purple spats.

As he came down the steps, I stopped and waited for him to pass. He stopped by me and said, "Can you imagine that? Here I am a devout Roman Catholic. I go to confession each Saturday and to mass on Sunday morning. I can't afford a contribution, but I keep my religion up. Now Father Schlag suddenly decides that I have to kiss his sprinkler. I won't do it even if it is Easter." My first impression was that some kind of joke was going on, a joke not comprehensible within my German sense of humor.

I hadn't the slightest idea what an aspergillum was. I couldn't even spell it then. So I said, "Hold it. What's all the fuss?" The thin man looked at me and said, "That priest has overstepped his commission. I won't kiss his aspergillum." I said, "Take it easy. Why won't you kiss his aspergillum?" I had the feeling I was being drawn into the kind of dialogue that I used to laugh at in the Marx Brothers movies. I know that Roman Catholics are always kissing funny things. It's the way the priests humiliate them and keep them brainwashed. If they'd stop kissing things there wouldn't be any parishioners. I'm a Lutheran so I don't know about this kissing business; Lutherans don't even kiss their wives. The thin man looked at me and said, "That aspergillum of Father Schlag has, like all of them, a sponge in it to hold the water as he sprinkles it around. That sponge hasn't been changed in twenty years. It's covered with mold, fungus, rot. Like his pocket book."

I smiled and said, "Why don't you come over to my apartment just around the corner on Vox Populi Street and I'll make you a cup of coffee?" The man agreed because, he said, he didn't get the wine or the wafer so he might as well drink some coffee. I took him into my kitchen, made some Folger's Instant Coffee, got out some Pream and we sat down at my breakfast table.

I introduced myself. I told him I was Gottlieb Otto Liebgott and that my special study was Italian military history. I told him that I was beginning a new career, that of a writer, and that my first project was to write the biography of the Italian war hero Giovanni Battista Salvatore. He said that his name was Dallasandro Vibini and that he was a private investigator and that he specialized in solving petty crimes. Vibini said he made his living by doing what no one else would do. "Vibini's the name; petty crime's my game." Then he said, "You're a writer?" And I repeated that I was trying to start a new career as a writer. I told him that my father Gottlob Gerebernus Liebgott had been a famous German novelist. Vibini laughed and said, "I need an amanuensis. I need someone to write down my investigations." I allowed as to how I could do that, but that at the moment I was involved in investigating sign language in the Ethiopian army and how their lack of sign language determined the outcome of the siege of Addis Ababa.

I was just beginning to tell him how important sign language was in the African campaign when the telephone rang. I picked up my phone and said, "Why, yes. He's here. It's for you." I wondered how anyone might know that he was in my apartment. Vibini wasn't the least surprised. "Yes," he said. "I'll be right there. It'll cost you $200." He hung up the phone and I said, "How did anyone know that you were here?" "They must have contacted my brother Culofaccia. He knows where I am at all times. He even knows what I'm thinking. Call a cab. I have a case to solve."

When the Quo Vadis cab arrived, I decided to go along and find out what this all was that had come to pass. I get my best ideas in cabs and I thought my time wouldn't be wasted. I asked Vibini where we were going and he said that we were going to Riverfront Stadium because someone had stolen the fungo bat and that the Reds couldn't warm up in the outfield until someone could hit them fly balls and that it couldn't be done without a fungo bat and that bat was missing and that he had to find it in one hour because the game was scheduled to start in two hours and the game couldn't start until the outfielders had warmed up by catching some fly balls hit off the fungo bat.

When we arrived at Riverfront Stadium, we were taken into the clubhouse. Fungus Schlag, the clubhouse manager, brother to Father Schlag I later learned, explained that the outfield coach Mold Schlag, brother to Father Schlag and Fungus Schlag, needed his bat that Father Schlag had sprinkled with holy water from his aspergillum or he, Mold Schlag, couldn't hit fly balls to the outfield. I couldn't understand how Mold and Fungus could lose sight of a bat. It wasn't as if someone could hide it in a pocket. Unless, of course, the bat was in sections and could be disassembled and put down a pant leg and then carried out past Rot Schlag, the security guard at the door and brother to Father Schlag, Fungus Schlag and Mold Schlag, all sons of Perfidy Schlag, who swept the floors at Our Lady of the Denunciation Church.

Vibini wasn't in the least distracted by the Schlags, took off his green beret and his red cape and went right to work. First he demanded a complete description of the fungo bat. Maury Schlag, son of Fungus Schlag and the bat boy for the day, said the bat was about forty-eight inches long. It had a diameter of about two inches. It was made of wood and had a sponge stuck in the end and the sponge was soaked in water and covered with mold, fungus and rot. Vibini asked when the bat was last seen. Maury said he last saw it when Mold Schlag was kissing the wet end of it and waving it around and drops of water were flying through the rotten air of the clubhouse before the players arrived with their boxes of pepperoni pizzas with mushrooms, onions, sausage, green peppers, black olives, green olives, mozzarella cheese, Swiss cheese, American cheese, cheddar cheese, provolone, anchovies, jalapeños and garlic on them. I wrote it all down and wondered what it all had to do with the size of the rocks in the fortifications at Brindisi, fortifications designed by Leonardo da Vinci and which stood waiting for the forces of Illyria. Which dimensions I didn't remember and which I would look up when the fungo bat had been found.

While Vibini scrutinized the team roster, I sat down to rest with Mold Schlag and asked him if he had ever been in the army. "Of course," he said. "I was in the Italian army at the battle of Brindisi where the Italian army stood firm before the forces of Illyria. That was June 6, 1945. Originally I was in the Wehrmacht, but I deserted when Mark Clark and Keightley moved up the boot. I ended up in Brindisi so I was there for the first battle of the Illyrian-Italian War. That was fifty years ago." I said, "There was no battle of Brindisi." "Of course," he said. "There was no battle. It was the only battle we ever won. The enemy forces set sail in rowboats from Split on the coast of Illyria, decided to stop off at Corfu for some Retsina and moussaka and decided not to sail on to Brindisi and attack. They didn't show up so they forfeited the struggle. We won." I decided to pursue my research elsewhere.

Vibini, meanwhile, was questioning Denny Schlag, the clubhouse attendant and cousin to Maury Schlag and son of Mold Schlag, who was brother to Father Schlag, Mold and Fungus Schlag and son of Perfidy Schlag. Vibini's questions were slick and pointed. "Where was the fungo bat last seen? Who's in charge of the bat? Where is it usually kept? What was the bat worth? How old was the bat? Was it sent out for repair? Was it sent to the cleaners? How old was the sponge in the end of the bat? When was the water last changed in the sponge? Was there mold and fungus on the sponge? Was the bat blessed on St. Emmanuel's Day?" Denny Schlag couldn't answer any of the questions. Vibini sighed and looked at his watch. I looked at my watch. He had thirty minutes to find the missing fungo bat.

Next Vibini examined the lockers of the players. Mold Schlag guided the tour. Vibini examined shoes, stretched the socks, picked through the pockets of the uniforms, threw batting helmets against the wall, picked up baseballs and, stretching out jockstraps, shot balls the length of the dressing room. Denny Schlag picked one up on the hop, whipped it to Maury Schlag, who fired it to Fungus Schlag for a double play. Rot Schlag called the runners out and Mold Schlag ran up to protest the call. When Mold complained too vehemently and used certain foul language, Rot Schlag threw him out of the game. "The Schlags aren't in this together, I can see," murmured Vibini. I said it reminded me of the Battle of Brindisi when the forces from Illyria didn't show up and the Italians won a questionable battle while the Allies were dividing up Germany and looking for war criminals. Vibini allowed as to how he hadn't lost yet and that his enemy had set sail and was just about to arrive at the gate and that he had fifteen minutes to go.

I could hear the crowd gathering in the stands. They were calling for the warm ups to begin. I could hear bottles breaking in the aisles. I could hear threats and curses from the faithful fans. I could hear, "Warm up or give us our money back." Chants of dire consequences unless the fly balls were hit to the outfielders. I could hear the motorcycles of the players arriving outside the clubhouse. I could hear their BMW's and their Mercedes sedans roaring up the ramps to the players' entrance. I could hear Vibini saying to himself, "Culofaccia, Culofaccia. Come in." I asked him who Culofaccia was and he said, "Not now, Liebgott. Not now. I'll explain later. I'm losing my $200. I've only got five minutes."

Muff Schlag, the manager, came in. Brother to Father Schlag, Mold, Fungus and Rot Schlag, and uncle to Maury and Denny Schlag and to Harry Schlag, the groundskeeper. Muff yelled, "Who are these nerds? Why are they in the clubhouse?" Mold Schlag told him that the fungo bat was missing and that Vibini had been called in for $200 to find it before the warm ups could begin and that he hadn't found it yet and that he had exactly sixty seconds to find it or he would lose his $200. Muff screamed, "$200? Who authorized this money? Find it yourself." Mold allowed as to how they had been looking for it for over two hours and that the fans were getting out-of-hand and that if the players didn't get out on the field and start chasing fly balls the whole stadium would erupt and the game be cancelled just like the Battle of Brindisi when the forces of Illyria didn't show up and the battle was forfeited while Harry Truman was getting ready to incinerate Japan.

Suddenly Vibini stopped and listened. His face took on a dreamy look. He stared into his final five seconds and said, "Thank you, Culofaccia." He turned to Mold Schlag and said, "Follow me." He ran out of the clubhouse and into the dugout. I waddled along behind him.

He slid and scrambled through the spit from the game the night before. He rushed up to the bat rack and pulled out the fungo bat. Mold Schlag grabbed it out of his hands, kissed the fungus and mold-spotted sponge in the end of the bat, swung it three times to the right and three times to the left. Little drops of water sprinkled over Vibini. Vibini knelt in the spit and said, "Check, please." Mold handed the fungo bat to Fungus Schlag, took out his checkbook and wrote out a check for twenty-five dollars. "Here," he said. "That will pay for your cab. Now get out."

In the Quo Vadis Cab on our way back to Vox Populi Street, Vibini told me about his older brother Culofaccia. How Culofaccia knew everything and could figure out things that no one else could see. How Culofaccia just sat in his apartment on Schadenfreude Street and meditated. How Culofaccia could send messages to him by telepathy. How Culofaccia was never wrong and never uncertain. When I said I'd like to meet the wonderful brother, Vibini said that Culofaccia never received visitors and never left his apartment. He sits and meditates and watches TV because he is writing a history of "The Price is Right." He told me that Culofaccia Vibini had been decorated with the Italian Order of the Yellow Heart and the Victor Emmanuel III Tin Cross with Garlic Cluster after the Battle of Brindisi for heroic action in the face of the forfeiting enemy on the day when the Russians were writing graffiti on the walls of the Reichstag and strolling along the Kurfürstendamm. Since then Culofaccia had been suffering from shell shock and would not go out into public where he was greatly admired.

Back in my apartment on Vox Populi Street, I asked Vibini if he'd like a cup of Folger's Instant Coffee. He said he was exhausted and would like one. I chuckled and said, "Mit Schlag?" and he said, "What does that mean?" I got out my German-Italian Italian-German dictionary, and read, "Panna montata." "That's whipped cream," I said. "You should learn some Italian. Then you could read about the Battle of Brindisi and the Victor Emmanuel III Cross and how the decoration for heroism was named after Victor Emmanuel III, whom Mussolini named 'Emperor of Abyssinia,' and how Culofaccia was so brave before the forces of Illyria while Konev and Zhukov were shipping Heinrich Schliemann's loot from Troy back to Russia and the nuclear bombs were on the way to Nagasaki and Hiroshima. He mumbled, "I will, Liebgott. I will. I'll learn Italian."

Vibini sipped his coffee. He became very quiet. He seemed withdrawn and tired. He said, "Liebgott, write it all down. Tell the whole world that when Vibini goes to bat he doesn't strike out." I thought, and suppressed the thought, "I'll write it all down, to be sure. But first you're going to stop using clichés, you have to learn to say 'dov'è il gabinetto' and stop smoking whatever it is you're smoking that makes you smell like the poison gas the Italians dumped on the Ethiopian bowmen and spear throwers at the siege of Addis Ababa."

The Hong Kong Umbrella

DALLASANDRO VIBINI is still trying to learn to speak Italian. He says that speaking Italian will help him in his "sleuthing." That's not why I encouraged him to learn Italian, but that's his reason. He says that Italian is the only language for the Prayers at the Foot of the Altar in the world of crime. To learn the language, he carries around with him a small box of cards. The box is a faded mustard color and is labeled: "Compact Facts. Italian Conversation. James M. Ferrigno, Ph.D. A guide to the use and pronunciation of everyday expressions in conversational Italian recommended for students and travelers. A Product of Vis-Ed. $2.50." Also on the cover, in the lower right-hand quadrant, is a small reproduction of Rodin's "The Thinker." Whenever he comes over to my apartment, which is now every day, he brings along his cards. So when I say to him, "Guten Morgen, Vibini," he takes out card number 33, "Meeting People," and says, "bwon JOR-no, Liebgott."

Vibini's Italian came into play and helped him solve one of his, for him, most famous and most labyrinthine of crimes, now referred to by him as "The Hong Kong

Umbrella Caper." The Introit was a phone call. (Don't all crime stories begin this way?) Vibini and I had just finished our breakfast of V-8 Juice and Barnum's Animals Crackers when the phone began to ring. Vibini says that a ringing telephone is the Kyrie Eleison of modern society and he will not touch one. He has no phone in his one room apartment over on Schadenfreude Street. He's already working out of my residence. I picked up the phone and said, "Doctor Gottlieb Liebgott here. This is the office of Dallasandro Vibini, private investigator of crimes committed by the vermin of this world. No, this is not Auschwitz. Please tell me why you are calling. Yes, he is available at this time. No, he will not speak on the phone. Just tell me what you need investigated and I will relay the message to him."

When I hung up the phone, Vibini said, "mee ah teh-leh-fo-NAH-to nehs-SOO-no?" That's card number 25. "Hotel Services." "Um Gottes Willen, Vibini," I said. "Does anyone ever call me? Nein. Ich habe keine Freunde. I sit by the phone day in and day out and wait for someone to call me to come out and pop a cyst or remove a butterfly tattoo from a left breast. But, nein, nein, nein. The people all think that just because I have my medical degree from Heidelberg University that I'm a money devil, a monkey diddler. They're all assholes. Shoot'em all, I say. It was for you." He leaned back in his LA-Z-BOY chair and said, "I don't want to think today. O mahl dee TEH-stah. (Card 43; "How Do You Feel?"). Non mee SEHN-to MOL-to beh-neh. (Same card). What did he want and how much will he pay?" "She," I said, and at that word Vibini leaped from the LA-Z-BOY chair and cried out, "sbree-GYAH-mo-chee." ("Amuse-ments"; card 64).

I took out my notes that I had taken during the telephone conversation and explained it all ganz klar und schnell. I told Vibini that the call was from Mindy Mohnkuchen, the manager of the Arlin's Bar and Garden. (I have to disguise some of the names in the Hong Kong narrative in order to protect the innocent.) "KEH TEHM-po FAH?" he said from Card 44; "The Weather." "Es fängt zu regnen an," I whispered and went on with the Dreckverzeichnis. "She says that she needs someone to find out who stole an umbrella that was purchased in Hong Kong." "Why," he asked, "would anyone want to hire a private detective just to find some cheap umbrella?" "Well," I said, "there's more to it than that." "What else?" he whispered. "PYO-veh." (Card 45; "The Weather.") "Hör mal," I bristled out. "Der Dieb hat den Regenschirm zurückgebracht."

Vibini turned to me angrily and said, "PAHR-lah een-GLEH-zeh?" (Card 7; "Basic Expressions.") "OK," I said, "The thief returned the H.K. umbrella." Vibini cried out, "He returned it?" "Or she," I corrected him. "Shouldn't close out suspects." Vibini was ecstatic. "Think of it, Liebgott. Just think of it. Not only did the thief steal the umbrella, but he or she brought it back. And just to befuddle Mindy Mohnkuchen. Gottlieb Liebgott, I'll need all your medical expertise in the forensic investigation. Umbrellas don't leave many clues. I'll need a minute description of the HKU and bios on all the customers that come into Arlin's Bar and Garden. We'll take fingerprints off the dirty glasses. That will give us a two weeks record of who was there during that time. Call Mindy and say I'm on my way. What a crime. To do it and then undo it. Liebgott, it's the Gloria of investigation. Mee-KYAH-mee oon tahs-SEE." (Card 103; "Taking a Taxi.") "You're a cab," I said and dialed the phone. And they say we Germans have no sense of humor.

It was indeed raining as we headed for Arlin's Bar and Garden. In fact, the rain was coming down like Italian words in a holdup. "This," Vibini said, "is the Collect for the fleeing criminal." I wondered what he meant by that but turned my attention to observing the buildings we were passing. I had to get myself back into the microscopic mind set of investigation. I get some of my best ideas while riding in cabs. Vibini had not entertained a crime since June. He was out of cash and out of stash. He needed work, no matter what the pay. Something I had forgotten to settle with Ms. Mohnkuchen. I didn't want to disrupt Vibini's happiness, now that he was back on the job. Besides, I figured to pick up a little medical trade, say, an abortion or two, or a lobotomy on the bartender, or maybe just remove a barstool from a customer's Arschloch.

We entered Arlin's Bar and Garden and asked the barmaid if Ms. Mohnkuchen was around. The barmaid belched and said that Ms. Mohnkuchen would not be in that day because she was on vacation in Nepal. I knew she was lying. I knew Mohnkuchen was the lady sitting at the end of the bar. They always sit there and pick their noses while trying to figure out who's stealing all the money from the cash register. So I turned to the lady and said to her, while she wiped her right index finger on her spotted blouse, "You're Mindy Mohnkuchen, aren't you? I'm Doctor Gottlieb Otto Liebgott and this is the famous private investigator Dallasandro Vibini. We're here to unravel the twisted skein of the theft of the HKU." "What's that?" she said. "What's what?" I asked. "That HKU shit. Don't come in here and talk that goddamned shit in initials. Come on back into my fucking office and I'll fill you in on all the shit that's going on around this fucking place." Vibini was taken aback by Mindy's language because that's the way his brother Culofaccia talks, especially when he and Dallasandro play duets, Dallasandro on the ocarina and Culofaccia on the Sousaphone.

Back in her office, Mindy pulled up three broken barstools and we climbed onto those wobbly mounts. Her legs didn't reach the floor, so she sat there with her legs spread and her hands in her crotch. Vibini's legs reached the floor so he tricycled through the Epistle of his investigation. I managed to ascend my stool and regretted it. Because the seat was cracked and I could immediately feel my German ass sinking in ridges into the chair, I concentrated on keeping my black penny loafers from falling off into the cockroaches. Vibini got out his notebook and began the interrogation.

"OK," Ms. Mohnkuchen. "What does the HKU look like?"

"Well, it's like a small beach umbrella. The cloth panels are alternately black and red. The ribs are black. The shaft is a shaft."

"Then there's nothing special to identify it. No name on it?"

"Well there is this little wooden thing at the bottom of the shaft. A handle like a priest's woody. About mouth-size. Fits right into the palm."

Vibini took out a card, "Taking Pictures," (#71) and said, "QUAHN-to KO-stah oon een-grahn-dee-MEHN-to? A joke there, Liebgott."

"Ganz schnell," I said and chortled at our wit while my pinched ass cried out in pain.

Vibini wiped the tears from his eyes and elbowed me in the ribs, causing me to nearly fall from the vertiginous chair and causing my butt to begin to bleed.

"Oh yes," Mohnkuchen said, "there's a label on one of the red panels that says, 'Made in Hong Kong.'"

Vibini continued his relentless questioning. His suspicions, I could see, were aroused.

He stared into the bleary eyes of Mohnkuchen and said, "OK. Spill it. Where's the HKU? We need it to see it and to take fingerprints off it." I realized just then that Vibini had grown up watching American movies just as I had.

Mindy chuckled and said, "There aren't any fingerprints on it. Only palm prints and a little ring of vaseline where the handle sort of attaches to the shaft. Also there are some streaks of what looks like printer's ink."

I could see Vibini was on to something. He took out card 16, "When In Difficulty" and read off, "CHEH oon oof-FEE-cho of-JET-tee reen-veh-NOO-tee? Where's the HKU?"

Mohnkuchen fanned herself with a napkin and said, "The owner has it back, I think."

"And who is this so-called owner and when did he retrieve the HKU?"

"The owner is Tom Nabal and I believe he got it back on Friday, June 23. It was hanging on the coat rack."

"Tom Nabal? That must be the devious Tom Nabal whom I convicted in the famous case 'Nabal vs. et. al.' He was caught stealing hotpot holders from the Ace Hardware." Card 110, "Shopping": "que-sto non mee PYAH-cheh. Is that Friday, June 23, 1995?"

"What the fuck year did you think it was, 1895?"

I could see Vibini's Gradual coming to the fore.

"And it disappeared on Wednesday, June 21, 1995, while Tom Nabal was here in Arlin's?"

"That's right. He was shit-faced and it was raining hard. That's why he had an umbrella. I don't give a fuck where it was made."

Vibini pondered a moment and then said, "If it was raining hard, how did Tom Nabal get home?"

"Oh," she said, "he took a black umbrella from the coat rack and walked away. Saklas took a brown one. Both of them had brought an umbrella and both of them took one, except the one they took wasn't the one they brought. All three of them were returned."

Vibini got off his tricycle perch and paced through the debris. Card 12, "Asking Directions": "do-VEH-eel gah-bee-NEHT-to pehr see-NYO-ree?" "Um die Ecke," I said and waited for him to return.

When he returned, he continued his inquisition. "All right, Mohnkuchen, tell me about the regulars."

"Which regulars?"

"Those who drink here all the time."

"Oh, I thought you meant the regulars in the gah-bee-NEHT-to. OK. There's, other than Nabal, Arch Pescadure."

25

"Ah yes. Arch Pescadure. I convicted him in the famous case of 'Pescadure vs. Unknown Victims.' He was caught red-handed in a parking garage. We trailed him there by following the scent of his pipe tobacco. He was carrying three library cards for the Clifton Branch Library and a letter from the president of the university saying he couldn't make it that evening. Who else?"

"Well," Mohnkuchen paused, "There's Rod Ready. Ugh. Yuck. Whooee. Can't keep him out. Always here. Just sleeps at home. U.C. prof. English. Drinks up all our Budweiser. He's got this idea that we all should be able to spell words correctly and punctuate correctly and write clearly and precisely. He thinks we should all speak in correct grammar. Just like him. He never makes a mistake, believe me. You see in him the effects of beer on a weak mind. Not dangerous. No convictions. Likes tongue-in-cheek activities. Walks around saying, 'mee LAH-shee een PAH-cheh!'"

Vibini looked disturbed as he said to me, "Know anything about this Ready, Liebgott? He must have a record if he's in Arlin's. Otherwise why would he associate with all these other suspicious people? I'll check with my brother Culofaccia tonight. Is that all the regulars, Mohnkuchen?"

"Well, there's this guy Mark Casanova. No one knows anything about him. Probably nothing to know except he's off umbrellas."

"OK, Mohnkuchen, that's all we need for now. But before we leave, Dr. Liebgott will get the fingerprints off the glasses so that we can know who's all been in here in the last two weeks."

"Well," Mindy Mohnkuchen sneered, "Detective Dallasandro Vibini, you and your fat and bleeding buddy there better hope your sweet ass that those lazy bastards behind the bar haven't made a mistake and washed them for a change. ah pyoo TAHR-dee." There was a mistake so we left sofort, or should I say, "prehn-DYAH-mo oon reen-FREH-sko?" Card 58; "In the Caffe." (sic)

After dinner, Vibini told me to call a cab so I dialed the Clifton Cab Company. Two hours later we arrived at the apartment of Culofaccia Vibini on Schadenfreude Street, who, Dallasandro told me, never leaves his bedroom. "Warum, denn?" I said. Vibini laughed. "Oh, he meditates day and night. He solves my crimes for me." It was to be my first and only visit to the secret room. I assumed it would be my only meeting with Dallasandro's mysterious brother. Vibini and I said an Alleluia and walked up the stairs.

I knocked on the door because Vibini won't touch doors just as he won't touch telephones. A soft voice said, "Entrez." There he sat, Dallasandro's famous brother, in his touch-and-go rocking chair. Vibini #1 got out card 43, "How Do You Feel?," and said, "KO-meh stah?" Vibini #2 answered, "Paris est la capitale de la France. Paris est situé sur la Seine. La Seine traverse Paris."

Culofaccia is huge. He must weigh 400 pounds. Vibini #1 had already told me that his brother just sits and meditates. He was a huge blur in his rocker. The only clear part of him was the tattoo across his forehead. There, in skyblue ink, was "Mother Teresa." Vibini #1 told me later that their parents had the tattoo put on so that they could remember which one was which.

We sat on the floor because there is no other furniture and the Vibinis went to work. Vibini #1 told everything to Vibini #2; the umbrella, the regulars at Arlin's, the confused umbrellas on June 21, 1995, A.D., the condition of the handle, the returned umbrellas. The summation was like Tract, Gospel and Creed all thrown together. "Mother Teresa" rippled across Culofaccia's forehead as he processed the information. I thought I could hear the synapses closing and opening. For ten silent minutes and then he spoke in a thunderous voice, "Cherchez la femme. There must have been a woman involved. I know there was a woman involved. But you haven't mentioned one."

"But how can you know?" Vibini #1 stammered.

"Mother Teresa" came to rest. Culofaccia smiled. "Complex, Dallasandro. Complex. It's the handle that says it all. You said the handle had a palm print but no definite fingerprints. That means the holder of the handle was small, weak, feminine. You said that there were traces of printer's ink on the handle. That means the person who held the umbrella worked in a bookstore. It's the ring of vaseline that brings it all together. The person who took the Hong Kong Umbrella was a thin female who works in a bookstore and who is given to exotic sexual acrobatics."

Vibini #1 leaped to his feet. "Liebgott, call Mohnkuchen at Arlin's. See if there was a woman involved."

I won't repeat all of what Mohnkuchen said to me because it would be too embarrassing. She did report a woman. I returned to the room where Vibini #1 was scooping wax out of Vibini #2's ears with a Q-tip. I told them that Mindy Mohnkuchen reported that on June 21, 1995, a certain Nora Baumzweig had come in with a brown umbrella and hung it up on the coat rack. She also said that Saklas brought in the black umbrella.

Dallasandro withdrew the Q-tip. Culofaccia set his rocker in motion and said, "I see it all now. Baumzweig brought in the brown umbrella. Saklas brought in the black umbrella. Nabal brought in the HKU. All three were hung on the coat rack. Who left first? Nora Baumzweig, of course. She took the Hong Kong Umbrella and she took it because she suffers from chronic, low-grade umbrella envy. That's it. That's it. And no one should take umbrage at such a switch because umbrella envy exists in the penumbra of consciousness. She took it as an offering to her weakness, she consecrated it and then returned it as a communion with her fellow sufferers. She was just reaching out to the other umbrella owners. C'est fini. Calais est dans le nord de la France. Calais est situé sur la mer du Nord. Strasbourg est dans l'est de la France. Strasbourg est situé sur le Rhin. Marseille est dans le sud de la France. Marseille est sur la Méditerranée. Brest est dans l'ouest de la France. Brest est situé sur L'Atlantique."

We left Culofaccia Vibini rocking alone in his old rocking chair. We left him with his skyblue "Mother Teresa" at rest. I closed the door behind Vibini #1 and we walked out onto the porch. It was raining. Card 45, "The Weather"; "OJ-jee FAH kaht-TEE-vo TEHM-po. KEH O-rah EH?" Number 46, "What Time Is It?"

I said, "Drei viertel eins. That's A.M."

"MOL-to beh-neh," Vibini said from #9, "Basic Expressions." "You can still call Mohnkuchen at the Arlin's Bar and Garden and tell her that the HKU caper has been unraveled. Tell her that you will come by tomorrow and collect my fee."

"Wir brauchen einen Regenschirm," I replied.

Vibini laughed and said, "It's all taken care of," as he reached the railing of the porch and picked up an umbrella and opened it. It was something like a beach umbrella. It had alternating black and red panels in the cover. The shaft was a shaft. The handle was about four inches long, shaped like a long peg and shiny with use. A dirty ring of vaseline melted down from the top.

"Vibini," I said, "was ist denn los?"

"Well," he laughed, "you remember when I excused myself at Arlin's and went to the rest room? There were three umbrellas hanging outside Mohnkuchen's office. When we left I helped myself to an umbrella out of the three that were there. You were too busy staring around to notice what I did. I need one just as much as those people do. I had my choice. There was a brown one, a black one and this one. I couldn't resist the Chinese pleasure of a spiffy protection from the elements. When the other two are taken the other two takers will share my passion."

He opened the umbrella. Held it high so that I too would be protected from the rain. We set out and I asked Vibini, "Where to now?"

"Back to your house," he said.

"Nach Hause?" I said.

"Of course," he said. "We can rest now. We are done. Solving a crime is the Nunc Dimittis of the private dick."

VIBINI IN LABOR

DALLASANDRO VIBINI has moved into my apartment. I didn't want him to, but he insisted. He explained that he couldn't afford to live by himself any longer. He did have a one room apartment over on Schadenfreude Street, next to the apartment of his brother Culofaccia. He simply pointed out that my retirement income from my medical profession was more than enough for me and that I was selfish not to share my wealth with a man of the people, such as himself. He offered to help pay the rent on my Vox Populi Street apartment whenever he solved a case and got some pay for it. I doubt that he will ever pay any rent. He has taken over my study and made it "his room." He just moved in his clothes and his LA-Z-BOY chair, his smoking chair. Mostly he sits in my kitchen and drinks my cranberry juice and eats my Fig Newtons. At least he plays his ocarina and smokes his marijuana in "my study."

Now that I'm stuck with him, I guess I'd better start taking seriously my recording of his exploits. Even though I was a medical doctor for thirty-eight years and even though I'm now sixty-five years old, I've got to think about how I'm going to write Vibini's stories, even though I've already recorded two of his exploits. All I know now is that most stories have a beginning, a middle and an end. There is a reason, an occasion, for a story. The action gets complicated. Something happens to make the action come to an end, to go away. And the reader sits and wonders why he read it in the first place. It reminds me of when I was a child in Wuppertal, Germany, and I used to sit and read *Grimms' Fairy Tales*. I never got the point of the stories. They seemed worth reading. A lot happened in them. Characters died, got their eyes pecked out, burned up. I decided to be a doctor.

I think my studies in Italian military history might give me a clue here. A story is like an Italian military engagement. There is a dispute, the Italian troops advance and shout at the enemy and then they retreat. Everyone goes home happy, no lives are lost and the dispute is over. That's it. That's the way a narrative works. It's all a lot of words with no damage done. Everyone feels a lot better when it's all over. The readers then sit around and tell jokes, like the first Italian joke. Culofaccia told it to Vibini, who told it to me. After the Risorgimento and Italy got its independence, Mazzini, who led the Giovine Italia, proposed to Garibaldi that the motto for the new nation should be "Dulce et decorum est pro patria mori." Garibaldi looked into his plate of calamari and said, "Are you out of your cotton-picking mind? You want young Italians to die for Sicily?" Culofaccia laughs and says that now, whenever Italian soldiers lean over their plates of calamari, people think they are praying. What they're doing is telling the calamari, "Dulce et decorum est pro patria mori." They do it in order to increase their appetites and get a good laugh out of their military training. It's not much of a joke but it was the first of a multitude.

I was thinking those things about narrative and wondering how I would write my stories when the phone rang. It was Monday, September 4, 1995, 2:45 P.M. I've realized that to have a good story it has to be given a precise time and place of action. I picked up my new beige touch-tone phone. Details, I've realized, must be exact. It makes the fiction seem real. The phone call was from my neighbor Guido di Pietro. He asked for Vibini. I wondered how he knew Vibini had moved in and then told him that Vibini was playing his ocarina, trying to learn the Italian national anthem. Guido wanted to know what the problem was and I explained to him that I couldn't explain to Vibini that "O Sole Mio" is not the Italian national anthem. "Get him on the phone," Guido screamed. "I got a serious labor problem."

When Vibini came to the phone, he murmured something I couldn't understand. The murmuring went on for a long time until Vibini said, "I'll be right over. Right. No witnesses. No Liebgott." I thought, "Why am I being left out? What happens to my narrative when I don't know what's going on?" Then I realized, "That's what point of view is. It's not knowing what's going on. If the point of view knows what is going on there can be no story." I asked Vibini, "What's going on?" He said, "Guido has a serious labor problem." "That I know. What is the problem? I got to know if I'm going to keep the record of your exploits." Vibini looked from his glassy eyes and said, "Liebgott, what are you writing

33

down? I didn't know you were doing that." That's not true. He's known all along that I'm making his narrative. When Vibini said, "Here's the problem," I knew that a story had begun.

Vibini began what I realized was a sub-narrative. It was a filling in of background to give the reader a context. "Guido has a secret business. He knows Vox Populi Street is not zoned for business. He carries on his business in his basement, known only to me. He has one employee who knows all about the business. The one employee is Emil Hasenpfeffer, who once was a guard at a Nazi prison camp. Emil can blackball Guido whenever he wants to. That's why Guido is afraid of Emil. Not only that, Emil has organized a union and insists on a written contract. He threatens to go on strike if his wage demands are not met. Guido and Emil are now in wage negotiations and Guido wants me to come over and be a fact finder in their dispute. It has something to do with fair labor practices law. I'd better get going before Emil is out on the sidewalk with a picket sign. That could ruin Guido's business. Then all the neighbors would know that Guido is breaking the zoning code."

I was nonplused. That, I realized, is a good condition for the point of view. So I said, "Emil Hasenpfeffer has a one-man union?" "That's right," said Vibini. "He has a one-man union and is affiliated with the AFL-CIO." I realized that the unions in America are getting smaller and that the Republicans are trying desperately to kill them, but a one-man union? And then I realized why, in narrative, data must be repeated several times for the reader to remember the facts. Then I said, "What is the dispute?" "Money. Emil wants a raise of one half cent an hour. He now gets four dollars and fifty-five cents an hour. He is demanding four dollars and fifty-five and one half cents an hour." "And you're to be the fact finder." "That's right. They will accept whatever I decide after I consider the facts." It came to me that here I had the conflict and the characters, the three characters of dramatic complexity. All I had to do as the writer was to sit back and watch how it all ended.

Vibini put on his green beret, his red cape and his purple spats. I knew he was ready to fact find or find fact, whichever came first. He was just going to leave when I asked, "Before you go, what is it that Guido di Pietro secretly manufactures in his basement?" Vibini sat down. I think he had to sit down. He was too high from the marijuana. He began a kind of maundering. "No one would ever guess what he makes. It'll be a surprise to you and to your readers. That should make the story more interesting. He manufactures lipstick for the Italian army. He has to do it secretly and not just because of the zoning laws. You see, ever since the Risorgimento and the rejection of 'Dulce et decorum,' the motto of the Italian army has been 'Nolo contendere.' They're the only smart soldiers in the world. They know that if you die for your country, you don't have a country anymore. They know that only stupid soldiers die for their country. They've sat back and watched the Germans, the Americans, the British, the French, the Spaniards, the Illyrians all slaughtering each other.

"The Italians win by not dying for their country. That's why Guido di Pietro's lipsticks are all shaped like bullets. The lipsticks come in various shades: olive, pepperoni, provolone, salami, pasta, onion, garlic. In the Italian army the last bullet in each magazine clip, in each belt of bullets for a machine gun, in each pistol, is a tube of lipstick made right here in Cincinnati on Vox Populi Street. So that whenever an Italian soldier runs out of bullets he still has his tube of lipstick to rely on. They're taught all this stuff in basic training. In spite of the jokes, the Italian army never surrenders. They know the Italian army lost the Battle of Caporetto when they ran out of lipstick." I thought, "My God, what do the men in the artillery have for lipstick? And the men in the air force with their bombs?" As if reading my mind, Vibini said, "The last artillery shell is a giant tube of lipstick and the men have to share it. The same way in the air force. The tube is huge. The men have to kneel around it and rub their lips against it to get it on their lips. That's why Italian soldiers are always smacking their lips. It all started when Caesar's legions conquered Britain. The Roman soldiers advanced on the Picts, who had never seen lipstick before. The legionnaires smacked their lips and the Picts ran and jumped over Hadrian's Wall. That's where the Romans learned the high hurdle."

I thought, "I can't ever put this in my story. No one would ever believe it. On second thought, I can put anything I want in my story. If the reader doesn't believe it, to hell with him. Because he's going to get more of it." Vibini went on, "You see, there's something called 'Italian camouflage.' Ever since the Risorgimento Italian soldiers have carried female clothing in their knapsacks. When the enemy attacks and the soldiers have to retreat, which is always, they hide away and get out that last bullet. They put on their designer dresses made in Hong Kong, their high heel shoes, their blond wigs, their lace panties, their lacy brassieres and their lipstick. When the enemy is engaged, the enemy soldiers don't take any prisoners because they can't find the Italian army and, besides, no one takes women as prisoners of war. That's why there are no suicides in the Italian army, nor are there any prisoners of war. The camouflage is an escape device. The soldiers just go home and leave the enemy in confusion. Sooner or later the enemy forces leave.

"When the Italian forces attack, they put on their camouflage and their lipstick. As they attack, they smack their lips and the enemy forces go nuts. If the enemy is British troops, the Brits go berserk and hand the disguised soldiers chocolate, gum and their guns. If the enemy is German, the Italian soldiers don't even shave their legs because they know the Germans like hairy legs." I interrupted to say, "Vibini, please." But he went on, "If the enemy is French, they put on some perfume. They have different strategies for different troops. But when the Italian forces attack in their female attire, they hide pistols in their hose and gelignite in their brassieres. They advance, rotating their hips and smacking their lips, and infiltrate the enemy lines. They make advances to the enemy soldiers and pick them up one by one. Then when they have the enemy soldiers in some upstairs room over a Gasthaus, a pub or a trattoria, they blow them away. It works every time. You see, the Italian soldiers would rather change gender than surrender."

Vibini got up and walked out the door. Or rather, stumbled out the door. I got to get these details right. As he went out he said, "I'll be right back." And he was. Ten minutes later he stumbled back in, eyes glaring and watery. All the main action of my story had happened offstage, as it always does in good fiction. "Well," I said. "Did you find the facts?" Vibini smacked some slobber across his lips and said, "Of course. I ruled in favor of the working class. The Vibinis have always stood up for working class people. We stood up for them before the Risorgimento, after the Risorgimento and we still stand up for them. That's why I moved over here on Vox Populi Street. Emil Hasenpfeffer now has a one half cent an hour raise. With a two year contract. Guido wasn't too happy, but he accepted it. Now they're back to work on a new contract. They have to make a lipstick shaped like a nuclear missile." "What shade?" I asked. And they say we Germans have no sense of humor.

Vibini whispered, "Veal parmigiana," and slumped into a chair. He was passing into one of his other states of being. His lips were moving. He was reporting, I was sure, to his seventy year old brother Culofaccia over on Schadenfreude Street. He mumbled something again. I said, "Vibini, I can't hear you. What did you say?" He mumbled, "Here's something for your next story. Did you know that my father Ruggiero Vibini was in World War I and that he got his penis shot off at the Piave?" I hesitated in confusion. "Vibini, how is that possible? Culofaccia was born in 1925 and you were born in 1945? The retreat to the Piave River was in 1917 after the defeat at Caporetto. Hemingway wrote about it. I know your father was born in 1898 and that he was in the Italian army in The Great War, but how could he have engendered you and Culofaccia without a penis?" As Vibini's head rolled slowly to the left, he murmured, "Don't ask. It's the second joke about the Italian army." I thought it was the best ending for a story that I'd ever heard.

HEMINGWAY'S VALISE

WHEN VIBINI HAD FINISHED solving the labor problems of our neighbor Guido di Pietro, he said to me, "Liebgott, I need a vacation. Let's go to Paris and relax for a week or two." I was surprised because Vibini almost never leaves Cincinnati. He stays at home and waits for the telephone to ring to call him out onto another case. I suspect that the reason he wanted to go on a vacation was that he had had no phone calls for over a year. Solving the case of the Hong Kong Umbrella had brought him no new customers. He was probably more bored than tired. So I said, "I'll go if you quit trying to speak Italian." He's been trying to learn the language for years. He still can't speak it, but he agreed to quit trying, at least for our Paris trip. I made the reservations for our flight from the Greater Cincinnati-Boone County-Northern Kentucky-Ohio River-Delhi-Clifton-and-Bevis Airport. I also made reservations through Marie Roget at the Bonne Chance Travel Agency for a hotel room in the City of Lights.

Vibini and I packed our bags, found a free ride to the airport and left Cincinnati on a Delta flight for Paris. We landed at Orly Airport at 10:00 A.M. on June 24, 1994, and took a cab to our room. On the way we passed the Quartier St. Roch three times, the Jardin des Plantes four times, the Place de la Bastille five times, the Eiffel Tower six times and Montparnasse seven times. Two hours and sixty-five dollars later we arrived at the Chez Vidocq in the Rue Morgue.

The entrance to the Hotel Chez Vidocq was in an alley. It was around a corner from one of the main streets in the Faubourg St. Germain. We carried our suitcases around to the door and rang the doorbell. At first we couldn't see who answered the ringing because she was so small. She said, from her stooped posture, that she was the concierge and that she was expecting us. She was seemingly crippled. Her legs were short. Her stomach protruded. She had swollen lips and tiny eyes. Her head and her whole body were covered with thin, silky red hair. We signed the register and followed her as she hobbled up the stairs to the third floor. When she climbed the stairs, she walked on the balls of her feet and the knuckles of her hands.

The tiny room included two small cots and a detached closet for clothes. There was a table, a chair and a mirror over the table. The bathroom was as small as the one on the passenger jet that we took to Paris. The bathroom would give Vibini no problem because he is just six feet tall and weighs only 150 pounds. I thought, "For me this is a problem." I'm five feet eight inches tall and I weigh 300 pounds. I wondered if I could even get into the tiny room. The one window onto the alley was covered with dirt. When Vibini closed the curtain, it made no difference. The room was just as dark as before. There

41

was a telephone and a pad with a note on it. Someone had written, "Call Al and Max."

The concierge Madame L'Espanye had no sooner showed us to our room than the telephone rang. We hadn't even unpacked our bags. Vibini said, "Well, answer it." For some reason I knew we shouldn't answer the telephone. I said in panic, "Vibini, don't answer it. We're on vacation." It continued to ring so I picked it up and handed it to him. Vibini smiled and said, "Dallasandro Vibini here. Yes, you have the right person. Yes, I do private investigations. That's my forte. Yes, I'm available. Yes, I have some literary training and I know just about everything about American literature. We'll settle the fee later. Where shall we meet you? How will we know who you are?" He made some more notes and wrote down an address while I sat and wondered how his reputation had preceded him to Europe. It seemed odd to me that someone knew about his abilities as a private investigator, that someone knew he was coming to Paris, that someone knew where he was staying, that someone knew his telephone number. Vibini didn't find it odd at all. He simply said, "Liebgott, call a cab. We're on our way."

We gave the cab driver directions and he began the long journey, he said, to the corner of the Rue de Babylone and the Rue du Bac. We passed the Arc de Triomphe three times, the Louvre four times, The Place de la Concorde five times, Notre Dame Cathedral six times and the Hotel des Invalides seven times. During the hour long ride, I asked Vibini how we would recognize our clients. He replied nonchalantly, "Wait and see. I have a full description." I was apprehensive. We were strangers in a strange town. We wouldn't know the difference between the corner of the Rue de Babylone and the Rue du Bac and the corner of Clifton and Vox Populi Street in Cincinnati. When the cab stopped, we got out and I paid the cab driver the fifty dollars he demanded. We looked around and Vibini said, "There he is."

Standing on the northeast corner was a man wearing a black bowler. He had ears whose lobes pointed down and whose flanges pointed up. He had dark eyes, a hooked nose and a thin black mustache. He wore a black dress coat over a black shirt with a black necktie. There was a large bulge in the left armpit of his coat. His trousers were black. He also wore black shoes that were covered by white spats. His white gloves spun through the air as we approached him and Vibini said, "Monsieur Dupin? Dallasandro Vibini here. And this is my colleague Gottlieb Liebgott." The man in black said, "My name is Max, bright boy, and my colleague is Al." Another man dressed just like the man on the corner stepped from the black Renault parked at the side of the street. We shook hands all around. "Max, meet Liebgott. Liebgott meet Max. Al, Vibini. Vibini, Al. Vibini, meet Liebgott. Liebgott, Vibini. Al, Max. Max, Al. Al, Vibini. Vibini, Al. Al, Al. Max, Max. Liebgott, Liebgott. Vibini, Vibini."

After the introductions Dupin informed us that we were to go with him and Al. Al would drive. But it would be necessary to blindfold us. We got into the back seat with Max and the car moved into the traffic. Max took out some strips of black cloth and blindfolded us.

43

We drove off. I became nauseated. The blindfolds were too much for me. I couldn't even play blind man's buff when I was a child because I would end up puking on my playmates. I tried to keep my mind busy in order not to throw up. I realized as we drove that the names of our clients weren't their real names. I also know that in the private investigation business you don't ask certain questions.

I concentrated on the voices. Vibini asked what Max and Al wanted from him and Max said, "We have in our possession some rare manuscripts that were written many years ago by a famous American writer. We called you because you might know something about American writers of fiction." Vibini replied, "Of course I know about American fiction writers. I'm the expert in the field." He's not an expert in anything. I'm the expert, but I didn't dare intervene. My attention became acute when Max said, "Have you ever heard of a writer named Ernest Hemingway?" Vibini cried out, "Of course I've heard of him. I know his works like the back of my hand " I cringed at the cliché. Vibini never even looks at the back of his hand; he's too busy staring off into space. I'm afraid I almost jumped out of my seat when Max said very softly, "We have found his lost valise. Or, as you say in America, his suitcase." Vibini was clearly flustered. He didn't know what Max was talking about.

As so often happens, I came to Vibini's rescue. I said, "Max is referring to the valise that Hemingway's wife had stolen from her in 1922. The valise had in it all of Hemingway's stories that he had written up to that time, except for two. The valise also contained the carbon copies of the stories. Hadley, Hemingway's first wife, was to travel by train from Paris to join her husband in Lausanne. When she went to board the train in the Gare de Lyon, someone stole the suitcase. It was a horrifying experience for Hadley and Ernest. They never forgot it. When Hadley reported the theft to Ernest he got on a train immediately and went back to Paris to their apartment. The carbons were not there. To this day no one has recovered the stolen valise. And no one knows exactly what was in it." Vibini said, "Oh, that suitcase. I should have known what you were referring to was early in his career. I thought you meant the suitcase he lost in Africa."

The Renault stopped. Max helped us out of the back seat onto the sidewalk and led us through a door. Once inside, Al took off our blindfolds. We were in some kind of warehouse, or so it seemed. We were led across the dirt floor and up a metal staircase to a steel walkway and then into a room that had a steel door and was made entirely of iron. The only furniture in the room was a table and four chairs. On the table was an obviously old suitcase that was about two feet by three feet in width and length and about six inches in depth. The handle was missing. The shriveling green leather was peeling from the corners and you could see the rivets and the thread. A copper colored dust lay around the suitcase. When Max picked it up, more dust fell from the layers of leather. Al said, "You sit over there, bright boy. And you sit over there, fat man." We drew up the four chairs and sat down around the table. Max laid the suitcase on its side, unsnapped the clips, undid the leather strap around the suitcase, and opened the lid. I said, "Where did you find it?" Al said, "We found it in a pawnshop." Max said, "Shut up. It's sloppy. You talk too much."

As Max was opening the valise, it occurred to me that, if the manuscripts were a scam, the whole ploy must have been thought of by a hundred fiction writers and scholars. The manipulation of the putative contents of the stolen suitcase is an obvious idea. I considered the possibilities of the forgeries, the fiction that could be written, the sensationalism that could be generated by a presumed discovery of the stolen manuscripts. Whether the manuscripts were real or not, I thought of all the money that could be made out of the idea of the discovery of the manuscripts. The idea, I knew, was available to everyone.

We all looked in. Inside was a pile of old paper yellow with age. The typing was faint but legible. When Al reached out to pick up one of the sheets, Vibini cried out, "Don't touch them. We need to test them for fingerprints." Max said, "Don't worry, bright boy. We already have. There aren't any. He must have worn gloves when he typed them. Isn't that right, Al?" "That's right, Max." The carbons were onionskin. They looked almost impossible to read. Monsieur Dupin, who was Max, said, "Shall we begin our negotiations?" Vibini said, "What do you have in mind?" And Al said, "$100,000." The other one said, "Shut up. You talk too goddam much." Vibini turned to me and said, "Liebgott, what do you say to that?" I said, "We don't have that much money with us." Max said, "We figured that, fat boy. What we want you to do is to contact an American university and arrange the payment. When we get the money you will then take the manuscripts to whoever puts up the money." I said immediately, "But these manuscripts are the property of the Hemingway estate. These manuscripts are stolen goods." Al and Max laughed and Max said, "That won't make any difference to an American university. Make the contact and you get ten percent. It'll pay for your vacation."

When I said, "We must prove their authenticity," Max said, "Go ahead and take a look." I put on my gloves and picked up the top sheet. It was a story called "In a Far Country." It began, "In the fall the war was always there, but we pretended we were wounded so that we would not have to go to it any more." The next story was called "The Assassins" and it began, "The door to Millie's lunch-room opened and two women came in and sat down at the counter." I was fascinated. Vibini was dumbfounded. The next one was called "Little Two-Hearted Lake" and it began, "The bus lumbered up the road and disappeared behind a hill of green pine trees." The next one was called "The Capital of France" and began, "Paris is full of young writers named Ernie, which is the diminutive of Ernest, and there is a Parisian joke about a father who came to find his lost son." The next one was truly amazing. It was called "Hills Like Skyblue Elephants." It began, "The two American women sat at a table in the shade and drank beer." The next one left me breathless. It was called "The Short Happy Life of Skyblue the Badass" and began, "It was lunch time and they were all sitting under the double green fly of the dining tent and laughing uproariously at what had happened that morning. The white hunter Grover Cleveland and the gun-bearers could hardly stand up they were laughing so hard. Tears flowed down the cheeks of Skyblue's wife."

The deeper we got into the pile of manuscripts the stranger things became. There was one called "On the Simplon-Orient Express." It began, "Fridtjof Nansen couldn't tell the difference between snow and rain. He couldn't tell the difference between Turks, Greeks, Armenians and Bulgarians." There was one about Schrunz. It was called "In the Madlener-haus" and was about skiing and snow that fell for a week so that everyone just sat around and played cards for money. There was one called "Merry Christmas" that was about a man who had bombed an Austrian train on Christmas day. There was one called "Alone in Constantinople" and had to do with lovers' quarrels and whoring. There were stories about the Schwarzwald and the Place de la Contrescarpe. An untitled story began, "We sat on the steps of the cathedral and wondered why the door was locked." Another, untitled, began, "In the Fall the Hirsch came down from the mountains to drink at the Isar." There was one about a half-wit chore boy who killed a man for taking some hay from a barn. The stories were astounding and I could understand why the loss of the suitcase was such a disaster. I told Vibini the manuscripts might be authentic.

Max closed the suitcase and said that we could not handle the manuscripts anymore because they were so fragile. Vibini turned to Al and said, "Did you say $100,000?" "That's right," they said in unison. Max turned to Al and said, "You see? I told you so. He's a bright boy. He knows the value of the dollar." Vibini turned to the two and said, "Listen, you Charlie Chaplins, we don't know yet if they are real. What if they aren't the real thing? What if they are forgeries?" I interrupted, knowing full well that if the whole thing was a scam they weren't the first or last to think of it, and said, "Vibini, it won't make any difference. We can take the chance." "OK," Max said. "Here's what you do. You go back to the Chez Vidocq in the Rue Morgue and send some fax messages to major American universities and see what happens. You know who to contact. We'll call you tonight at 10:00 P.M. and see what you've come up with. If you get the $100,000 we'll make the exchange tomorrow morning. We'll phone you the directions. Now get moving. You got a lot of luck. The offer won't last forever."

Again we were blindfolded and driven back to the corner of the Rue de Babylone and the Rue du Bac. The blindfolds were removed and Al and Max drove away. We stopped a cab and began our drive back to the Rue Morgue. As the driver started to take us to our hotel, I said to him, "Monsieur Ubu, we've had the grand tour. Just get us back to the Chez Vidocq." We arrived there five minutes later. The fare was $4.00, including tip.

When we got back into our room, Vibini closed the door and said, "Liebgott, what did you mean by that remark about it not making any difference about the authenticity of the manuscripts?" I said, "Vibini, don't you understand? American literary scholars would sell their souls to get their hands on those manuscripts. Just

49

think a minute. If they are authentic, all the Hemingway biographies would have to be rewritten. All the literary scholarship would suddenly be out-of-date. Just think of all the publication that would come from the discovery of those manuscripts. Just imagine all the university promotions and tenure that the scholars and critics would receive. Just think of the amount of money they would make from the manuscripts. And if they're not authentic just think of the controversy they would cause. There would still be the same effect as if they were authentic." Vibini's nostrils flared and he whispered, "But, Liebgott, that would be unethical." I laughed and whispered back, "Unethical? Vibini, were you born yesterday? Do you think for a moment that literary scholars and critics care about ethics? Don't make me puke." I almost apologized for the cliché, but I have to use them to communicate with the great Dallasandro Vibini.

He paused and said, "What now? What should we do?" I didn't hesitate. "Wire the Constellation Bank in Cincinnati and tell them to send us $100,000. They're still open because of the time differential. We'll borrow the money. They have a branch here in Paris. Then we'll buy the manuscripts. When we get back to the U.S. we'll sell them for at least $500,000. The University of Texas will pay that much for them even if they are forgeries. That way we'll make 500 percent, not ten percent. When Max and Al call this evening we'll tell them that we have a buyer. If it's a scam, we won't be the first to exploit the idea. We'll pick up the valise tomorrow morning and take it on the lam." Another cliché, for which I'm sorry.

Vibini needs some mystery in his actions. "Right now I'll call Delta and make reservations for a flight out of here tomorrow afternoon. We'll be back in Cincinnati by tomorrow night. Then we'll contact the universities."

Vibini paced the floor and looked out the window. Speaking to the window, he said, "We got to keep amused, haven't we? Get the reservations." I smiled at his back and picked up the phone.

THE THRALL STREET CONUNDRUM

THE $100,000 THAT VIBINI wagered and lost on the Hemingway manuscripts left him flustered and frustrated. When he fell for that scam in Paris, he thought he had $400,000 in his pocket. Everybody knew the manuscripts were forgeries. Not even the University of Texas would bite on his offers to sell them. Now he has the old suitcase and the manuscripts sitting on his old chest of drawers in his bedroom. He sometimes looks at them and says, "Liebgott, I should have known that Al and Max were crooks. Why didn't you warn me?" I sit back and say, "Vibini, why were you so innocent? Didn't you know that everyone in this world has had the same idea? The idea was obvious to every fiction writer in this world. Didn't you know that the contents of his lost suitcase opened up a plethora of fictions *hic et ubique terrarum*?" When we got back from Paris, he sat for weeks waiting for a phone call. He sat and smoked marijuana and played the ocarina. He didn't even call his fat brother Culofaccia Vibini for some advice.

Hearing the phone ring last Wednesday, he jumped from his LA-Z-Boy chair and yelled out, "Gottlieb, answer it. I'm sure it's for me." I picked up the receiver and handed it to him. "Hello," he said, "Dallasandro

Vibini here. Yes, I'm an expert on petty crime. Vibini's my name and petty crime is my game. Your name is Barry Vermis? Yes. Your problem is that someone has stolen your deck? Yes. You made it yourself and someone stole it while you were at the University of Giancaldo lecturing on 'Roman Whoopy Cushions?' I think I can handle the problem. Yes, I can be right over. Liebgott," he said, "call a cab. We have a case. Get out the garb."

Ecstatically I hustled my fat self over to the wardrobe for my green beret and my black cape. I put on my Wellington boots, my gray silk gloves and my scarlet bandana. For Vibini I got out his orange tam, his yellow cloak and his red leather gloves. I knew he would also want his black penny loafers and his purple spats. I wanted him to dress for the chase. I wanted him ready to solve a case so quickly that he would revive his spirits, start eating blood sausages again and again take up his Chianti and calamari, learn some more Italian. His six-foot frame looked too thin for criminal investigation. His weight I knew was down to 145. All because of one false move in Paris that cost him $100,000.

Timely as the call was and even with his enthusiasm I couldn't understand why he had not asked about his fee. When we got into the Quo Vadis cab, the driver turned to us and said, "Quem quaeritis?" We gave him directions and headed for Thrall Street, a part of the historic Clifton district. When we came to Vermis' house, I was amazed at the place. It was painted in one of those colors that paint companies call "Foxglove," "Insipido" or "Ecce Homo." Nothing about the house was suspicious until we met the owner and went inside.

Hairy Barry Vermis answered the doorbell. He was about five feet tall and had viridis hair that hung down over the back of his neck and covered his ears and his forehead. His flat chest and flat stomach made him look, I'd say, "Caesarean." He was wearing a Roman helmet and pink pajamas. His sandals flapped against his peeling heels as he opened the door. He was holding a glass of rubicundus liquid. I thought it was probably a mixture of bella donna and Seven-Up. Vermis said, "Ave atque vale." Vibini said, "Cogito, ergo sum. I'm Vibini and this is my friend Gottlieb Liebgott. We work together." "Come in to the atrium," said the Vermis. "Here's my problem." When he started talking about his problem I looked around and knew that his problem was not his deck.

Inside, the walls of the house were covered with sculptures of female breasts. There were monstrous breasts, flat breasts, cupcake breasts. More breasts than Alexander the Great or Virgil had ever seen. It recalled to me the mosaics at Pompeii. Some of the breasts were made of purpureus clay. Some were made of fulvus styrofoam. Some were made of fuscus wood. One pair that fascinated me was made from two plastic bags from Keller's grocery. The two plastic bags hung side by side. At the bottom of each bag were cans of anchovies, tuna and sardines. Above the cans were rolls of toilet paper, paper towels and packages of frozen cod. The groceries were packed in the plastic bags with studied elegance, obviously the work of an expert at packing groceries. At the outside bottom of each bag was a nipple made from a dried mushroom. All those things that go into mothers' milk. I felt as if I were being hugged by the Diana of Ephesus. The composition was called "Ave Maria" ($4000).

"Est deus in nobis," Vermis said. "I notice that you have noticed my wife's sculptures. Please meet my wife Tallulah." Tallulah stepped from behind a huge poster for a brassiere ad that at the top said, "Ex oriente lux," and at the bottom, "Ex occidente lux." Tallulah was short and fat. Her skin was gray, her hair aereus and she was flat chested. Her headband had a large pin on it that read "Juncta Juvant." She rolled her glaucous eyes and said, "Alta petit. They're all for sale. This one made from composted cow manure is called 'Mirabile dictu.' It is modeled on the breasts of the Venus de Milo and is for sale at $5000. This one is called 'Novus Ordo Seclorum' and is made from recycled, acid free newspapers and is modeled on the breasts of Joan of Arc. You can buy it for $8000. This one is made from Barry's unpublished manuscripts and is called 'In Hoc Signo Vinces.' It is a reprise of the breasts on Michelangelo's 'Pieta.' It goes for $10,000." Vibini allowed as to how he was strapped for money and could not, at that time, buy wall hangings. Tallulah said, "De profundis clamavi," and went back behind the brassiere ad. Barry said, "Ad astra per aspera. She's temperamental. Don't worry. Before you leave she'll give you some tits. She never lets a man leave this house without touching her mammaries."

Funky Barry stroked a couple of the nipples on "Ad Maiorem Dei Gloriam" ($11,000) and led us out into the backyard. There was a precipitous drop just outside the kitchen door. That was where the deck was. "Look,"

Vibini said, "before I begin this case I have to know what I'm to be paid. I usually receive $1000 for these difficult cases." Barry looked through his fingers at the empty space and said, "Why, the deck only cost me $500. I paid for the wood and built it myself." Vibini laughed and said, "Caveat emptor. That was your first mistake. No one should do his own work. That's why it was so easy for the thief to detach the deck from your house. It probably was sloppy work." Barry laughed and said, "Ex officio, I was thinking of something along the lines of $200. And you don't get paid unless you solve the case and get my deck back." Vibini said, "Nihil obstat," accepted the offer and went to work. I looked away and thought, "Veni, vidi, vici."

"Initially," Vibini said, "I need all the background. Who are you and what do you do? Why did you build your own deck? When did the deck disappear?" Barry glanced around to see if his wife Tallulah was listening and then said, "I'm a professor of Classics at the University of Cincinnati. I work very hard to keep my wife in clay. She can't sell her tits and I have to keep her happy. Before you leave I'll make you a deal. Carry out the $15,000 one called 'Beatus Vir' and I'll pay extra for your services. I can't stand to have all that crappy phony flesh hanging on my walls."

Serenely, Vibini looked up to the sky and said, "Forget the tits. What do you write?" "Oh well," Barry remarked, "they're not too important. My famous articles are 'The History of Roman Buttons,' 'The Physiology of Latin Tongues' and 'Fingernail Hygiene in Virgil's *Georgics*.'" "Does anybody read them?" I asked. Vibini said, "Have you been gone?" and Vermis admitted that he had been gone for six weeks while he lectured on "Whoopy Cushions in the Roman Senate" at the University of Giancaldo in Sicily. While away, he admitted, his son Boris had stayed in the Thrall Street house and had been there when the deck was carried away. His son admitted that the deck was purloined one piece at a time while he smoked dope and ate his parents' frozen cod one piece at a time.

Tired already, while Vibini examined the nail holes on the side of Vermis' house, I sat with Vermis on some lawn chairs and told him about my studies. He took off his Roman helmet. I took off my green beret and my black cape. I told him that I too was a scholar, that my special field was Italian military history. I told him that I had discovered that the motto of the Italian army was "Nolo Contendere" and that the Italians hadn't won a war since Julius Caesar. The reason for that, I told him, was that the Italians were smart enough to realize that wars aren't worth the trouble. They decided a long time ago to let the Germans, the British, the Americans and the Russians go out and get killed while they stayed home and drank Chianti and ate pasta primavera.

Happiness is all, I thought, as I told Vermis that the sanity of the Italian military came from their literary past. "Just look," I said. "Italian literature is filled with books about the horrors of death. Italian is a language consummately fit for talk about mortality. It's the language of the dead. That fear runs all the way from Dante to Primo Levi, from Thomas of Celano to Alberto Moravia. The Italians know how fearful dying is so they learn to say before the gun, 'We surrender.' They know a dead man can do nothing. Vibini," I said, "is trying to learn Italian. He still hasn't learned to say in Italian, 'Nicht schiessen.'"

Abruptly Vibini cried out, "What's this?" Vermis and I jumped from our chairs and ran to where Vibini kneeled in the dirt. "It's just a pile of leaves," Vermis laughed. Vibini looked at him with scorn. "No wonder you can't get a real job. Don't you see? Quod vide. The pile of leaves is our first big clue." He kicked the pile of leaves aside. Underneath the pile was a black bowler. "So what?" Vermis remarked. "Don't you get it?" Vibini cried "It's the sign of Caelum Caeruleus. He never strikes without leaving his mark. He's absconded with your deck and left you with bare dirt in your yard. He's like that. Opere citato. No mercy. Nomina stultorum parietibus haerent. That'll be $200 for my services."

"Time out. O tempora! O mores! Wait a minute," Vermis said. "Videlicet. We haven't got the deck back yet. E pluribus unum." "Don't worry," Vibini replied. "Tell your wife to write the check. The deck is in your neighbor's garage. Vade mecum." And, indeed, it was there. In pieces. We carried the pieces back into Vermis' backyard. We stacked them neatly.

Courtly Tallulah came out, handed Vibini a check for $125, shoved into his arms a pair of tits carved out of Ivory soap entitled "Annuit Coeptis," said "Nunc dimittis" and called us a Quo Vadis cab. Vibini looked at the check and said, "Wait a minute. We agreed that my fee would be $200." Tallulah smiled and said, "I charged you $75 for my art. It's my first sale ever." As we got into the cab we could hear Barry and his son Boris pounding nails into the side of his house. We could hear the pieces of the deck banging together. We could hear Barry singing, "Gaudeamus Igitur." Vibini leaned over to me and said, "At this rate I'll soon be out of debt." "Yes," I thought, "if you can get 800 more calls for stolen decks."

Luckily I had paid our phone bill. And I was even, at that moment, ready to go out and steal a few decks myself just to get Dallasandro Vibini back on track. It's in cabs that I have my best thoughts. I even, for a moment, imagined wetting and rubbing my hands over "Annuit Coeptis" and washing my hands in the Ivory suds around the nipples while singing "Salve Regina."

Upon arriving back at our domicile on Vox Populi Street, Vibini threw the tits in the trash and I began to question him as to how he had solved the case so quickly. Never had his mind worked so quickly and decisively. Vibini took up his marijuana pipe and said, "Festina lente. It was Culofaccia who sent the message."

"Mea culpa," I said. "But Culofaccia Vibini was not at the scene of the crime. He couldn't have known about the black bowler."

"Simply put, Liebgott, it was by telepathy. When I saw the pile of leaves I knew that it was a false lead because tenebrae ficti sunt. I contacted Culofaccia by telepathy and he said I was correct. Caelum Caeruleus had nothing to do with it. Simply put, the thief left a false trail. In principio, Caelum Caeruleus would never cover his black bowler with dead leaves. Perhaps in tenebris, but never in venite adoremus. You didn't see me whisper to Vermis the real name of the thief."

"You see, summa cum laude, I didn't understand."

"And," Vibini continued, "Culofaccia told me by telepathy of the terra incognita that you will enter when you record the solution of the Thrall Street Conundrum."

"Useless to be semper paratus," I said. "Tell me."

"The story is the fiction of oblivion. Semper timidum scelus."

"Happily in a memento mori," I replied.

"Only Culofaccia would realize that writers often tell more than they realize. He knows what cacoethes scribendi is."

"Right. Let me guess. I will reveal in my narrative who the thief was and I will not know that I did it."

"Don't worry," Vibini replied. "Narrative is the lifeblood of the dead. Or, so says my brother. And you know that his motto is 'Saepe falsus sed nunquam incertus.'"

"All that I can accept because fiction is the folly of the pure in heart."

"Let only the secret messages in your stories tell the truth and reveal the calamity of order."

"Likely most all of that," I guessed, "came from the dies irae of the Culofaccian mind."

"All kings and queens have guessed as much. It was all hidden in Tallulah's knockers, tits, boobs, jugs, hooters or lungs. Whatever they are called nowadays."

"Surely I'm confused," I admitted.

Without flinching, Vibini said, "Nota bene. It's as the comedian Father Guido Sarducci says. You have to find the Pope in the pizza.

"In nomine. Dominus vobiscum. It'll all be right out

front. Anyone will be able to see it. They'll only have to get the big picture. Ratiocination will do it. Like Poe's purloined letter."

Explaining it to myself, I said, "Let me get this straight. When I write the story of your latest exploit, I will reveal the name of the thief without realizing it."

"But remember, Liebgott, as you once said, suspicion is the Eucharist of the unimaginative.

"Exeunt omnes. I think you got it. The mind of a great writer exceeds the limits of reason. He stutters into the world of the oppressed and says, 'Fiat lux,' and all becomes clear. The reader's epiphany is the culmination of the art that hangs on the walls of the physically obsessed. At least, that's what Culofaccia Vibini says. He also says, 'Cave canem.'"

VIBINI AND THE SPECTRE FATHER-IN-LAW OF THE BRIDE

I WAS DEEP INTO my study of the Battle of Isola di Capo Rizzuto, where the armed forces of Illyria once again, in October of 1946, attempted an invasion of Italy after having had lunch at Corfu and after having given up on attacking Brindisi, when the little red light on my beige touchtone telephone started blinking and the phone began ringing. I picked it up and listened to the panic of the caller. It was a summons for the services of Dallasandro Vibini, who was needed to find Don Robin Pugh, whose son Ron Robin Pugh was being married that afternoon at 4:00 P.M. The woman who was calling said that Don had disappeared that morning about 10:00 A.M. and hadn't been seen since. The wedding that was supposed to begin in two hours could not go on without him. His future daughter-in-law was in tears, his son was sweating up his pink tuxedo and his wife, as I had guessed, was on the phone, screaming for Vibini. I assured the wife that Vibini was available for $200 and that he would be over to their home on Thornburg Lane in ten minutes. It was 2:00 P.M. on Saturday, October 7,

1995, when I put in a call to the Quo Vadis Cab Company and went into my study, the room that Vibini had commandeered for himself when he moved into my apartment on Vox Populi Street. He was watching the Penn State football team destroy the Ohio State football team. He was laughing through the haze of his marijuana smoke and yelling things like, "Kill those Buckeyes. Smash those nuts. Break those legs before they break yours. Come on, Paterno, get those Nittany Lions chewing up some yards. Come on, State College." I tapped his right shoulder and told him about the phone call. He looked around and said, "Not now, Liebgott. I can't leave this game." I smiled and said, "Yes, Vibini. You're going to go out and find that missing future father-in-law of the bride. You owe me money for some rent. Let's get going. The cab's on the way." Vibini got up and said, "Don't turn the TV off. We'll be back before the game's over."

He got up slowly, stubbed out his joint, and put on his uniform. Red beret, green cape, lavender shirt, orange pants, black penny loafers and purple spats. "Liebgott," he said through his glazed eyes, "I'm ready. Call a cab." "I already have and it's honking outside right now. Let's go." I helped him down the steps and into the cab for what I didn't know was a ride of four blocks. Right around the corner from Vox Populi Street.

The house on Thornburg Lane was one of those ominous monstrosities in the historic district of Clifton. The stone retaining walls around it sagged and water leaked through the cracked mortar. Our shoes stuck to the gray paint on the steps that led up to the front porch that sagged and looked as if it might fall away any time. The house was painted that kind of yellow that is the color of the Italian medal awarded to the Italian soldiers for being wounded in combat, the Order of the Yellow Heart. On the porch were pots of wilted impatiens and geraniums. A dog barked and the front door opened. We entered chaos.

Vibini began his questioning. The dog started jumping against his legs. I wrote down what I could in order to record another exploit in the Vibini saga. Phyllis Amaryllis Pugh, the mother of the groom, said that she had last seen Don Robin Pugh that morning around 10:00 A.M. The dog jumped against Vibini's leg and Phyllis smacked the dog with a rolled up newspaper and screamed, "Down, Penelope." The dog continued to jump against Vibini. Vibini murmured, because he always murmurs when he's on a trail, "What was he doing before he disappeared? How was he dressed? Any erratic behavior? Did you notice anything special about him?" Phyllis grabbed the dog and laughed. "Don was sitting on the front porch. He was smoking a cigar. He was drinking his fourth martini for the morning. He was reading *Skyblue's Essays* and spitting over the porch railing. He was wearing his usual boxer shorts with the little pink kitty cats walking toward his crotch. He had braided the hair on his chest into dreadlocks. He had shaved the hair away from his tattoo on his left breast so that you could read where it said 'Lewie' over the head with the nail through it. The last thing he said to me was that he was dressed for the wedding and flipped his cigar ashes into the Rose of Sharon." The dog jumped up on Vibini as he said, "How many cigars did he have with him?" "I think six," Phyllis added thoughtfully. "Ah," Vibini murmured, "that means that at one cigar per hour, the usual rate of smoking for future fathers-in-law, Don Robin Pugh has enough to last him six hours, that means, from ten to four. One hour and thirty minutes from now he will be on his last butt."

"Where's the groom?" Vibini asked as he kicked the dog away from his leg. "Over there. In the toilet. Getting his hair in order." I wondered how Phyllis Amaryllis Pugh could know that, but I didn't ask as the groom opened the door and walked in. He was a sight, I must admit. His tuxedo was the pink color that the Illyrians paint their rowboats. It's the same pink that is the color of the first of the vertical stripes on the Illyrian flag, followed by the skyblue and the chartreuse stripes. It's the same pink that so baffled the Italian forces at the Battle of Isola di Capo Rizzuto and at the Battle of Paterno in Sicily.

That pink is, I discovered in my research, Illyrian camouflage. When they paint their boats that pink and then wear their pink uniforms it's difficult to see them when they row in under the fortifications designed by Leonardo da Vinci. Certainly it confuses the Italian defenders because they can't tell how many men are in the boat. That's why so many Italian soldiers got the Order of the Yellow Heart at the Battle of Isola di Capo Rizzuto because when the forces of Illyria landed they landed on a pink beach and no one could see them until they walked into the trattoria and demanded some Grappa, which the trattoria was out of so the women of the village put on their pink dresses and fraternized and served up so much Chianti that the soldiers from Illyria got back into their pink boats and rowed back to Corfu, sicker than dogs that constantly jump up on the legs of guests. Now, on the anniversary of the Battle of Isola di Capo Rizzuto, October the Seventh, the women of the village wear pink ribbons and the soldiers wear their Yellow Hearts.

Vibini blinked at the bright pink and asked Ron Robin Pugh if he had noticed anything strange about his father that morning. Ron laughed and said, "How could you tell? My father gave new dimensions of meaning to the word 'strange.'" I wondered if I should write all this down, but Vibini went on. "What do you mean? I've got to find your dad in one more hour. I need information." "Well," Ron began, "he doesn't like to wash his feet. That's why he goes barefoot so much. He is obsessed with a pinball game called 'Terminator 2: Judgement Day.' He associates with the local drunks and some university creeps. His Volvo never runs. He drinks martinis and Harp Lager.

"Dad's father Conrad Robin LePugh, who was from Picardy, was military advisor to the Italian forces at the Battle of Capo d'Otranto when the armed forces of Illyria landed and tried to bifurcate Apulia in 1946. His father was awarded the Order of the Tin Star with Garlic Cluster after the women of Otranto saw the pink boats on the beach and let out their Gothic yell. The Illyrians decided when they heard the noise to go back to Corfu for some feta cheese and wine. It was a great victory for LePugh, who immediately dropped the 'Le' from his name and set sail for Saginaw, Michigan, where he was promised a job in a meat packing plant.

"Captain Conrad Pugh never made it to Saginaw. In fact, he ended up in Cincinnati where Don Robin Pugh was born on a pink morning in June of 1948 to Conrad Robin Pugh and his new wife Maribel Elsie Floss, who had just arrived on a refugee boat from Pachino in Sicily where she had been abandoned by the American armed forces when they invaded Sicily and brought along their own U.S.O. show. I remember her singing 'September Song' while pink tears rolled down her pink cheeks and dropped onto her pink dress, which she always wore in memory of Queen Martha Von Stoepf the First, the tyrannical ruler of Illyria, the Marxist menace to the peace of the Adriatic Sea, the Strait of Otranto, the Golfo di Taranto and the Golfo di Squillace.

"That's part of the Pugh family history. And that's why we all wear pink on any occasion. It is, for us, the color of fear and the color of heroism. I'm wearing it for my wedding, as you can see. My bride is wearing chartreuse which is the color of the Stretto di Messina, which grandma swam across in order to get from Villa San Giovanni to Messina on Sicily so that she could rejoin her U.S.O. troop which was abandoned by the U.S. armed forces in Pachino where she got on a refugee boat and headed for Cincinnati and where she met my grand- father who was the main wiener man at Kahn's Meats."

I wrote down all of that that I could. I hope I got it all right. Vibini just listened, astounded at the overload of information he was receiving. He looked around. "Where's the bride?" he asked. Tiffany Regina Broccolini stepped out from behind a large screen that was covered with a large photo of the dead bodies of American soldiers washing up on the beach at Salerno. She smiled her yellow smile and said, "Did someone call me?" Ron Robin Pugh spun around and yelled, "Shut up, you pig. No one wants to talk to you. Don't interrupt me when I'm talking about my family history." Tiffany sneered, "Piss on you, you dumb shit. I've heard all that crap before." When I heard that little exchange between the bride and the bridegroom I knew perfectly well why neither Vibini nor I was married. I wondered who would put up with such behavior, even on a wedding day and even with the future father-in-law of the bride missing and Vibini cold on the trail even with the dog jumping against his leg. He had forty-five minutes before that beastly organ in that beastly church would rock out the beastly wedding march.

Tiffany's veil had little yellow stars spread through it. It made it appear that her red eyes glowed behind the chartreuse lace. It made her face look like the face of Queen Martha von Stoepf the First, the Marxist Medusa, that is on the five kocki coin from Illyria. That face was on all coins and all bills until it was realized that the coins and bills with that face on them were rotting so it was decided to leave the face only on the five kocki piece because you can't buy anything for five kocki in Illyria anyway.

The decaying money disrupted the system that Queen Martha had installed when she took over from the German army in 1944 so she could help German war criminals escape to South America. When the Germans left, she set up a feminist system of Marxist money: 100 peckers equal one kocki, 100 kockis equal one labia, 100 labias equal one utera and 100 uteras equal one mamma. It was that monetary system that got the war started because it took so much Illyrian money, 100 mammas, to exchange for one Italian lire. It took a whole boatload of mammas to buy a meal of fettucini.

The Illyrians couldn't stand to be so financially inferior to the Italians so they attacked the coast of Italy, first at Brindisi in 1945 and then at Isola di Capo Rizzuto in 1946 where they grossly underestimated the valor and cleverness of the Italian army. The armed forces of Illyria landed on the Italian coast, waved their pink, skyblue and chartreuse striped flags with the two black crosses in the upper left-hand corner and their motto "Marx Mit Uns" and then rowed back to Split where Queen Martha von Stoepf the First gave them all a stick of Wrigley's Juicy Fruit Chewing Gum and a lecture on fiscal responsibility.

Tiffany Regina Broccolini turned to Vibini and said, "I guess you want me, don't you? I mean to answer some questions." "Yes," Vibini said. "I have only thirty more minutes to find the missing future father-in-law of the bride. That's you, by the way. Your marriage is off if I don't find him." Tiffany laughed and said, "Shoot. I don't need him. He's probably just over shooting pinball and drinking Harp Lager."

Vibini kicked the dog away, waited a bit and then said, "Did you notice anything peculiar about Don Robin Pugh this morning, or any time for that matter?" Tiffany pulled down her chartreuse veil so that she talked through it and said, "'Peculiar' isn't the word. Just after his breakfast of bacon, eggs and sardines, he finally put on his boxer shorts with the little pink kitty cats walking towards his crotch. If that dog jumping up on your leg is bothering you, I'll throw it out the door. When he got up to spit over the railing, he dropped his cigar into the Rose of Sharon. Then, I guess he'd had enough, and he said, 'That's it. I've had enough.' That's the last I saw him.

"I sat down and cried for a while until I remembered Queen Martha Von Stoepf the First from Illyria, how she took over after the German soldiers retreated into Austria, how she left her native village of Schweinfütterung in the Salzkammergut and hiked through the Gurktaler Alps to Illyria where she announced a feminist-socialist revolution and made the kocki the basic currency of the newly minted realm where she sits and stares enviously at Italy, which is why Venice is sinking and Italy is turning to stone. I realized that with that inspiration I could bear the absent future father-in-law, but I didn't count on Phyllis Amaryllis Pugh. She's a screaming blob. She'll ruin it all and my memories of Queen Martha von Stoepf the First, who made Illyria into a major world power by attacking Italy at Brindisi, Isola di Capo Rizzuto, Capo d'Otranto, Paterno in Sicily and San Benedetto del Tronto. All my memories of Queen Martha will fade away into Phyllis Pugh's scummy bitching. Find Don Robin Pugh. Maybe the wedding will happen after all."

Vibini looked at me and said, "Liebgott, let's get shaking. We have fifteen minutes. I think I know where Don Robin Pugh is hiding out." I immediately surmised that Vibini had contacted his brother, the fat and immobile Culofaccia Vibini at his apartment on Schadenfreude Street. But it wasn't so. Vibini explained that Culofaccia would be watching the Penn State-Ohio State football game and would not allow any interruptions. I said, "You mean Culofaccia watches football games?" Vibini laughed, "Of course he does. He's an Ohio State fan. He says the games break his heart. He can't stand the coach named Cooper. He says the coach is a loser, but he sits there and roots, as they say. I saw him once get so excited during a football game that he stood up. That's the only time I've seen him stand since he moved into his apartment on Schadenfreude Street. You can tell by that how he gets involved. But come on, Liebgott. Let's go get the spectre future father-in-law of the bride."

Vibini kicked the dog off his leg one more time and we walked down from Thornburg Lane and turned towards Ludlow Avenue. Vibini, who is tall and and thin, walked fast and I waddled my 300 pounds along behind. We turned down Thrall Street and passed the house of Barry Vermis, the house painted a color called "Ecce Homo." I remembered how Vibini had solved the Thrall Street conundrum. Tallulah Vermis stood on the porch and waved to us as we passed. She held up a piece of sculpture she was scraping on. It was a pair of female breasts made out of frozen ocean perch. Tallulah called out, "When they melt they sag." Vibini called back, "Get them a bra made out of hot ice. They'll stay lifted and sweet." We turned down Telford and crossed to the other side of Ludlow. Vibini walked into Arlin's Bar and Garden and there at the pinball machine was Don Robin

Pugh in his boxer shorts with the pink kitty cats walking towards the crotch. He was smoking a cigar and a mug of Harp Lager stood on the table by "Exterminator 2: Judgement Day."

While Vibini went over to speak to Don Robin Pugh, I sat down at the bar and ordered a bottle of Budweiser Beer. The barmaid chomped on her gum, lit a cigarette and said, "I suppose you want a glass." "Of course," I said. "Life is like a bottle of beer. You never know what's in it." And they say we Germans have no sense of humor. The barmaid didn't get the joke, chomped on her gum, and I drank my beer and began writing down notes for my chapter on the battle of San Benedetto del Tronto. It was one of the most important of the battles in the Illyrian-Italian War.

It was at San Benedetto del Tronto in 1948 that the Italian forces, seeing the pink boats of Illyria heading toward the shore, stood firm behind their fortifications designed by Leonardo da Vinci. Their commander Mario della Picollo ordered the Italian flag raised. The flag went up and proudly floated, for the first time, the new great seal of resurgent Italy with its new motto which was taken from Dante's Commedia. The voice of the people of Italy selected by popular vote the line that Dante speaks to Virgil just as they emerge from the "Inferno." "Dov'è il Gabinetto" flew for the first time in the Italian flag against the pink forces of the Marxist Menace Queen Martha von Stoepf the First as the Illyrians landed their boats and walked up the beach towards the fortifications of San Benedetto del Tronto designed by Leonardo da Vinci.

The Italian forces were ordered, from the headquarters in Rimini, to wipe out the armed invaders from Illyria, but as they got ready to fire their weapons, a strange event happened. The Italian soldiers suddenly started leaping into the air and yelling, "C'è della posta per me?" and "A che ora si serve la prima colazione?" After the war that particular response to threat was labelled the Victor Emmanuel III Syndrome. It is an uncontrollable, neurological-chemical response of the body when the person inhabiting that body does not want to die for Sicily.

When the commander Mario della Picollo ordered the Italian troops to drop their weapons and put on their female camouflage, the leaping and shouting ceased. The soldiers got out their female clothing kits, put on lipstick, dresses, wigs, high heels and perfume and walked down to the beach. There they mingled with the Illyrian soldiers, punched holes in their boats and told them to go home and be good little boys. The disguised Italian soldiers gave the Illyrian forces bottles of wine and salami sandwiches for their trip back to Split, guided them to their boats and helped them push the boats back into the sea. The cross-dressing soldiers waved to the parting Illyrians and watched with tears in their eyes as the pink Illyrian boats sank slowly beneath the waves. It was then that Mario della Piccolo put up his famous message for his commanders in Rimini. The troops smacked their lips and cried out, "C'è un buon ristorante qui vicino?" as Mario della Piccolo wrote on the fortifications designed by Leonardo da Vinci, "Go tell the Italians, you who read; we ignored your orders, and we're still alive."

When I looked up from my notes, Vibini was standing beside me. "Liebgott," he said as he handed me a five dollar bill, "get some quarters." I managed to get the barmaid to stop chomping on her gum and smoking her cigarette long enough for her to hand me twenty quarters. I got up and waddled over to "Exterminator 2: Judgement Day." Don Robin Pugh was standing ready to play the pinball game. I could see his bare feet and could see the dreadlocks in the hair on his chest. I could see, on his left breast, the "Lewie" tattooed over the head with the nail through it. Vibini put the quarters on the top of the glass cover of the machine. "Vibini," I said. "What about the wedding?" Vibini turned to me and said, "Pugh and I are going to play some pinball. We got about two hours to kill. Go ahead and shoot, Pugh. I've seen your future daughter-in-law."

VIBINI ON THE E-MAIL

LIKE ALL THE TROUBLES in this world it began with a good idea. Put in E-Mail and save the forests, save the trees, save the secretaries who can't spell or punctuate. Direct communication with the department. Thoughts fluttering along the electronic system. Exchange ideas. Avoid meetings of the faculty. Save time and money. Malformed ideas twitching along from office to office in that great daydream where technology substitutes for intelligence. A new form of togetherness without the problems of bad breath, sweat-stained garments, obnoxious voices, stupid arguments with no intelligence and no thought. Put-downs and put-offs anaesthetized by computer screens. Ugly faces and ugly minds denatured by computer keyboards. It is the new collegiality.

Unfortunately, saving those trees had a downside. That's why James Christian Fortescue called and asked for Dallasandro Vibini. I said, "Gottlieb Liebgott here. Amanuensis, formerly M.D. and now Schriftsteller." It was Wednesday, June 5, 1996, and 4:30 P.M. Vibini was out anyway so I explained that he was out and couldn't come to the phone. Vibini was out on marijuana, snoring in my study, his head resting among my notes on the battle of San Benedetto del Tronto where the Illyrian Queen Martha von Stoepf the First sent her Marxist hordes against the pink defenses designed by Leonardo da Vinci. I had just discovered that in that battle the Italian military gained one of its greatest standoffs with the Adriatic menace and awarded fifty soldiers the Victor Emmanuel III Medal of the Order of the Lead Star with Fettucini Cluster.

While Vibini slobbered on my notes, I asked Fortescue what the problem was. He explained that someone in his English Department was sending pornographic messages over the E-Mail. The Citizens for Community Values had found out about it and were demanding that the culprit be deceased. I asked how the CCV knew about the messages, and Fortescue explained that someone was printing the smut and selling it on lower Vine Street. I couldn't understand what would drive a faculty member to smut but I informed Fortescue that for $200 Vibini would solve the problem. I set up the appointment: 8:30 A.M., June 6, 1996.

I went into my study and slapped Vibini until he awoke. I said, "Vibini, you've got a case." Vibini jumped up and cried out, "Call a cab, call a cab. Liebgott, let's get going." I explained the appointment and the case. Vibini, who is still trying to learn Italian, muttered, "Cinque, dieci, venti, trenta, trentasei, quarantatre. I hope Culofaccia knows something about computers, because I don't." "Don't worry," I said. "If university professors can figure them out so can you. It doesn't take a whole lot of intelligence. Get some rest and be ready in the morning. You need to make some money to help pay the rent." Vibini has never paid any money for the rent on the apartment on Vox Populi Street and I want him to stop the freeloading.

Vibini mumbled, "Se vuol ballare, Signor Contino," stumbled into his room and went to bed. I sorted out my notes and went back to the Battle of San Benedetto del Tronto. It was all in the *Annali Calabresi*, Volume 33, number 41, pages 99-100. The whole narrative was written by Fra Bartolomeo Masaccio, who chronicled the assaults of the Illyrian hordes on the eastern coast of Italy during the final days of World War II and the beginning of the long peace that shattered the dreams of Fiat, Lancia, Ferrari, Maserati, Alfa-Romeo and Lamborghini when the Japanese and the other Oriental manufacturers of automobiles stole the world market and left the Italian auto industry fizzling and got the Illyrian socialists to try the Yugo, which also fizzled. That narrative all written in longhand by a Benedictine brother who fled Subiaco when General Mark Clark's Fifth American Army moved up the Italian peninsula in 1943 towards the Gustav Line, leaving a trail of dead soldiers, while chasing the Hun or, as the French call them, *Les Boches*, through the bloody battle of San Pietro and up to Monte Cassino where the Allied bombers took care of 1000 years of Italian history so that *Les Boches* could move into the rubble and use it for an observation post and teach the Benedictines that culture means nothing to an American general. Fra Bartolomeo Masaccio managed to get south from Subiaco and slip across the Rapido River and move east to the east coast of Italy where the British Fifth Corps under Keightley broke out across the Pescara

River and moved on up to the Tronto River and retook Asccli and San Benedetto del Tronto where Fra Bartclomeo stayed until the Germans left, some of them via Illyria with the help of Queen Martha von Stoepf the First, who directed them to Argentina, Uruguay and Brazil.

So Fra Bartolomeo was in San Benedetto del Tronto, never having returned to Subiaco, when, in the spring of 1948, the pink boats of the Illyrian military forces appeared off the coast and Capitano Giovanni Salvatore, commander of the Apulian fusiliers, stood on the breast-works of the fortifications designed by Leonardo da Vinci, raised his right fist in front of his face, slapped his left hand across his right elbow and cried out, "Avanti. Avanti, you Illyrian dogs," and raised the new Italian flag with the new motto of the new Italian nation, "Dov'è il Gabinetto," while the new Italian army hid behind the fortifications designed by Leonardo da Vinci and put on their female camouflage and let their oregano-flavored perfume waft across the little waves into the nostrils of the bloodthirsty Marxists who wanted to reduce Italy to a Marxist utopia under the heel of Queen Martha von Stoepf the First, also called "the squinter," and "old rotten butt."

Fra Bartolomeo Masaccio writes in the *Annali Calabresi*, Volume 33, number 41, pages 99-200, the volumes now stored in the restored Monte Cassino and now available on Internet, where the first 1000 years of Italian history were destroyed by American bombers and were now being replaced by a new history that began the next 1000 years of Italian history, that

Capitano Giovanni Salvatore for waving the new flag and for delaying the Illyrian armed forces long enough for the Italian soldiers to put on their female camouflage received the Victor Emmanuel III Royal Order of the Tin Cross with Ravioli Cluster for his bravery and the Order of the Yellow Heart for the shell shock he endured as the result of standing in the sun so long on the stone fortifications designed by Leonardo da Vinci. When Capitano Salvatore disappeared from the ramparts and the armed forces of Illyria poured over the fortifications and onto Italian soil, all they found were women, actually the Italian soldiers in disguise, who, feeling peppy, goose-stepped up for the first time and fondled the Illyrian soldiers, took them into the Trattoria Nastagio degli Onesti, filled them with Grappa and then blew them away. After which, the Italian soldiers, the new forces under Capitano Giovanni Salvatore, took off their high heels, put their trousers back on, wiped off the lipstick and marched down to the Illyrian boats, punched holes in their bottoms and pushed them out into the Adriatic where they slowly sank out of sight while the new Italian soldiers cried out, "Dov'è il Gabinetto, you suckers. We'll teach you what war's all about." When I first found the *Annali Calabresi*, I wanted to find and embrace Fra Bartolomeo Masaccio. Such a great historian. That's right, "embrace." Men can do that. They can't hug. I'll bet you won't get history like that on the E-Mail.

The next morning, I rousted Vibini out of his slumber. That's right, "slumber." Vibini doesn't sleep; he slumbers. You slumber when you sleep without moving or snoring. Vibini slumbers and it took me ten minutes to get him out of it and onto his feet. I said, "Dress for work," and he walked to his closet, put on his black beret, his black cape, his black trousers and shirt, his black penny loafers and his purple spats. He looked in the mirror and said, "Liebgott, giovanni liete, fiori spargete davanti al nobile nostro signor. Call a cab." I asked him why the black dress. "We're going to the university, aren't we? I want to look academic." I think he took his cue from me. I had earlier put on my black shoes, black socks, black three-piece suit, white shirt, black tie and my black homburg. I had also combed my gray mustache and beard and my gray hair. To make it all just right, I wore my gold pocket watch in my vest and let the gold chain hang out across my fat belly from one pocket to another. I wanted to show those American university professors what a professor ought to look like.

The Quo Vadis Cab arrived and we headed out of Vox Populi Street onto Clifton Avenue. The weather reminded me of the weather that was reported on the day of the Battle of San Benedetto del Tronto. That day, and on June 6, 1948, at 8:30 A.M. the weather was balmy. That's right, "balmy." There was a zephyr. That's right, "zephyr," a light, warm, westerly, springtime wind, the kind of breeze that blows at the openings of novels and poems, the kind of breeze that wafts its way across the Adriatic Sea from Italy to Illyria. That's right, "wafts." Zephyrs waft; they don't blow. So a zephyr wafted its way down from the Apennines, across the fortress of San Benedetto del Tronto, across the beach and over the Adriatic Sea to where the pink Illyrian war boats were being rowed into the wafting zephyr because the

Illyrians need a straight out hard wind from the east to blow their boats across the waters in order to carry their Marxist aggression to the shores of the Italian Republic. The zephyrs also carried down and out the oregano perfumes of the Italian soldiers as they donned their female attire and prepared to waddle down to the beach to meet the Illyrian soldiers and confuse them into going back to Split. The Italian soldiers well knew from experience that the Illyrian soldiers couldn't resist Italian perfume wafted on a zephyr across the slumbering waters of the Adriatic Sea. The Illyrians fell for it every time. That's right, "donned." That's right, "attire." You put on clothes; you don attire. I'm going to get this literary language right. I need to get it right for my recording of Vibini's exploits. Even though I was a medical doctor most of my life, I think I can now become, in my old age, a member of the literati. That's right, "literati."

The Quo Vadis Cab turned onto the University of Cincinnati campus at the main gate. A raven-haired maiden stopped the cab and asked the driver what he was trying to do. That's right, "raven-haired" and "maiden," just like in the great literature. Our driver said he was dumping us off and she said, "Dump and get." He dumped and got. We stood by a large, red brick building. Over the archway was their motto: "Wisdom is the principal thing therefore get wisdom." It sounded like something that was written by a committee. What caught my attention was the white cupola on top of the building. It was obviously an empty cupola but it was capped by a weather vane that was exactly like the weather vane on top of the keep in the castle of Queen

Martha von Stoepf the First, the Marxist Medusa, in her capital city of Split. I had read in the *Annali Calabresi*, IX, 36, pp. 35-36, recorded by Fra Bartolomeo Masaccio, refugee from Subiaco, that Queen Martha von Stoepf the First put that weather vane on her keep so that it would guide her pink boats out and away towards the Italian shore even when the wind was blowing from Sicily to Siberia. I took the weather vane to be a portent of things to come. That's right, "portent of things to come," as if you could have a portent of what had already happened. I'm finally realizing how those famous writers filled up those pages.

We entered the hostile building and climbed up to the second floor. It was exactly 8:30 A.M. We knocked on the locked door of the English Department. No one answered. We waited. At 9:30 A.M. a secretary wandered up and unlocked the door. She looked at Vibini, smirked—that's right, "smirked"—and said, "What do you want?" Vibini flipped his cape over his right shoulder and said, "Non piu andrai, farfallone amoroso. I'm Vibini and this is my amanuensis (that's right, "amanuensis") Gottlieb Liebgott. We're here to see James Christian Fortescue about the smut." The secretary scratched her butt and said, "All our classes in Victorian Literature are closed." "Oh no," I said, "it's about the E-Mail messages." "Well," she said, "he won't be in until 11:00. Why don't you wait in the lounge?" We decided to wait. We sat and imbibed the atmosphere. That's right, "imbibed the atmosphere" which was like the atmo-sphere that Fra Bartolomeo Masaccio describes that he experienced when he was in the castle of Queen

Martha von Stoepf the First in Split. There was an oppressive mood of quiescence, like the moment before death. The leaden hand of mortality lay heavy on the air. It was, as Fra Bartolomeo Masaccio writes in the *Annali Calabresi*, XV, 39, pp. 10-58, like being in an alabaster chamber in Split where the ominous waves laved the feet of the petrine elevations. I can fill pages with that kind of writing.

At 11:30 A.M., exactly, Fortescue came in. He was about five feet and four inches tall. He had straight black hair that hung down to his shoulders. He was wearing a red and green plaid shirt and denim trousers. If you've ever seen the drawing of the head of General Volsung Volsunga, commander of the Illyrian military forces, you'll know what his face looked like. The drawing is in the *Annali Calabresi*, IX, 95, p. 73. The drawing is part of the record of the battle of San Benedetto del Tronto, which Fra Bartolomeo Masaccio recorded in 1948. I stood up and said, "I'm Gottlieb Liebgott and this is the famous private dick Dallasandro Vibini." I figured that "private dick" stuff would impress the head and let him know that I was "ganz modisch." Fortescue introduced himself and said, "Come into my chambers." That's right, "chambers." I'm sure I'll use that word in one of the Vibini episodes.

He explained why he had sent for Vibini and Vibini said, "Per finirla lietamente, let's see." We rolled our chairs close to the computer screen. Fortescue sat at the keyboard, punched something in and up on the screen popped the opening of a story called "Robin's Nest, or, Springtime in McMicken." It began, "In the springtime, the old cock robin peeks into the windows and watches as the old professor turns his thoughts to amorous intentions. Old cock robin can see, even through the slats of the venetian blinds, that the old professor has locked his door and has pulled out his pencil." "You see," Fortescue explained, "that's what came over the E-Mail the first time. As you can see, it's signed 'Lock.'"

He punched some more buttons and up came "Elizabeth Finds It Hard Going." It began, "Elizabeth Finger, editor of *Female Frenzy*, a feminist rag, sat at her desk and waited for her all male staff to come in and fill her in. She sat at her desk, huffing and puffing, sweating in her thighs, until the door opened and in came her office boy. He was six feet and eight inches tall and weighed 290 pounds. His hairy arms were encased in a pink t-shirt. His hairy thighs protruded from his athletic shorts. He threw everything off her desk and said, 'Let's get to work.'"

Fortescue punched some more buttons and up came "Why Gillian Grunts." It began, "The springtime zephyrs wafted gently across the verdant hills to where there was grunting in the copse. It was the shepherdess Gillian and her swain playing a game of Hey-diddle-diddle. His staff was stuck in her pocket and she was crying out, 'Pull it out, you stupid shepherd. Pull it out.'"

Fortescue said, "Here's the fourth and last one to appear." He punched and up came "Bertha Beats All." It started out, "Bertha Ballway felt a tickling in the palm of her right hand. It was a sign, she knew, of things to come. She dialed her phone and said, 'Frederick? Come on over. Let's handle this afternoon better than we did last night. I need some more hands-on experience.'" I recognized that it was lousy pornography. I knew I could do better with a little practice, just as I could and would someday write better than the literati. I was learning fast.

Fortescue turned to both of us and said, "That's enough of that. You get the idea. All the messages are signed 'Lock.' So far we can't divine (that's right, "divine") who the culprit (that's right, "culprit") is. Your job, Vibini, is to find out who is putting this stuff on the E-Mail. We've tried to trace it down and we can't. It's now up to you." Vibini smiled and said, "Che stupore. Give me a list of all your faculty members. That's the place to start." I asked him trenchantly, "What can you tell from a list of the faculty members?" I like that "trenchantly" so I'll add "rejoined." That sounds literary. "Well," Vibini trenchantly rejoined, "we can eliminate suspects. We know, for instance, that the faculty members who teach British Literature can't write. They don't know what a sentence is, so that leaves them out. We know that the faculty members who teach criticism have no sense of humor, so that leaves them out. We know that the faculty members who teach American Literature aren't interested in sex, so that leaves them out. We know that faculty members who teach business and technical writing communicate only by telephone, so that leaves them out. We know that the secretaries can't spell or punctuate, so that leaves them out." I enjoined, "Then who's left?" I enjoyed saying "enjoined" while Vibini said, "Sono in trapolla. Complicated, Liebgott. Complicated. It has to be a linguist. It has to be a faculty member who thinks he knows something about language and doesn't." "But how do we find him?" I asseverated. That's right, "asseverated." "We don't," Vibini asserted. "Son tre stolidi, tre pazzi. We call Culofaccia. He'll know."

We went downstairs to a pay phone. I dialed. Culofaccia answered. It was difficult to hear him because his TV was on so loud to "The Price is Right." "Culofaccia," I yelled, "turn down the TV. Dallasandro wants to talk to you." The TV stopped. Vibini took the phone. "Culofaccia," he murmured, "here's the evidence." Vibini murmured on. "Yes, yes. Son venuti a sconcertarmi," I heard him say. "Yes, they're signed 'Lock.' Yes, of course. Of course. It's got to be him. But he's retired. He's not on the faculty anymore. OK. I'll report it to the head. Thanks, Culofaccia. Sorry to interrupt your program." He then turned to me and said, "No doubt about it. It's Peter Solomon Seiltanzer. It's Skyblue. He's getting in from the outside. I didn't think of it but it has to do with the black bowler. 'Lock' is the name of the company that first made them. Only Skyblue would leave such an exotic clue. Now we can get my money and head home. Son confuso, son stordito." I had no idea who Culofaccia and Vibini were talking about, but the case was over and it didn't matter.

After reporting the solution to Fortescue and explaining the enigma and after collecting Vibini's $200, which I put in my pocket, we took the Quo Vadis cab and headed back to Vox Populi Street. I get some of my best ideas while riding in a cab, and I began to think about Fra Bartolomeo Masaccio's cryptic remarks about Baron Lucien Samedi, who was, according to Fra

Bartolomeo, the head of "Die Singende Jugend," the Illyrian secret police. Fra Bartolomeo devotes ten pages of the *Annali Calabresi,* Vol XXV, number 75, pages 472-482, to the undercover work of the agents of Baron Samedi, who was trained by the Gestapo in France in World War II. Fra Bartolomeo also records that one of the boats captured at San Benedetto del Tronto had in it a hand-drawn map of Rimini, Riccione and San Marino. Arrows showed lines of attack. With the map was a note to Baron Samedi from Queen Martha von Stoepf the First, old squint eye, old rotten butt herself. It instructed Baron Samedi to find Leonardo da Vinci, the guy who designed all the hard rock fortifications, and kidnap him back to Illyria so that he could show them how to build fortifications without cutting down all the trees. I mentioned the tree problem to Vibini and he said, "Aprite un po' quegli occhi." I thought, "Another good idea. Another set of troubles. Save the forests. Start a war. While the world slumbered." That's right, perdono, perdono, "slumbered."

Vibini and the Indian in the Woodpile

D OSTOEVSKY, FOR INSTANCE, in *Crime and Punishment*. He's one of those writers who has the idea that the criminal and the policeman form a kind of secret spiritual brotherhood. He has the idea that the criminal and the policeman need each other. They depend on each other for a kind of spiritual absolution of communal guilt. They thus seek each other out to complete their scenario of absolution. The criminal commits the crime. He needs to be caught so that he will be punished. He sends out "strong vibes" that the policeman can tune in on. They seek each other out eventually and, often clumsily, form a sacred union of guilt and absolution. There is a kind of mystical affinity between the hunter and the hunted. When the crime is punished both the criminal and the policeman have a clear conscience. They are "brothers under the skin." They are, as the saying goes, "on the same page." I love to use language like "strong vibes," "brothers under the skin" and "on the same page." It makes me feel literary because I'm incorporating everyday language, the language people really use, into my narrative. When I was a medical doctor, if we'd have said "brothers under the skin" it would have meant infection.

I mention Dostoevsky because in my belated career as a writer, I am trying to be a sophisticated stylist. I am trying to sound like a writer. I need all my newly acquired skills to tell the stories about the career of Dallasandro Vibini. I need all my literary skills now because Vibini, the great solver of petty crimes, has himself committed one for $200. The great defender of "the public weal" has gone over to the other side. He has crossed that foggy border that separates the detective from his immanent brother the criminal. He has said to law and order, "In your face," a phrase which I learned recently and which I was determined to use in one of my narratives. So there it is, reader; "get a life." Notice too my use of "public weal." You don't hear that phrase very often anymore. It shows that my linguistic borders are expanding.

Vibini's recognition of his inherent impulses began with a phone call on April 1, 1997. "April fool," you want to say. But don't. Try to be a little sophisticated. I've learned already not to write the obvious. I've learned not to trust my initial response. I'm trying to be different. You do the same. I was on the World Wide Web and cleared into the Web site at Monte Cassino. I had just called in "Fra Bartolomeo Masaccio" and discovered more than five hundred entries. Too much to handle right then. I tried *Annali Calabresi* and got 2000 entries. Still too much. So I entered "Capitano Giovanni Battista Salvatore" and got 125 entries. I was ready to begin my biography of Salvatore, the greatest of the Italian war heroes in the Illyrian-Italian War of 1945-48 when the Illyrian forces of old buttless Queen Martha von Stoepf The First, the Marxist moll from Split, sent her army against the east coast of Italy and Capitano Salvatore stood on the fortifications designed by Leonardo da Vinci at San Benedetto del Tronto, extended his right fist, slapped his left hand across his right elbow, raised his right fist in the air and yelled, "Dov'è il gabinetto," the new national motto of the newly liberated Italian nation, and received his wound because his shirt was missing two buttons so he got sunburned on his plump belly for which he received the Order of the Yellow Heart for his being wounded and the Victor Emmanuel III Royal Order of the Tin Cross with Ravioli cluster for his bravery.

I "moused" in "place of birth," because I didn't know where he was born and grew up. I like that "moused in." Nice variation in my diction. And, while waiting for my information to pop up, was just thinking what could be done in 1945 for sunburn, my medical training causing me to always be concerned about healing the wounded and the ill, when the phone rang and I answered as usual because Vibini has a paranoia about phones and won't answer them unless I call him to the phone, which is always a problem because of his bad habits.

The woman on the phone, a Sharon, or was it Susan, Holiday Inn Towel wanted to speak to the great Dallasandro Vibini. I told her that there was no "great" Vibini here, but that I'd connect her to private investigator Dallasandro Vibini, who specializes in solving petty crimes. I told her that if she was fortunate he would be with her "shortly." There's another of those words you hear a lot nowadays. No one says "soon" any more. It's always "shortly." Sharon, or was it Susan Holiday Inn Towel, said she'd wait. I should have said that Vibini would call her back. I knew it was a mistake to tell her to hold on and that he'd be with her shortly. I don't understand why I never seem to be able to remember Vibini's habits.

It was a mistake because when I opened the door to my study, the room which Vibini took over in 1995 when he moved from his apartment on Schadenfreude Street and moved into my apartment on Vox Populi Street, for which he has never paid any rent, I was greeted by a funky cloud of marijuana smoke and the ear-blistering noise of Kiri Te Kanawa singing the "Laudate Dominum" from Mozart's "Vesperae solennes de Confessore." I walked over to the CD player, turned down the music and said, "Vibini, you have a phone call. The bottom line is that you have to get out and make some money so you can help pay the rent. You know, cash flow and all that. Answer the phone. Get up out of your stupor and get to work. Haul ass." Vibini, who was real laid-back, waved me off and hissed, "Liebgott, never interrupt a 'Laudate Dominum.'"

I waited until the aria was over and said, "Vibini, it's a Miss Sharon, or Susan, Holiday Inn Towel. She wants to speak to you now." He rolled his bleary eyes at me and said, "She must be a native American Indian." I was surprised by his response and said, "Why should you think she is a native American Indian?" "Because," he

91

said, "Indians name their children after the first thing the mother sees after the child is born. Culofaccia told me that so it must be true." I didn't pay attention to what he was talking about then because I was proud of myself for using "bottom line," "cash flow" and "haul ass." Vibini took a deep drag on his little cigarette and sighed, "Liebgott, life doesn't get any better than marijuana and Mozart. As the philospher says, 'While there's life there's dope.' I'm on my way. Hold the phone. Hang the traitors. Throw caution to the wind. Live and let live. Where there's smoke there's dope. Where there's dope there's Mozart. And where you got Mozart and dope you got me and the war on crime can't go on without me and dope and Mozart and Miss Sharon, or was it Susan, Holiday Inn Washrag, or was it Towel."

When Vibini got to the phone, his client was still there so I went back to my computer to get more on Salvatore. There it was. Internet to Monte Cassino Web site and you could know that Giovanni Battista Salvatore was born on March 21, 1925, in Castelluccio Inferiore. His father was a cobbler named Gesualdo Fuscaldo Salvatore and his mother was the virgin Tinea Cruria Girandola. Giovanni was baptised in the Lao River by Father Pietro Tagliacozzo Gleet, a defrocked priest who was excommunicated because he refused to acknowledge and pay for the six children he had fathered in Policastro Busentino. The record also shows that when it came time to baptize the squalling Giovanni Battista, the Lao River was dry, so the parents, the priest and all the neighbors spit in a chalice and that was the water used to consecrate the child.

I was just starting to read about Giovanni's education and life experiences when Vibini put down the phone and stared off out a window. "Vibini," I said, "what's the new gig?" I didn't know if he knew what a "gig" is, but I was anxious to try out a new word in my Wortschatz, my vocabolario, my glossaire, my vocabulario.

Vibini wiped the sweat off his forehead with one of my linen handkerchiefs and outlined for me a petty swindle. He began by telling me that Holiday Inn Towel was not the lady's real name. I allowed as to how I had guessed as much. He said that the lady said that she used that name because she thought it made her sound like a native American Indian. I told Vibini that I remembered reading about Indians named "Fencepost" and "Two Dogs Fucking." That I knew the joke. I said, feigning innocence, "Why does she want to sound like an American Indian?" I'm learning how to play the straight man. I think that's got to be part of my equipment if I'm ever to be a writer. Vibini continued, "She wants to be a native American Indian because she's a writer. She hasn't been able to publish anything so far. She thinks that if she were to be a member of some oppressed minority she would be guaranteed publication no matter how bad her writing. She said she'd been reading stuff by so-called native American Indians and that she knew she could write better than they do. She says those so-called native American Indians all grew up in Chicago, San Francisco, New York, and went to Harvard, Bryn Mawr, Radcliffe, Columbia. She says they became Indians by sending in a coupon from a matchbook. She wants me to find an Indian in her family history. As she put it, she'll pay me

$200 to find 'the Indian in the woodpile.' She wants me to find for her an Indian ancestor so she can claim to be a native American Indian. Her real name is Sharon Rose. Her ancestry is pure Caucasian, as far as she knows. She wants me to find her a literary career."

Without saying it, I knew the spiritual brotherhood between the cop and the criminal was about to come out. I looked at the dope-streaked face of the fifty-two year old detective and said, "You're not contemplating fraud. You're not meditating deceit. You're not going over." Vibini looked at me, grinned and said, "I got to pay the rent, don't I? For $200 I'd find an Italian in her ancestry. For $200 I'd find a hedgehog in her ancestry. For $200 I'd make her a genealogy. Which is what I'll probably do. It would save a lot of work. At any rate, I'm interested in native American Indians. Culofaccia knows a lot about them. He can tell me what to do. Besides, just look at those native American Indians in Connecticut. Those Pequots have set up a gambling casino on the Mashantucket Pequot Indian Reservation and are making a fortune and you can get a cut of the profits and become rich if you can prove that you're one twenty-fourth Pequot. You don't even have to send in a matchbook coupon."

It was curious to see Vibini go to work to commit a petty crime for $200. He dressed in his green beret, his red cape, his yellow trousers and his purple spats. He set out on his search like a conquistador looking for gold. He got books from the Public Library of Hamilton County. Piles of them. I have no idea what it cost for all the rides he took on the Quo Vadis cabs. It made me wonder how many crimes are committed because we can read books for nothing. A lot of crimes must start at the check-out desk of the library. I bet you can go to most libraries and check out a book on how to rob banks. I bet you can go to a library and check out a book on how to commit rape. Not to mention embezzlement, counterfeiting, larceny, blackmail, divorce, child abuse. I've heard you can even check out books that will tell you how to build an atomic bomb.

Vibini read for two weeks. He consulted his brother Culofaccia. He checked old maps. He went to the Historical Society. He gave up marijuana. He listened to no Mozart. He became obsessed with satisfying his client by creating a background for her that did not and could not exist. He said one day to me, "Liebgott, look at this. Fake Indians at Haskell Indian Nations University in Lawrence, Kansas. I got it off the Internet in the Hamilton County Library. Here we go. People pretending to be Indians so they can get a free education at government expense. Look at this. Here are the names of the guys who were expelled when they pretended to be Indians. Paul General Hospital. George All My Children. John The Price is Right. Ringo Channel 36 Weather Report. They must have thought there were TV sets in the delivery rooms in the hospitals on the reservations." I said, "Vibini, wherever you go there's an Indian in the woodpile. You just got to find him."

Vibini smiled and said, "I have. I have found exactly the right native American connection to give to Ms. Sharon Holiday Inn Towel. She's now a member of an oppressed minority. She's from Cleveland. I almost tried to do something with her being a Cleveland Indian, but I remembered your command not to mix detective work and humor. From now on her Indian name is Susan Crack In Ceiling and her mother is Frances Flat Tire. Her father is Carl Budweiser Can and she is an enrolled member of the Sitting Stone Sioux Indian Reservation in South Dakota. I found the address in a matchbook. It cost twenty dollars to turn her into a member of a tribe."

I said, "Vibini, I don't want to hear a word of this. Stop this right now."

There was no stopping him. He went on, "Now here's how it all works. I can document it all. There are records to prove everything in this genealogy. I got all this stuff from the Historical Society Library in the Union Terminal. When the Bigfoot Sioux were wiped out at Wounded Knee on December 29, 1890, one of the soldiers, a Gerald Broadax from the Clifton area of Cincinnati was one of the troopers, Seventh Regiment, Company D, Troop C. He kept a diary of all that went on. It's there in the historical library. Just as the blizzard began to move in after the slaughter, he helped four Sioux women to escape. He hid them in a cavalry supply wagon and took them back to Fort Pisscall in Nebraska and put them onto a train back to Omaha. One of those women was a Belle Buffalo Dung who managed to get to Cincinnati and set herself up in business as an interpreter of dreams. She already knew that White people have this idea about Indians that they have some special relation with the dream world. She was very successful at her business because the people of Cincinnati were suckers for dream literature. They all thought it was just swell.

She went by the name of Dreamboat Rose. Her motto, written in Sioux signs across a piece of driftwood fished out of the Ohio River, was 'Ad Majoram Dei Gloriam.' It was a PR coup. The German Roman Catholics of the city paid her so much money for her dream interpretations that the Roman Catholic clergy tried to get the city council to pass a city ordinance against dream deciphering, against what they called 'oneiromancy,' because they were losing all their Sunday income."

"Vibini, please," I said. "Enough,"

He continued, "They shouldn't have concerned themselves because Dreamboat Rose made a big mistake. She predicted to Boss Cox that if he extended the city sewer lines to his private home on Jefferson Avenue the ravens would come and bury the city in bird shit. Boss Cox built the sewer. The birds didn't come. And Broadax, who had been dishonorably discharged from the cavalry for sodomizing his mule Katie, returned to Cincinnati in 1900 where he was given a hero's welcome. After the parade up Ludlow Avenue to Mt. Storm Park, Broadax helped Dreamboat escape once again. Except this time he went with her to Cleveland, where they got married and had a family of fifteen girls. They kept the name of Rose, dumped the name Broadax because it sounded so stupid to them, and went once again into the dream interpreting business. One of those girls, Philistine Rose, gave birth to a daughter. And that's where Broadax's diary ends."

"All right," I said. "OK. That's it."

"No," Vibini said. "There's more."

"I'm sure," I said. "I'm sure there's lots more."

Vibini went on, "Now, there's that anonymous daughter who was born to Philistine Rose, I'd guess, about 1920, because Dreamboat, the anonymous daughter's grandmother, was only sixteen when she first came to Cincinnati in 1891. She and Broadax went to Cleveland in 1900. So the mother of Sharon Holiday Inn Towel was born about 1920 and Sharon was born, by her own admission, in 1940. There you have it. Sharon is the great-granddaughter of Bigfoot Sioux, that is, of native American Indians, who suffered that terrible oppression at Wounded Knee. Does that make her a kind of octoroon? I don't know about that. You can check it out. The Broadax diary is available to anyone. Whoever wants to see it can see it in the Historical Library. You can still find pieces of driftwood along the Ohio River. The citizens of Cincinnati still can be swindled by any drifter who comes to town. They still listen to charlatans. That's why they continue to vote Republican."

I leaned back and looked at Vibini, who lit up a joint while he wrote out a bill for $200 for Sharon Holiday Inn Towel. I said, "Vibini, you're not going to do this. You're joking. This all sucks. You're not going to set up this would-be writer?" Vibini looked at me and said, "You can bet your sweet ass I am," and I knew I had to get him off Ludlow Avenue because he was starting to talk like the bartenders at Arlin's Bar and Garden. Then I thought to myself, "It's that fucking Internet. What oh what has that fucking Internet done to our fucking world?" and realized that I too at the age of sixty-seven had gone over.

A month later, during a rainy, dull, lifeless spring day, Vibini was hidden in a cloud of smoke. Mozart's

"Great Mass In C" was blasting across the limits of decibel possibilities. I was on the Internet and hooked into the Monte Cassino Web site and the file for Salvatore. I had just read in Masaccio's *Annali Calabresi*, XXI, 36, pages 86-94, that Capitano Giovanni Battista Salvatore was monorchid, that is, he had only one *testicolo*, that in 1948, after the defeat of Queen Martha von Stoepf The First and her Marxist horde, he married Beatrice Gallina Farona in Falconara Marittima. He opened there a fish market and sold squid to the impoverished Illyrians who crossed over and, in complete awe of the great capitano, paid double prices just to get squid from his barrel. Giovanni and Beatrice subsequently had seven sons, all of whom, Bartolemeo Masaccio remarks, looked remarkably like Illyrian soldiers.

The Berlin Radio Symphony Orchestra and the St. Hedwig's Cathedral Choir under the direction of Ferenc Fricsay had just begun the "Qui tollis peccata mundi" when the phone rang. It was a woman. She said, "Is this Gottlieb Hakenkreuz Flying in the Wind?" I said it was and she said, "This is Butterfly Dancing on the Breeze. Let me speak to Chief Dallasandro Vibini." I put down the phone and signaled to Vibini. He turned down the Mozart. He came to the phone. I handed it to him and said, "It's for Chief Dallasandro Vibini." Vibini said, "Hello, Heap Big Chief Vibini, also better known as Dallasandro Vomit on the Floor." An ear-busting war whoop came over the phone. I could hear it clear across the room. Vibini said, "Congratulations. Now please send me my $200. That's the bottom line."

Vibini and the woman talked for a long time and when he hung up the phone I said, "Vibini, who was that?" He said, "That, my dear Dr. Liebgott, was Sharon Holiday Inn Towel. Her novel *The Sacred Buck* has been accepted by Gitchee Gumee Press and she will receive a $50,000 advance. She says the reviewers are already calling it a major novel dealing with the oppressed native American Indians. When I asked her what the book is about she said that it's all about Indians and their dreams, how they enter the dream world and return, how they talk to animals, how there is a spiritual affinity between the hunter and his prey, his wild brother, who brings spiritual enlightenment to the hunter by presenting himself to be killed by the hunter. She says there's a lot of that Ghost Dance crap in the book. She says the book is really just a bunch of South Dakota fairy tales and the Gitchee Gumee Press is buying it. She says she's just writing what White people think Indians are like. She says the biography that I discovered for her is printed in the back of the book and that she's dedicated the book to me. The dedication doesn't give my name. It just says, 'For D.V., who found the Indian in the woodpile.'"

I thought, "Dostoevsky, in your face. You and I are now on the same page."

VIBINI AND THE VIRGIN TONGUE

TAKE JOSEPH CONRAD, for instance. When he writes his stories he uses a literary language that is clear, simple and precise. I did see a place where he says a barge leaked "like a sieve" and sometimes his language is awkward and pretentious. He was, after all, like me, not a native speaker of English. But usually he writes English prose about as well as anyone ever has. I'm studying his writing, along with the other great writers, because as I get further into my writing career I'm trying to find the best literary language I can. I want to develop a style that does exactly what I want it to do. I need a language that is not burdened by past usage. I need a language that is not burdened by connotation. I need a style that is not worn out with repetition and is new and my own. I need that style because Dallasandro Vibini is in love. The idea overwhelms me. I need a language that disciplines my thoughts, a language that will not mislead me or pervert my feelings. I need a virgin tongue.

On Thursday, May 1, 1997, it was cold and rainy. There was a strong breeze. The day before, April 30, it was springtime. The sun was shining in one of its 100 days per year that it shines here in Cincinnati. The flowering trees were gorgeous. The redbud, the dogwood, all glorious in their flowering. The temperature was seventy-five degrees Fahrenheit. That night, about midnight, a cold front moved in with high winds. The temperature dropped rapidly. The winds cleaned the petals from the flowering trees. On May the First we were back to wintry weather.

I need to tell you all this because it was on that day, Thursday, that my story begins. It was late in the evening. Vibini sat in my study, the room he now calls "his room," smoked marijuana and said complacently to me, "Liebgott, I've fallen in love for the first time in my life. Her name is Saponata Santarellina and she's a librarian at the Clifton Branch of the Cincinnati Public Library. I know she's seventeen years old because I heard her tell another librarian that today was her seventeenth birthday and her father had given her an air flight ticket to Rome, Italy, so that she could visit the ancestral home of the family in Falconara Marittima and eat the local squid, and I'm taking her out to dinner on Saturday evening."

I was busy tracing out the life story of the Italian war hero from the Illyrian-Italian War of 1945-1948, Giovanni Battista di Gesualdo da Castelluccio Inferiore Salvatore. I was hooked into the Web site at Monte Cassino and was reading through Volume XXVI, number 42, pages 345-392 in Bartolomeo Masaccio's *Annali Calabresi* when Vibini's mention of Falconara Marittima caught my attention and diverted me from the fact that Masaccio mentions, in passing, that all the men in the Salvatore family, from the earliest records to 1948, were monorchids, that is, each had "uno testicolo." Masaccio had just described the Salvatore family crest, a gold circle inside of which and from the top of which hangs a black thread with a pink ball at the bottom end of it, a thread which passes between the open blades of a red scissors, and beneath the golden circle the motto of the Salvatore family, which is "One for all and all from one." When Vibini said something about Falconara Marittima and squid, I turned from my computer screen and paid attention to what he had to say.

I looked through his marijuana smoke and said, "How could you? You're fifty-one years old. You've never been married. You've never had anything to do with women, except as clients. If you pursue this woman, you'll be robbing the cradle." I immediately realized that I had used a cliché and I apologized. Even if Conrad did use a cliché once, that doesn't give me the license to do it. Then the phone rang. I answered it, of course, since Vibini won't pick it up for any reason. It was Father Gottlob Schlag from Our Lady of the Denunciation Church. He wanted Vibini. I handed Vibini the phone and said it was Father "Praise God" Schlag. I heard Vibini say, "I won't kiss your aspergillum, if that's why you're calling." I heard an explosion of language from the other end of the line and Vibini smiled at me, made kissing motions with his lips, waved his left hand at me and didn't hang up.

While Vibini talked to Father Schlag, I thought about the day before, Wednesday, April 30, when the weather had been so gloriously springlike. I had taken a walk along Vox Populi Street in the afternoon. The flowering trees had all survived the early April freeze when the temperature dropped to the lowest reading ever recorded in April in Cincinnati. The trees were loaded with blossoms. The white petals covered the sidewalks. I walked around the neighborhood, bathed in the bounty of spring. Redbud. Dogwood. All in bloom. As I walked, I realized why May the First is the time of revolution, of sexual license and new love.

As I thought about that walk and while Vibini talked on the phone, I realized that he had been conned by Mother Nature. I realized that he had fallen for that great annual swindle we call spring. It was appalling to me that a man of Vibini's intellect would be taken in by the smell of daffodils, the wafting breezes and the tender butt of a seventeen year old girl. But why not? Our literature is full of the victims of springtime. Just think of the infinite number of innocent writers and readers who have been brainwashed by the literary conventions about spring. If Vibini had grown up in Wuppertal, Germany, as I did, he'd not get taken in by those literary conventions. Springtime in Germany doesn't fool anyone. There's flowers and soft breezes, all right. But in Germany no matter how many daffodils you lie down in, you can't cover up the stench of those winter-cured armpits. The springtime zephyrs in Germany carry to your tingling nostrils the odors of rotten crotches and death.

That's why I'm so concerned about my language. How can I tell the story of a fifty-one year old man who falls in love with a seventeen year old librarian? How can I avoid the clichés, the stereotypes, the prescription plots? What do I have? Dallasandro Vibini, the great detective and solver of petty crimes. I have Saponata, librarian. Lovers in springtime, virgins, dogwood in bloom. How can a writer match with language that delicious moment in human existence? I know already that there is no language that can do it. I know the writer is doomed to forget it all or distort it. The writer is doomed to forget it and thus deprive mankind of that glory of first love or to try to articulate it and create a lie because of the imperfections and shortcomings of his linguistic vehicle. No wonder writers use indirection. No wonder they avoid direct confrontation with the ecstatic moment and divert the reader's gaze to Italian military history. No wonder they realize the ineffability of the human condition and sell out by avoiding trying to tell it at all. No wonder they betray their high calling and insult the reader by referring him to the mundane, the diurnal refuse of his existence. That's why, I now realize, at moments of high emotional interest in a narrative, writers fall back upon clichés and into iambic pentameter. They wouldn't do that if they had available to them a virgin tongue.

Vibini hung up the phone. I stared at my screen. I noted that someone named Massimo Santarellina had written in the margin of the *Annali Calabresi* volume that I was reading that the oldest son of Giovanni Battista Salvatore, Sigismondo Pandolfo di Giovanni da Falconara Marittima Salvatore, had emigrated to the United States and had settled in Cincinnati, Ohio. I jumped at the note. No. I carefully read the note. Joseph Conrad would never have anyone jumping at a note. The note was not in Masaccio's handwriting. The note made it all too evident how clear and pure Masaccio's style was. The note clearly was not by Masaccio. I thought, "If Salvatore's son is in Cincinnati, I must find him. He can give me direct information for my biography of his father. What a great break for my research. I've got to get on it right off."

Vibini turned to me and said, "Liebgott, I have a commission. Father Schlag wants me to find him a saint for his church." When Vibini makes a statement like that, I go into my straight man act. I suppressed my laughter and said, as innocently as possible, "Why does Father Schlag want you to find a saint for his church?" Vibini took a long drag on his joint and explained it all to me. "Father Schlag's church is called 'Our Lady of the Denunciation.' It's called that because it's named for Peter's threefold denunciation of Christ. Father Schlag doesn't like the negative implications of the name. He wants an upbeat saint, one his parishioners can be proud of, a saint that no one else has taken for a patron saint." I stopped him and said, "Why not just look in The *Golden Legend*, the *Acta Sanctorum, The Lives of the Saints* or *The Penguin Dictionary of Saints?* I mean, there are whole lists of saints and martyrs. Just close your eyes, open a book at random and point to one. Divine wisdom will select what you need." "No," Vibini said, "Father Schlag wants a modern saint, someone who answers to modern needs. He says all the relatives and friends of Jesus have been used up. All the Apostles and Disciples have been used up. He wants a saint all his own, a saint no one else has." I said, "Sounds to me like he wants one of the Beatles, a

106

senator from Kansas, a football coach from Notre Dame, a congressman from Georgia, a leader of the Medellin Cartel."

Vibini looked at me with disgust. "You Lutherans don't understand Catholic beliefs. You just make a joke out of our religion. You tried to blow the Roman Catholic Church out of the holy water of history and now you refuse to understand what we stand for." I said, "You got it wrong. We Lutherans didn't try to blow the Roman Catholic Church out of the holy water of history. We tried to blow the holy water out of the history of the church." And they say we Germans have no sense of humor. Vibini continued, "Father Schlag wants to find more than a saint for his church. He wants me to find a candidate for beatification and later canonization. He wants to start from scratch. He wants to create his own saint. He says that if the Pope can canonize a Gypsy, his church can find someone. I'm to find a candidate for sainthood and then find the evidence for his beatification and canonization." I said, "How much will he pay you?" "Father Schlag says that he will pay me the offering from Quasimodo Sunday when I find the candidate and the evidence. And if I find that candidate and he is made into a saint, I won't ever again be asked to kiss his aspergillum."

I said, in phony innocence, "Won't Father Schlag need a saint's relic from this saint, whoever he is? Shouldn't he ask for a saint who still has a piece of him lying around somewhere so Father Schlag can put a piece of his saint in his altar?" "No," Vibini said, "Father Schlag tells me that there is a martyrs' parts catalogue published by the Vatican and he can order a piece from Rome." I couldn't resist. I said, "Which part do you think Father Schlag might prefer? It might make a difference in your choice if only certain pieces still exist." Vibini smiled and said, "Father Schlag wants, for his saint's relic, the proximal, the medial and the distal phalanges from the middle finger of the right hand. He wants, he says, the bones involved in the Italian salute." My respect for Father Schlag went up immensely and I said, "I bet those bones are scattered all over the sites of martyrdom. They're probably still hooked together after two thousand years. They're probably the cheapest ones in the catalogue. You could probably find them at the site of the great battle of San Benedetto del Tronto where Giovanni Battista Salvatore repelled the Illyrian invasion by giving them the Italian salute and crying out, 'Dov'è il gabinetto.'"

Vibini's eyes were glazed over from his marijuana. He said good night and locked himself into "my study," or, as he calls it now, "his room." He put on a record of Mozart's "Gran Partita," turned up the volume and soon that sweet smoke of meditation drifted through the cracks under and around the door. I thought about what that library had done to Vibini. I remembered my earlier meditations on the ways in which a free public library is a dangerous thing. I realized that any crazy can go in there and find what he wants to find. Someone can go into a free public library and check out a book on how to blow up this world, how to overthrow a nation, how to torture animals, how to find a candidate for sainthood, how to fall in love and when.

I was surprised, I must admit, that it never occurred to me that a free public library might be an emotional trap for a fifty-one year old man. It never occurred to me that a librarian might be one of the dangers of a library. It never occurred to me that a free public library might also offer free public love. I'm sure the founders of the public libraries never had love in mind. I'm sure the founders of the institution never realized that spring and a librarian might be a dangerous combination, but look what happened to Vibini. Perhaps, I thought, if Vibini continues his love affair he might become that martyr that he seeks. He could be the patron saint of librarians. Perhaps, I thought, I might be that martyr if I don't find that virgin tongue I need to tell this story. I could be the patron saint of failed authors.

Somehow, when I think of spring, love, perfect sentences, narratives full of grace and dignity, the lovely hands of the librarians checking out books, stamping the dates in the backs of the covers, running the little light gun over my library card and saying thank you when returning the card and smiling, I think of sleep. It was late and I felt drowsy. It occurred to me that somehow sleep is the natural state of man. Maybe I thought about sleep again because libraries are great places for the induction and imposition of sleep. Wherever we are, we long for sleep all day long. Wakefulness is a burden and is therefore an unnatural state of being. God and sleep have something to do with each other. When God created all things, the universe was asleep. God woke up the universe. He separated light from darkness, that is, He separated wakefulness from sleep. Our birth is a waking from the sleep of the womb. Our death is a return to that sleep. After all, our lives are but brief moments when we consider how long we slept before we were born and how long we will sleep when we die.

Most of our existence, then, is a condition of sleep. Sleep is our normal state of being; wakefulness is abnormal. Our brains develop when we sleep, not when we're awake. God rewards us with sleep when we suffer. For instance, when we are bored God sends sleep to relieve our suffering. Sin came into this world when man first awakened and came to consciousness. There is no sin, war, suffering, when we sleep. Michelangelo shows God touching Adam's finger to awaken him to a life of disobedience, suffering, murder, war and boredom. We pay a great price for our unnatural state of wakefulness. It's in wakefulness that we fall in love, suffer from the blandishments of spring, are assaulted by bad fiction and bad poetry, suffer the obsessions of priests, worry about writing good prose, contact the sources of Italian military history, find the data on the lives of Italian war heroes.

The next morning, Vibini called a Quo Vadis Cab. That was last Friday, May 2, just two days ago. He said he was headed downtown to the main library to do some research. After he left, I booted up my computer and got onto the Internet. I was hot on the trail of the oldest of Giovanni Battista Salvatore's seven sons, Sigismondo Pandolfo, the one who had emigrated to the U.S. and settled in Cincinnati. I got onto the Monte Cassino Web site and right into the *Annali Calabresi,* volume XLV, where I discovered that Bartolomeo Masaccio had recorded a lot of information about Giovanni Battista

Salvatore. I read that the young war hero had taken as his family motto, "A squid in the barrel is worth two in the sea." I saw that his family crest was "Aut lolligo, aut nihil." I read with extreme interest that Giovanni Battista Salvatore's great-grandfather Cristoforo Mali Acquistato Salvatore may not have been a legitimate son of his father Lodovico Allesandro di Mariano Salvatore. Masaccio records that it was a widely circulated rumor around Castelluccio Inferiore that Giovanni Battista's great-grandfather Cristoforo was stolen from Gypsies when he was a baby and raised by Giovanni's great-great-grandfather as his own son because he had no sons, just fifteen daughters, none of whom would or could leave home because he could not afford to pay any dowries.

That Cristoforo Mali Acquistato Salvatore was stolen from Gypsies would account for the fact that the Salvatore males from then on all have just that one *testicolo*. I discovered also that that child stolen from Gypsies had a tattoo on the left cheek of his butt. The tattoo was the number eighteen with an arrow through it pointing from upper right to lower left. That tattoo, Masaccio writes, was the sign of the Illyrian Gypsy King Piccinoscroto the Eighteenth. Wherever that tattoo came from, the Salvatores, to this day, tattoo their sons in the same way on the day they are born. That way they know that if their sons are stolen by Gypsies the family will be able to identify them, even if it is thirty years later.

I found out also in that Volume XLV, that Giovanni Battista Salvatore had called together the veterans of the Illyrian-Italian War when Queen Martha von Stoepf the

First had called a halt to her attacks on Italy in 1948 and decided to retire and spend her last days eating squid in Split. Giovanni Battista gathered the veterans at a meeting in Falconara Marittima on Sunday, June 20, 1948. There they decided that September the Eighth would be henceforth Italian Army Day and that on that day every Italian war veteran would fly a white flag from the front porch of his house. They decided also that on that day they would all wear their medals of the Royal Order of the Yellow Heart and their Victor Emmanuel III Royal Order of the Tin Star with Ravioli, Fettucini or Garlic Clusters. The veterans also decided that henceforth the Italian national anthem would be the "Dies irae, dies illa" of Tomasso a Celano arranged in four part harmony for a male quartet. After the meeting ended, the veterans indulged themselves in a huge meal of Apulian tortellini al dente and ate smoked calamari, all prepared by Franciscan vegetarians.

Just before closing out my computer, I noted with great surprise that among the list of veterans who attended the meeting was Ruggiero Vibini, father of Culofaccia and Dallasandro, although Ruggiero was a veteran of World War I. Probably the young veterans invited him because Ruggiero made the supreme sacrifice in World War I when he got his penis shot off at the Piave during the retreat from Caporetto in 1917. Maybe they invited Ruggiero because his wife had given birth in 1945 to his second son Dallasandro, even though it had been a long time since the first son Culofaccia was born in 1925 and so it had been some twenty years between the times when Ruggiero had dipped his wick, or what was left of it. Culofaccia was not listed as a guest even though he had suffered shell shock at the Battle of Brindisi in 1945. Perhaps he had already left for America.

I spent all day Friday on the computer and had a wonderful day. Just after six o'clock I was just starting to relax when I heard the Quo Vadis Cab squeal to a halt in front of my apartment. I heard the door slam. I heard someone pounding up the stairs. It was Vibini. He burst through the door and cried out, "Liebgott, you should see Sudsy's nape. You would cry out in ecstatic wonder if you could but gaze upon that nubile skin under her dirty collar." I thought, how can I write all this? How can I find a language commensurate with Vibini's craziness? How can I find a tongue capable of articulating Dallasandro Vibini's surreal capers? Then it came to me. Why didn't I think of it before? It's always there. It's always available. When you have to talk about insanity, German is your perfect language. With Vibini off his rocker, I can, if necessary, just go back to my first language. I can tell it all and get it all right in German, the language of confusion, the language of the nuthouse. It wasn't chance that Wagner, Marx, Kafka, Freud and Hitler wrote in German. Maybe later. I'll try English first.

"Wait a minute," I cried out. "Vibini, who is this 'Sudsy?' And what's this stuff about a nape beneath a dirty collar?" "Oh Liebgott, you should see her. She's so lovely." I thought, it's this accursed springtime. This would never happen in Wuppertal where the winter slathers foul smells across the skin and no one wants to stand next to anyone else, not even in church. Vibini blurted out, "Sudsy? Why that's Saponata Santarellina,

113

the librarian at the Clifton Branch of the public library. I told you about her yesterday. The librarians call her 'Sudsy.' Today she helped me at the 'Cinch,' the computer where you can look up all the books in the main library and in the branch libraries and call for any one of them. I was looking for books about martyrs and she came up and leaned against me and showed me how to do it. I thought I'd die right there on the keyboard. And then when I did check out a book, I did it just so I could watch her lean over the check-out desk and scan my library card with her little light gun and ring the book up in the computer and while she did that I looked right down the back of her blouse and saw that tender, dirty nape. When the little light gun beeped, she looked up and smiled at me and said thank you. Here's the book I checked out. It's called *Going to the Mountain*. I checked it out because Sudsy recommended it. You can read it if you want to. I'm not going to read it. I'm just going to return it tomorrow and then check out another book. Oh, Gottlieb, I'm hooked, I'm afraid."

I thought I would change the subject before Vibini started sighing and weeping, so I said, "Surely you didn't spend all day at the Clifton Branch of the library. It doesn't open until 1:00 P.M." "Oh, no no no," he said. "I spent all morning at the downtown library. I found nothing there. The librarians there were rude and wouldn't help me at all. They all looked as if they were about to fall asleep. And did they stink. After I checked out my book at the Clifton Library, I went over to see a Biblical scholar. Sudsy told me about him. I was trying to find my stuff in the regular library collection and she said to forget it. She said, 'Go see the expert. Go see Aristarchus Skiamachos over on Shekinah Avenue. He's called Ari the Hermeneutist.' She said that he comes in all the time and checks out books about golf, intestinal disruptions and the Bible. He's a sports nut, evidently."

I interrupted him and said, "I assume you went right over to his house."

"I did indeed. I walked over to his house and he received me most cordially. When I told him that I was looking for a martyr who could be made into a saint for Father Schlag's Church of the Denunciation, he knew exactly what I wanted. He took me into his library and said, 'I think what you should look into is *The Gospel According To Oholibamah*' He explained to me that *The Gospel According To Oholibamah* is a pseudepigraphon, a scripture that was never accepted as canonical by the Jews, the Christians or the Roman Catholics. The early Christian Oholibamah seems to have written it about forty-five A.D. Or, as Ari said, 'C.E.' That, he explained, makes it earlier even than *The Gospel According To Mark*. When I asked him why the *The Gospel According To Oholibamah* was never recognized as canonical, he said that it may have had to do with the fact that Oholibamah was a leper who tried to get Jesus of Nazareth to heal him and that when Jesus laid his hands on Oholibamah's left arm it fell off. Which was O.K. because Oholibamah was right-handed and could still walk to Decapolis and there write down the first of the Gospels. What is important about that first Gospel, Ari pointed out, is that it contains the first of the birth narratives. In it you will find the first story we have about Eutychus of Troas."

115

I was getting lost in the details. I was getting lost in trying to follow all of Vibini's data. I was being overcome by the fact that I had no language adequate to the task of recording the whole story and making sense of it. I said, "Wait a minute, Vibini. Let me get a drink of water and then you can go on." I got my glass of water, even though I wasn't thirsty. When I came back into the room, Vibini was already talking. "Now. Listen to this." I said, "Wait a minute. I thought the library didn't have any books you wanted." "They didn't," he said. "Skiamachos loaned me his copy of *The Gospel According To Oholibamah* and Bruce Rumbumsen's *Sleep and Its By-Products*." I noticed he used "loaned" instead of "lent." I took a sip of that lousy Cincinnati water and thought, "I'm afraid to ask what this is all about. Here I was concerned about a virgin tongue and the fact of Giovanni Battista Salvatore having *uno testicolo* and Vibini comes up with all this stuff." I decided not to ask about *Sleep and Its By-Products*.

Vibini continued. "Just listen to this," he said and he began to read from *The Gospel According To Oholibamah*, chapter 2, verses 8 and forward. I've copied it all down for posterity. I wouldn't want anyone to miss it.

"In the year when Yobab was first ruler of Pseudo-Syria, the boy Eutychus was born in the city of Abydus in the region of Troas. He waxed strong in his youth and his father, an executioner by trade, instructed him in the art of a wandering minstrel. When he was eighteen years of age, the youth left his father's house to travel through the known world. He was received in many homes and mansions where he played upon his harp and told the stories of the ancient world. In the year when Caesar Augustus declared that all the world should be taxed and Cyrenius was the governor of Syria, the youthful Eutychus was passing through Judea. When night fell upon him and there was no light to guide him, he paused in his wanderings to question a group of shepherds who were sitting on a hillside, keeping watch over their flocks by night. He asked of them the road to Bethlehem. The shepherds said one to another, 'Lo, it is late and darkness is on the earth. This man cannot find his way to the city. Let us entreat him to tarry with us until the dawn.' Eutychus thanked the shepherds for their kindness. For their generosity he sat by their fire with them and told them a story so that they might remain awake and guard against the evils of the night."

I wanted to hear this uncanonical story by Eutychus so I leaned back and listened. Vibini continued, "The wanderer Eutychus laid down his harp and spoke: 'When the Grecian hero Odysseus returned to his kingdom in Ithaka after his long exile because of the Trojan War, his wife Penelope was besieged by suitors. Odysseus destroyed the suitors and began his life again as a husband and as a ruler. When three years had passed after his return, Penelope was taken from him by the gods and Odysseus began the life of an aging and wifeless king. His son Telemachus was also taken from him by the gods when he was killed in the Vale of Peneus by an enraged unicorn and the ruling king was left with no heir. When the hero Odysseus visited King Alexikakos on the Island of Cephallenia, the aging Odysseus was smitten by the beauty of Alexikakos' young daughter. He asked for the hand of the seventeen year old Oneirodynia and was given the maiden in marriage. But when the fifty-one year old man took the seventeen year old maiden home to his island kingdom of Ithaka, she invited many young men into her house. The young men drove the ancient king out of his island and onto the mainland. He wandered across Acarnania, Aetolia, Thessaly, Macedonia and Thrace until he came to the Hellespont where he crossed to the windy plains of Troy. He came at last to the ruins of the once great city where he had once fought so valiantly and there he laid himself down and died. After his death, the gods took Odysseus into the heavens and made him into a star. His star appears very bright in the sky and can be seen only above the place where a seventeen year old virgin has just given birth to a king.'

"Eutychus finished his story. The shepherds remained wakeful. The heavens filled with winged messengers. Angels' voices came upon the shepherds. The voices cried out, 'Go to Bethlehem and see the child who has come to redeem the world.' The shepherds cried out in fear. The angels said not to be afraid and to go. Eutychus told them to believe what they had seen. The shepherds did as they were commanded. As they left, they gave thanks to Eutychus, who had kept them awake so that they might receive the voice of God and welcome in the Messiah, the Savior of the World. Eutychus sat alone by the fire and watched the sheep until the shepherds should return. He realized in his heart that he was now the servant of the Lord."

"Vibini," I said, "what does this all have to do with the price of squid?" "Wait," said Vibini. "There's more. In *The Gospel According To Oholibamah* the narrator tells how Eutychus searched all of his life to find that savior who was born that night in Bethlehem when he, Eutychus the Minstrel, sat out there in the cold and froze his harp and fingers, but he was without success. Until, when he was a sixty-seven year old man, Eutychus came home to Troas where one night he chanced upon a man preaching in the third floor of a house. He was preaching the 'Gospel of Jesus of Nazareth,' born in the City of David, called Bethlehem, and Eutychus knew his journey had ended. Unfortunately, Eutychus, being of great age, fell asleep while he sat and listened. Because he was sitting in a third floor window, he fell to the courtyard below and was severely injured. But the Apostle Paul, who was the preacher, healed the old man and baptised him and Eutychus officially became a Christian."

I was getting anxious for Vibini to get done with his recital so I said, "And there's that other book that Skiamachos lent you. I'll bet that book's important too." "That's right," Vibini said. "It's just what I was looking for. It's called *Sleep and Its By-Products* by Bruce Rumbumsen. See, it's recent. It was published in Gnadenhutten, Ohio, in 1996, by the R.E.M. Press." "So what?" I said. "Who cares?" I wanted to get back to my computer. But Vibini was not to be stopped. "Look," he said. "Here's chapter 12 in the book. The chapter is called 'Sleep and Religion' and in it the author quotes a long passage from what is called *Celestine's Book of Martyrs*. In this chapter 12 the author quotes from the *Book of*

Martyrs, which was compiled in 1198 C.E. by Fra Sonnifero Dormiglione a Poggio Mirteto. The book was put together at the request of Giacinto Bobone, Pope Celestine III, who was Pope from 1191-1198 C.E. It was this Pope who baptised the young Francis of Assisi, who later became a saint.

"Now here's where *Sleep and Its By-Products* becomes interesting. In *Celestine's Book of Martyrs,* the compiler includes the martyrdom of Eutychus of Troas. Fra Sonnifero Dormiglione a Poggio Mirteto writes that after his baptism by the Apostle Paul, Eutychus, even though he was sixty-seven years old, was sent out to convert the Scythians, as he writes, 'to the northward of the known world.' Eutychus went there to baptize the heathens in the name of the Father, the Son and the Holy Ghost. When he arrived in Scythia, he played his harp for the heathens and began telling them about how Jesus of Nazareth raised people from the dead and how Jesus himself rose from the dead after being crucified and after being in the tomb for three days. Eutychus didn't even have time to say his prayers or drop his harp before he was hanging on a cross himself. After he died the Scythians cut off his head, which is their custom. They peeled the skin off his skull and made it into a handkerchief, which is their custom. They cleaned the meat off his skull and used the skull for a drinking cup, which is their custom.

"Now here's what's important. When the early Christians learned about the martyrdom of Eutychus, they began to pray to him to help them in their insomnia because he had kept the shepherds awake. They began to pray for his intercession when they wanted to fall asleep and when they wanted to stay awake. He was prayed to, for instance, before the *Pervigilium Veneris*."

That was all on Friday, May 2. The next morning, Saturday, yesterday, Vibini was up early. His Quo Vadis Cab came by at 8:00 A.M. and he was off to do more research. I asked him what he was looking for that day and he said he needed to find evidence that real miracles had happened when people prayed for the intercession of Eutychus of Troas. He said he was off to Mariemont and the Roman Catholics. They, he said, believe in miracles. They, he said, believe that if you pay a sales tax of one half cent on the dollar two stadiums will rise up by the Ohio River. They, he said, believe that if you pray strenuously enough the Cincinnati Reds will win baseball games. They, he said, believe that if you pray sincerely the poor people in Cincinnati will all move to Dayton, Ohio. They, he said, believe that if you pray hard enough God will forgive the Republicans who lied in order to get elected. They, he said, believe that if you pray seriously enough and long enough the University of Cincinnati will turn into an educational institution.

When Vibini in his red cape, his black beret and his purple spats had gone away from me, I returned to my research and happened onto Masaccio's remarks about St. Hermenegildo in Volume XLIX of the *Annali Calabresi*. There I learned that St. Hermenegildo was the protector of testicles and was the patron saint of the Salvatore family. That all seemed fair enough for a family of monorchids. I also learned that the head of St. Hermenegildo was on one side of the holy medals that Italian soldiers pinned to their skirts in the Illyrian-Italian War when they cross-dressed and camouflaged themselves as women in order to infiltrate the enemy ranks, seduce the Illyrian soldiers, lead them away from the battlefield and blow them away in a trattoria. The other side of the medals, which were sold in order to pay for the rebuilding of Monte Cassino, had the face of an Italian soldier above two crossed white flags. Those medals had all been blessed at Monte Cassino to help the soldiers win a battle or help an Italian golfer win a golf tournament.

Everything that happened yesterday is still clear in my mind. With Vibini gone, I decided to walk over to the library and see this bibliographic beauty, Saponata Santarellina, who had captivated the aging heart of Dallasandro Vibini. I dressed in my black three-piece suit, put on my gold watch with its gold chain across my fat belly, clapped my black homburg on my head and waddled down Vox Populi Street to Clifton Avenue, along Ludlow and entered the library. I was disgusted at first. The place was filled with derelicts. A man, I believe, sat at one table and made scratching lines across a sheet of a yellow legal pad. One fat man with gray hair and dirty, bagging trousers yelled at the librarians to get him the new newspapers. One old lady slumped over a table and rubbed her nose in *The New York Times*.

I looked about and wondered which of the librarians could be Sudsy. I didn't realize at first how conspicuous I was. Everyone was looking at me. I was the only clean person in the building. I tried to look down the back of the blouse of one of the librarians. She was old and freckled down her spine and smelled like cut cabbage. I sidled up beside another librarian who was younger than the first one I saw, but who had on a clean collar. I could see that lower down her faded pink bra strap was frayed. She gave off the odor of old socks. Another of the librarians wore no bra and I could see clearly when I glanced down the front of her blouse that the nipples on her breasts pointed east and west. As I held my breath and tried to get a better look at the collar on her blouse, I heard someone say, "Sudsy, call the cops." I was pressing up against another librarian for an on-site inspection, a woman whose hair smelled like vinegar and whose hair looked electrified, when someone tapped me on the shoulder. A man's voice said, "Mister, we don't allow no creeps in here in Clifton." I turned to the short, young man who had sandy hair, a red complexion and a large belly, and said, "Sir, I am Dr. Gottlieb Liebgott. I am no creep, I assure you. I am retired from the medical profession and I'm here to do research for my narratives." The young man who smelled like tires said, "Yeah, and I'm Sherlock Holmes. I saw you ogling the librarians. I saw you looking down their blouses." I said, "Are you a policeman?" He looked out the dirty window and said, "I'm Horton Stayne. I'm Clifton's watchdog. I'm paid by the Clifton Town Meeting to keep creeps like you out of our neighborhood. Now get going." I said quietly, "I just wanted to meet Saponata Santarellina. She's a friend of my boarder Dallasandro Vibini." I heard a tiny voice say, "I'm Saponata. You must be the idiot that Vibini lives with." I turned and my language failed me.

Saponata Santarellina was, in a word, "beautiful." She was young, fresh, tempting, you name it. I was astounded. She looked exactly like the figure of Flora in Alessandro Filipepi Botticelli's "Primavera." Like Botticelli's Flora, she looked gravid with immanent lust. She had thin, long blond hair, the same heavy eyelids, the same pale green eyes, the slightly opened mouth, a slight flush around her neck as if she were in the early stages of some kind of overwhelming and inexorable erotic ecstasy. It was her skin that was the most sensual of all. Pale white. A slight touch of pink. Perhaps incipient freckles. I gazed down the dirty white gauze collar. I breathed in her delicate aroma of hyacinths. She said, "So you're the fat slob who lives with Dally." I noted the "lives with" and I said, "No, madam. I'm Dr. Gottlieb Liebgott and Vibini lives with me. He lives in my apartment and in my study." She giggled and turned away. Horton Stayne grabbed my right elbow and pushed me towards the door. "You've bothered these ladies enough. Go stare at some other ladies' tits," he said and shoved me out onto the sidewalk. I walked away with all the dignity I could practice. I decided I'd better join the Clifton Town Meeting.

When Vibini returned yesterday evening, he was ecstatic. I seem to be using that word "ecstatic" a lot lately. "Liebgott," he said, "Mariemont is the perfect place for finding evidence for sainthood. The place is loaded with miracles. All I had to do was start knocking on doors. At practically every house someone said he or she had prayed to such and such a martyr or saint and miracles had happened. After twenty stops I had enough evidence for Father Schlag and his campaign to find a new saint for his church. I've got enough evidence to insure the beatification and canonization of Eutychus of Troas." I said quietly, knowing full well that I couldn't avoid hearing it anyway, "Let me hear the evidence." Vibini grinned and took out his notebook.

"First," he said, "was a Mr. Fred Hoden. I knocked on his door and said, 'Any miracles lately?' He said, 'Why sure. Just last Friday I prayed to Eutychus of Troas to help me and I was able to stay awake through a two hour sermon by the Reverend Billy Graham.' That was just the beginning of prayers for help from Eutychus. I didn't write down all the other martyrs and saints that had been prayed to for intercession and a miracle had resulted. A Mrs. Henrietta Fotze prayed for help from Eutychus and she was able to read a whole copy of the Sunday *Cincinnati Enquirer* without falling asleep. Mary Beth Scheide asked for Eutychus' aid and she was able to listen to a whole speech by Senator Dole and never once fell asleep. A Mr. Sydney Geil read the biography of Jesse Helms, with the help of Eutychus, and never fell asleep. A Mrs. Hildegarde Brustschwarze summoned Eutychus and she read a whole novel by (fill in any name here) and never fell asleep. She said that if those Disciples of Jesus had prayed to Eutychus, they wouldn't have fallen asleep in the Garden of Gethsemane. A Philip Schamlippen read a volume of poetry by (fill in any name here) and Eutychus kept him awake the whole time. Gottlieb, I've got some more. But we only need six verifiable miracles and all these people are willing to document their experiences. Father Schlag has the evidence to get his saint for his church. When it's all done, the church will be named for St. Eutychus of Troas, the patron saint of all those with sleep disorders. It'll be just as famous as St. Richard of Chichester. And I will get the credit for it all and will also receive the total offering for Quasimodo Sunday."

I closed my ears to Vibini's discourse. I hoped that was the end of it all so I could end my story. I hoped that was it for Saturday and I could get back to my computer. It wasn't. Vibini leaned over to me and said, "Liebgott, can you lend me some money? I'm taking Saponata out on the town this evening." I was so pleased that he used "lend" instead of "loan" that I handed him $100 in cash and said, "Go. Enjoy. It's spring. She's lovely. Buy her a clean blouse."

I don't know how he spent the $100 that I lent him. He did later admit that he spent fifty-five dollars for cab fares with the Quo Vadis Cab Company. I should mention, for the record, that Vibini dressed for the evening in such a way that even I was impressed. He put on his black beret, his black cape, his black shirt, black trousers, black shoes and white spats. I lent him my gold watch and gold chain so he could let the gold chain hang across the front of his chest. With his tall thin frame and his hooked nose, he looked like a chic Savonarola. He asked me if I knew any place that served squid. I didn't. When he left in the Quo Vadis Cab, he left behind the scent of azaleas. I don't know what he and Sudsy did that evening, but when he returned at 2:45 A.M. this morning, he woke me up and said, "Liebgott, I've got to talk to you. I need the expertise of a doctor."

I got up from my bed, put on my red robe over my pink pajamas and shuffled into my parlor. I made myself comfortable in my chair. Vibini sat down on the couch and lit up a joint. The smoke drifted around the lamps and up along the ceiling. Vibini looked at me and said, "Dr. Gottlieb Liebgott, tell me about women. You were once married. You have children. Tell me." I was startled. I've never told him about my former family. I didn't know he knew about them. I looked at him and my innocent tongue said to me, "Virgin." I said, "What do you want to know?" "Well," Vibini said, "explain the openings." I said, "Which openings?" And he said, "The ones between the legs." I said, "There's only one" "No," he said, "I found two, one behind the other. Which one do I use when I make love to her?" I said, "Where did you find the second one?" "Why," he said, "in the back seat of the Quo Vadis Cab." I said as professionally as possible, "Vibini, use the front one." He said, "Why are there two?" I realized that spring has come and Vibini hasn't. All I could think to say was, "Vibini, have you ever gone bowling?" And they say we Germans have no sense of humor.

When I finished my explanations at 5:34 A.M., I was too awake to go to sleep. I considered praying to Eutychus of Troas to put me to sleep, but I'm not religious. Vibini was asleep on the couch. He had his notebooks ready to carry to Father Schlag after the early mass. Which he did, and I'm sure that Father Gottlob Schlag is now reading them avidly. But, this morning, instead of trying to go to sleep, I switched on my computer and surfed to the Web site at Monte Cassino. I tracked to Volume LXXI of the *Annali Calabresi*. I read Bartolomeo Masaccio's wonderful prose. In his own virgin tongue he had written a passage that I leave as my gift to you for staying awake during the whole of this narrative.

"On Wednesday, June 6, 1945, Giovanni Battista di Gesualdo Salvatore left Castelluccio Inferiore and walked north along the coast of the Tyrrhenian Sea. World War II was over and he was headed toward Subiaco where he hoped to study manuscript illumination with the famous illuminator Fra Agnello Costipazione a Tagliacozzo, a member of the Order of Skiagraphoi, which was founded by Pope Celestine III. The temperature was seventy-five degrees Fahrenheit. The wind was southwest and the sky was clear.

"When he came to the crossing of the Rapido River, Giovanni noticed a grove of trees at the foot of a hill away from the road. He was very tired and thirsty. He decided to rest. When he entered the grove, he could not see clearly at first because of the deep shade. When his eyes adjusted to the absence of the sun's glare, he saw a white unicorn lying under a pomegranate tree. A squirming squid was skewered on his corkscrew horn."

La Folle Journée
ou le Nozze di Vibini

BECAUSE I HAVE LEARNED that to be a writer I must use exact dates for my narratives, I wrote the date down. It was Wednesday, June 17, 1998, 3:00 P.M. The phone was ringing in my study. I rushed in to grab it before the caller hung up because Dallasandro Vibini has not had a commission for almost a year. When I raced into the room for the phone, I nearly stumbled over Vibini, who was kneeling on the floor. I grabbed the phone and said hello. Behind me I heard Vibini say, "Five, ten, twenty, thirty, thirty-six, forty-three." I said to the caller, "Yes, this is the office of Dallasandro Vibini. Yes, he solves petty crimes. He's right here." Vibini got up from the floor and took the phone. He said, "Yes, I could find out for you who's marrying your daughter. But not now. Call me back in a week. This Saturday I'm getting married myself," and hung up. It was the first I heard about a marriage.

I turned and saw Vibini again kneeling on the floor, holding a metal measuring tape and measuring the distance from the east wall of "my study" out to a spot in the middle of what he now calls "my room." I said,

"Vibini, what are you doing?" "I'm measuring," he said. "I can see that," I said, "but why?" "It's to see if my bed will fit." "What bed?" I asked. "Isn't your cot good enough? You snore loudly enough when sleeping on it." "Liebgott," he said, "I'm getting a new queen size bed." You will understand my confusion when I say that Vibini not only did not need a queen size bed, he also did not have any money to pay for it because he'd had no cases to solve since he found the name for St. Eutychus of Troas, for which Father Schlag paid him the offering on Quasimodo Sunday, which turned out to be $52.36.

Ever since Vibini moved into my apartment with me on Vox Populi Street, I've tried to let him know that I pay the rent, that he is a guest, that I don't exactly appreciate his freeloading. I said last Wednesday, "Vibini, why do you need a new bed?" "Liebgott," he smiled, "it's for my wedding. Saponata Santarellina and I are getting married next Saturday. When she moves in with me we will need a bed big enough for two. I've already ordered the bed. I'm just making sure it will fit into the room. It's coming tomorrow."

I have become accustomed to Vibini's willy-nilly capers when he solves petty crimes, but this maneuver took the cake, as the saying goes, because I knew as soon as Vibini mentioned marriage that I was going to get stuck with the bill, so this marriage would take the wedding cake and I'd have to pay for it. I know that "take the cake" is a cliché, but I wanted to use it so that I could make that little play on taking the "wedding cake." And they say we Germans have no sense of humor.

I said, "Vibini, you did not ask my permission to do this. You did not ask me if Sudsy could move in. You did not ask me if you could put a new bed in here. What will I do with my computer? How will I carry on my research for the biography of the Italian war hero Giovanni Battista Salvatore?" Vibini looked up, smiled and said, "My new bed will fit in just fine. The head end just under the window where Sudsy and I can catch the morning breezes, the birds singing, the children chatting on their way to school." "Yes," I thought, "and the exhaust fumes from the busses, the horns from the sports utility vehicles and the screams of the dying pedestrians." I said, "Vibini, is this all real? Are you really going to marry that eighteen year old librarian from the Clifton branch of the Cincinnati and Hamilton County Public Library? You, a fifty-two year old man? Are you aware that you will be fifty-three years old next Wednesday?" Vibini pressed the sides of the tape holder, the long metal measuring tape slithered into the slot like a burnt tongue. "Yes, Liebgott. We're getting married this Saturday and you're going to be the best man."

I admit I was a bit flattered at first. It would have been an insult to me if Vibini hadn't asked me. I immediately went to work and got out my formal suit, I shined my shoes, shined my watch chain, got out my old homburg, began trying to think of a gift for the happy couple. I decided that my gift would be the bed. I decided that I would bless the marriage and move my computer out into the living room. I got out the pictures from my marriage back in Wuppertal in 1951 when Gertrude and I experienced the happiest day of our lives. I better get that right. It should be, "When Gertrude and I experienced the only happy day of our lives."

Now, as I write this down, I'm not flattered, I'm not happy about it all, but I'm ready. It's 10:00 A.M., Saturday, June 20, 1998. There's the exact data I need for my narratives. My black coat is clean, my white shirt is starched, my cravat is in a Windsor knot, my gleaming watch chain hangs richly across my big belly. I'm ready to go over to Saint Oholibamah's Chiliastic and Universalist Church of the Redeemer and All Saints of the Full Space-Time Continuum for the marriage of Dallasandro Vibini and Saponata Santarellina at 11:00 A.M. It's only a couple of blocks away. I can get there in a few minutes.

I'm not only ready to go over to St. Oholibamah's and be best man for Vibini, I also am ready to make it all into one of my narratives from the life of the great detective. I can see how the narrative will shape up. I will begin my narrative from this moment. I will begin my narrative as near to the end as possible. I will begin it just before the denouement. I will start *in medias res* and loop back to the beginning. I will begin at the penultimate moment, just as great narratives must begin. That will compress the time so that the actual time consumed by the narrative will be only the time from this moment to when I leave my house on Vox Populi Street and go to the church to be the best man in the wedding. That way I can put in whatever preceding events I want in order to titillate the reader. I will not tell about the wedding itself in this narrative. I will leave the reader in suspense as to what happens at the wedding and after. I will save that material for another story or stories, and the fact that they had no rehearsal for the ceremony.

I will begin by writing that it was Wednesday, June 17, 1998, at 3:00 P.M. that I entered my study and discovered Dallasandro Vibini kneeling on the floor and measuring with a metal measuring tape the distance from the wall to a spot in the center of the room. I said, "Vibini, what are you doing?" Since you already know this part of the story, I'll skip to Thursday when the bed arrived. The delivery truck from the Nighty-Night Bed Store arrived at 1:00 P.M. The driver and his helper brought the bed in and set it up in my study. I helped them put it together. The bed was a metal frame, a box spring and a mattress. There was nothing with the bed to soak up the various liquids that might ooze, leak or spurt from the horny bodies of the newlyweds while in the throes of fornication on their wedding night. Vibini and the delivery men helped me move my computer into the living room. The bed fit nicely into one corner of my study and everyone sat down to rest.

Vibini said, "Now that I'm going to be a married man, I'm going to have to learn how to entertain guests." He got out four marijuana joints and handed them around. I passed. The others lit up and soon the room was filled with the smoke of celebration. We all sat on the floor since Vibini doesn't own any chairs and I speculated as to how much his chairs would cost me. And a table, and a clothes closet, and a night stand. The driver OshKosh B'gosh and his helper L. L. Bean both said they needed a rest because they had just delivered a king size bed to a Sigismondo Pandolfo di Giovanni da Falconara Marittima Salvatore just down the street. I was startled. I said to OshKosh, "Who did you say?" OshKosh said, "He's called 'Siggy.' He lives just up the street from here." I said, "Right here on Vox Populi Street?" "That's right," OshKosh said, and inhaled. The little ash dropped on the floor and I squirmed because that was the name of Giovanni Battista Salvatore's oldest son. Could it really be that such good luck would come my way? Could it be that my war hero's oldest son lived right on the same street with me right here in Cincinnati? Could it be that a prime source for my biography of Salvatore could live right on my street right here in Clifton? Sigismondo, like Vibini, was born in 1945, the first of Giovanni's seven sons. He'd now be fifty-two or fifty-three. Still young enough to have his mind and his memories. I was ready to give some money to Vibini and tell him to go out and get more dope.

When the furniture movers had left, Vibini carried in two suitcases full of Sudsy's belongings. I went into my bedroom, took the white sheets off my bed, took my pillows and put them on Vibini's new bed. I made the bed neatly. I smoothed the sheets. "Vibini," I said. "You can't lay a bride on a bare mattress. Your bed's ready. You and Sudsy can put your own designs on the sheets." He pressed his fingers into the mattress and said, "It's good and hard. Just the thing for our first night." He opened the suitcases and said, "Liebgott, can you find a place for all this?"

With the new bed in place and Sudsy's clothes hung on a wire from the front window to the west wall, and with her cosmetics and underclothes stored in my chest of drawers, and when Vibini had recovered from his trip, I asked him about the coming wedding. "First of all," he said, "we won't be married in St. Eutychus of Troas." "What," I said, "you won't be married in the church you found the name for?" "No way. Father Schlag, the jerk, won't let us be married there. It has something to do with announcing the wedding six weeks ahead of time. I asked him yesterday and he said he wouldn't allow us to be married in his church. So I arranged to have the wedding across the street in St. Oholibamah's Chiliastic and Universalist Church. The minister said he'd do the job for seventy-five dollars, chapel included." Since I'm always the straight man in these Vibini dialogues, I said, "Who is this minister?" "He's called Thomas the Gymnast. His full name is Thomas Takianopoulos. He says he's from Patmos. He's a defrocked Patriarch from the Eastern Orthodox Church. He says he's licensed to perform marriages and funerals. You've probably seen him around Clifton. He's bald with a thick fringe of gray hair that sticks out, like a tonsure gone berserk. He wears thick glasses. He's always smiling. He always looks surprised. At what I don't know, but he always looks surprised. You've probably seen him in Keller's I.G.A. He's always buying bananas." Since I didn't want to get Vibini started on a discussion of bananas, I asked him about Thomas the Gymnast.

I said, "Can this Thomas the Gymnast perform the ceremony?"

Vibini said, "Why not?"

"He's defrocked."

135

Vibini laughed again and said, "That doesn't make any difference. Once a priest always a priest. He's a perfect priest."

"I didn't know there was such a thing."

"Sure. He's perfect. He's a thief, a lecher and greedy. Aren't all priests like that? He's just like Father Schlag at St. Eutychus of Troas."

"Right," I said. "How did he get defrocked?"

"He was caught stealing."

"So what? What's the matter with that? They all steal. You said he was a thief. Priests have been stealing from the churches and their parishioners since time began. They especially like to steal from poor people."

"Well, this Father Takianopoulos was caught stealing an icon from the Dionysiou Monastery on Mt. Athos. He told me all about it. He'd gone to Greece on a pilgrimage. He went to Mt. Athos and needed a souvenir. It seems that he collects icons and he wanted a certain one for over his fireplace. So he took an icon of St. Pruritis the Kynosargite, stuffed it into the front of his cassock and tried to leave. The guards caught him as he was walking out. He blessed them and they let him go."

"But he still got defrocked?"

"Not until he went back. He went back disguised as a delivery man. He pretended he was delivering a bed to the Archimandrite at Mt. Athos. After delivering the bed, he was leaving and the guards caught him with the icon of St. Pruritis in his underwear."

"You mean St. Pruritis was painted in his underwear?"

"No, no. Takianopoulos had the icon in his underwear."

"You said, Vibini, 'St. Pruritis in his underwear.'"

"I meant that the icon was in Takianopoulos' underwear."

"That's not what you said. You know, Vibini, how senstitive I've become to these linguistic nuances. Always remember that I'm now a writer, not a doctor."

"Sorry. I misspoke. So anyway, the Archbishop in Thessaloniki brought charges against Father Takianopoulos but he beat the charges."

"How'd he do that?"

"He got a lawyer from Israel."

"Got a lawyer from Israel? How could he do that? Can a lawyer from Israel practice in Greece?"

"Sure. They have some kind of organization, sort of like the American Bar Association except it's international. Father Takianopoulos explained all this to me. Israeli lawyers practice law wherever they want to. If anyone questions their credentials or tries to prevent them from practicing law, they call in their organization. It's called something like 'Moses,' or 'Mustard,' or 'Mozart,' or 'Hassad,' or 'Mosadim,' something like that."

"Where'd he find this lawyer?"

"In *The Book of Genesis*."

"In *The Book of Genesis*?"

"That's right. He closed his eyes, opened the Bible at random, put his finger on the page and he was pointing right at Genesis 10:29 right to the name Jobab."

"How did Takianopoulos get this lawyer?"

"He called his friend Father Sciron Alexikakos in Jerusalem and said, 'Send me a lawyer whose first name is Jobab.'"

"And this Father Alexikakos in Jerusalem found him a lawyer whose first name was Jobab."

"That's right. His name was Jobab Dershowitz and he got Takianopoulos off."

"How'd he do that?"

"He cited the sanity clause. The Greek judge didn't have the slightest idea what the sanity clause is so he dismissed the charges. Father Takianopoulos walked out a free man and came back to America with no icon but with a new wife."

"He got married?"

"Sure. Eastern Orthodox priests marry. And this wife was part of the deal."

"I hate to ask this, but what was the deal?"

"It seems this Jobab Dershowitz had an unmarried daughter named Leah. He agreed to take the case only if Takianopoulos would marry his daughter if he got Father T. off."

"This daughter Leah must be awfully ugly or something."

"Not at all. The only thing wrong with her was that she wasn't married mainly because Jobab Dershowitz said that no daughter of his was going to marry a man who wore a black hat. She's handsome and she has tender eyes. She's very smart and she wanted to become a U.S. citizen. Her name means 'wild cow,' just as Rachel means 'ewe, female sheep.'"

"And Father Takianopoulos told you all this. Well, then, why did he get defrocked?"

"The Patriarch in Thessoliniki was pissed off by the court's decision. He defrocked Takianopoulos and sent him back to the U.S. Takianopoulos came back to the U.S. with no foreskin and a new wife."

"What's this foreskin stuff?"

"I forgot. Jobab Dershowitz said that Takianopoulos would have to be circumcised before he could marry his daughter. Father Takianopoulos' lawyer cost him his foreskin and his freedom, instead of two million drachmas."

Probably I should leave this dialogue out of my story. No one would ever believe it.

It's now 10:20 A.M. I still have forty minutes before the ceremony and thirty-five minutes to write down the rest of these preliminary notes that I'll need for my narrative. It wasn't bad enough that Vibini had to get a defrocked Patriarch to do his wedding. There was the assumption that I would be the best man. I'll try to get all that into my story.

I tried to talk Vibini out of getting married, period. I discussed all the problems of a fifty-two year old man marrying an eighteen year old girl. I even tried to talk him out of having me as his best man. I sat him down last night and I said, "Vibini, I respect your wishes and your future. I would not do anything to hurt you. You understand that don't you?" He nodded. "You want me to be your best man, but you don't know anything at all about my past. If you knew about my past life you wouldn't even want to live here with me. Are you sure you want to bring an eighteen year old girl in here to live with two old men? Do you realize what you're doing?"

Vibini looked at me and said, "I don't even want to hear about it."

I said, "You're going to hear about it because it has to do with your future and my future. First of all, you have to know that Gottlieb Otto Liebgott is not my real name. I've never told anyone this before, but you must know that I'm really the son of Joseph Goebbels and my real name is Helmut Goebbels. My father was the propaganda minister for Adolf Hitler in Nazi Germany."

Vibini lit another of those infernal little cigarettes and said, "You don't expect me to believe this do you?"

"It's all true. You know I was born on October 2, 1935, in Berlin. My father was Joseph Goebbels and my mother was Magda Quandt. She'd been married once before and she had a son Harald by that first marriage. When Johanna Maria Magdalena Friedländer married Günther Quandt in 1921, she was eighteen years old and Herr Quandt was fifty-two. He already had two adolescent sons named Hellmuth and Herbert. Günther and Magda got divorced in 1929 because she was a nymphomaniac and he wasn't up to it because he was too old. She then married my father Joseph Goebbels in 1931 and she got pregnant every time he made a speech on the radio. She and my father had five daughters and me, their only son. The daughters were named Helga, Hilde, Holde, Hedda and Heide. I was the third child."

Vibini smiled at me and said, "Liebgott, I don't believe a word of what you're telling me. The Goebbels children were all killed in the Führer bunker when the Russians took Berlin in 1945."

"That's the official story. That's not what happened. No one knows what happened to the bodies of the children. No one knows where they are buried, if they are. The Russians left no record as to what they did with the bodies of the children. They photographed the dead bodies of my mother and father, but not the children. As you can see I survived. I'm here. Here's what really happened on that evening of May 1, 1945. I was only ten years old, but I remember it all clearly."

Vibini lit another of those little cigarettes, puffed once, let the smoke circle his head, and laughed. "Go on, Liebgott," he said. "Tell me the story I have to listen to. You're paying for the bed and the wedding so I guess I have to pay attention."

I gasped and said, "Paying for the bed and the wedding?"

"Of course," said Vibini. "The best man always pays for everything."

I was not put off. I went on. "As the Russians moved into Berlin, my father took all of his family down into the Führer bunker. It was April 22 and we moved in two limousines. I and my five sisters were given a little room to sleep in. The room had three double-decked bunks that we were to use. I remember that on April 29, Hitler got married. That was at 1:00 P.M. and afterwards there was a banquet. His new wife Eva Braun was dressed in white gauze and carried a bouquet of yellow and red flowers. She wore a coronet of pink flowers. White stockings and white shoes. Pale blue ribbons floated from her flowery crown. I remember her heavy eyelids that she seemed unable to keep open."

Vibini interrupted. "Liebgott, where could they get flowers? The Russians were destroying Berlin. They were all around."

"I don't know," I said. "But they did have flowers. The next day, in the afternoon, I saw the men carry out the bodies of Hitler and his wife. Later I heard them talking about the burning. That evening my father and mother comforted us by talking about our family vacations at Heiligendamm on the Mecklenburg coast and about motor boat rides on the Wannsee where we had an estate on an island. The place was called 'Schwanenwerder.'

"Then, I remember looking at my father's big head and his tiny body, his prosthetic support on his left foot, as he told about his boyhood in Rheydt. Then mother told about how Hitler had urged her to leave the bunker, fly to Bavaria, take us children to safety, how she refused, because she wanted us six little Goebbels not to live for Germany but to die for Germany. She told how her son Harald had been captured on Crete and was now in a British prisoner of war camp. She said she'd written her last letter to him on Saturday, April 28. Was she getting even for getting suckered into the Nazi Party? Was she getting even with that screaming little clubfoot? Was she taking revenge for listening to his mindless ranting? Was she taking revenge for him poking his ugly Nazi penis into her Wagnerian body?

"We hid in the bunker and listened to the bombs going off, the noises of war and destruction. Hitler was dead and, I heard, burned. On Tuesday, May 1, in the evening, Dr. Kunz came in and gave me and my sisters morphine injections. He said it was to make us sleep. He stuck the needle into my arm but he didn't push the plunger. We were lying in our bunk beds when mother and Doctor Ludwig Stumpfegger came in. Mother took little glass capsules and broke one open by each of us. She poured the liquid into the mouths of the girls. She stopped by my bed, broke open a capsule, dumped it beside my pillow and whispered to me, 'Helmut, you must live for Germany. Pretend to go to sleep. Someone will come for you.'

"Later, as I lay in the dark, Naumann, Rach and Schwägermann came in and carried me out into the darkness. They dressed me in the clothes of a street beggar. We went out into the courtyard where I could see two bodies burning. One was my father. I could see the steel leg brace on his left leg turning in the flames. There was a huge explosion and the doors jammed. We got back in and went out the top exit. We sneaked out into the night. There was fire all around, and lots of explosions.

"How we traveled I don't know. All I know is that we got to the West. I ended up in Wuppertal. There a family named Liebgott adopted me and gave me the name of Gottlieb Otto Liebgott. They raised me and sent me to medical college in Heidelberg. I became a medical doctor. I was successful. I met and married Gertrude Schneespiel in 1956 and we had four wonderful children. When she committed suicide in 1980, I decided to leave Germany and come to the U.S. I came to Cincinnati because I heard that it was a German city with lots of Neo-Nazis. I was told that I'd feel right at home in this fascistic city, and they were right. The citizens of Cincinnati thought I was a good doctor because I was German. If we ever have an American Hitler it will happen right here.

"So you see, Vibini, it's not a good idea to bring Sudsy into my home. My past is so awful that it can't but influence her innocent mind. Try to find your own apartment. I'll help you look. I'll pay the first month's rent."

Vibini laughed, no, sneered. "Liebgott," he said, "do you think I was born yesterday? I don't believe a word of what you've just told me. You're one of the nicest men I've ever met. You're just a great guy. You'll have a wonderful influence on Sudsy. She'll love you and your learning. She'll help you type your manuscripts."

Vibini knows how vulnerable I am to flattery. "First of all," he said, "you got your dates mixed up. You were born in 1930. Besides," he said, "you forgot that Saponata works in the library. She told me that you had checked out *The Last Days of Hitler*, *In the Shelter With Hitler* and a biography of Goebbels. When you returned them, she looked into the books and read the passages which you had marked. She reported them to me. And, Liebgott, Joseph Goebbels' prosthetic support was on his right foot."

Vibini took a deep drag on his little cigarette and there was a flash of light in the cigarette, as if it were loaded. I thought, "There goes another seed. No progeny for that plant ovary. Dead in Vibini's high." Vibini held in the smoke, looked at his exploded and smoldering joint and said, "Liebgott, I know all about your past. I've researched everything about your life. It's all on the Internet at the public library. Sudsy showed me how to use it."

I thought, "There's that damned public library again. It's ruining my life. It just ruined my best fiction." I realized that I had a lot of improving to do in my narrative skill. I have to learn to get my data correct. I can't let some reader unmask the fiction. I realized that if you can't fool a dope-saturated, love-sick detective, you aren't much of a writer.

Later last night, about, I guess, eleven, Vibini knocked on my door. I got up, put on my robe and opened the door. He came in and sat down by my bed. I lay back down. I was tired and sleepy. The next day was already weighing on me. Vibini leaned close and said, "Liebgott, you're a doctor. Tell me about her." "About whom?" "Saponata Santarellina." "What is it you want to know? You surely know her better than I do." "No," he said, "tell me about this woman stuff." I remembered when he asked about what he found when he poked around in her forbidden zones. I remembered that Vibini had never been married, maybe never touched a woman.

I said, "What do you want to know?" He looked down and said, "Last Sunday, Sudsy was feeling bad. I asked her what was wrong and she said she was having her period. I said, 'Are you sure it's not a comma?' When I said that, Sudsy looked at me and said, 'You don't know, do you?' Well, Liebgott, what's a period?"

I twitched and felt a terrible pity for Vibini. I realized what a horrible thing it is to grow up in Cincinnati. I said, "It's not a mark of punctuation. But it is sort of like a comma in that it is a pause in the sentence of life." And they say we Germans have no sense of humor. "Liebgott," Vibini whispered, "that doesn't help. You've got to realize that I attended religious schools. My grade school was St. Thomas Santoliquido and my high school was St. Leah Gravida. They didn't teach sex education in those schools."

"OK," I said, "it has to do with the reproductive cycle in a woman's life. A woman ovulates about once a month; she lays an egg in one of her ovaries. The egg descends the fallopian tubes. If it is not fertilized while in the tubes, it enters the uterus and does not result in a baby. If it is fertilized it attaches itself to the wall of the uterus and a baby results. Once a month, or so, if the woman is not pregnant, the uterus sloughs its lining that is prepared to receive the fertilized egg and the woman bleeds from her vagina. That's called her period. You must learn to know when that is and expect it and respect it."

"My God," Vibini said, "that's what those things were for I felt in her panties. Those pads."

"That's right," I said. "You need to be aware of a woman's menstrual cycle. Your married life will be governed by it."

"But how, Liebgott, does the egg get fertilized? Don't you have some pictures so you can show me how it happens?"

I devoutly wished that I did have pictures. They might have made him cancel the wedding. "Vibini," I said, "I don't have any pictures because I threw away the book with those kinds of pictures after my wife used it to commit suicide. The book had footprints on the cover. I couldn't even sell it at a used bookstore."

Vibini looked confused so I went on. "Vibini, you are aware that you have testicles, the sack with the two eggs in it between your legs." "That's right," he said. "And they've been aching lately." I realized that Vibini was beginning to believe what I was telling him so I changed my narrative. "That pain is because your body is producing sperm. Your testicles produce these little wiggling, worm-like animals that have one goal in life and that is to find that egg in that fallopian tube and get lost in it. Your testicles produce millions of them.

"Let's say that one of those millions of sperms is called 'Figaro.' Now this little Figaro swims, along with millions of his friends, from your testicles out through a tiny tube called the vas deferens into your prostate gland, which is just above your penis. There he gets mixed into a foul-smelling gummy liquid called semen. Are you following me so far?" Vibini nodded so I went on, thinking only in Cincinnati could this scene take place. "Now when you get an erection this little Figaro gets all excited. He wants to leap out into the vagina of a woman. When a man ejaculates into the cave you've been sticking your finger into between Sudsy's legs, Figaro and all his pals fan out in all directions. They wiggle their little tails and swim madly around and in and over and under, anywhere, like blind and insane squid. Each one tries to find that fallopian tube where that egg is floating in the darkness and waiting for one of them. They try every possible entry. Remember that Figaro and his pals are all blind and searching in absolute darkness. It's a kind of hide-and-seek for the blind, except there are millions of seekers and only one hider.

"Let's call that egg 'Susanna.' Now when Susanna leaves her home in the ovary there's only one place she can go and that is down and into the dark tube. There she hides for about twenty-four hours, waiting to see if anyone will find her. Let's say that Figaro finds the tube by chance in the absolute darkness and swims up it and finds Susanna, who doesn't have the slightest idea who he is because she's blind and can't tell him from any one of his pals. When Figaro finds Susanna, he says, 'Knock, knock,' and she says, 'Who's there?' He says, 'Almaviva,' and she says, 'Come in. I've been expecting you.'" I hope my readers will know that "Almaviva" means "life-giving" or "life-fostering," or my little German joke will go awry. I continued, "Figaro then burrows into her and shuts the opening behind him so no one else can enter. Figaro does what men have been doing since time began and that is to re-enter the female body and return to the womb. That's what a man does when he copulates, that is, he tries to re-enter the female body and return to the womb but because he is too large to enter completely he sticks a hard part of himself in, leaves a deposit and goes away satisfied." I shouldn't have used the word "copulate" but I continued anyway. "After Figaro re-enters Susanna, the two of them float down into the uterus where they hook onto a wall, grow a kind of snorkel tube for feeding, mix their chromosomes and turn into a fetus." I shouldn't have used the word "fetus," but it was too late.

Vibini looked up and said, "Is Figaro in that sticky, crusty stuff that I've been finding in my pajama pants in the morning after I've had a date with Sudsy the night before?"

"That's right," I said. "And if that Figaro doesn't stay in your pajama pants and gets into Sudsy's tubes, he'll find a Susanna and you'll become the father of a little Rafaello and, unless Gypsies steal the baby, you'll have to go out and find your own apartment because I'll allow no children in my study. So keep Figaro under control by keeping him in your pajama pants." Vibini didn't ask how he was supposed to keep Figaro under control and I felt relieved. I'm sure I'll have to explain that to him later, hopefully before it's too late.

Vibini said thank you and left the room. I lay on my bed and thought about my courting of Gertrude Schneespiel in Wuppertal. I remembered our wedding on June 24, 1951. I remembered how lovely she was in her white, gauzy gown. I remembered the white lilies she carried. The white stockings and white shoes with high heels. I remembered the skyblue ribbons that flew from her crown of yellow daisies.

I remembered our wedding night, how Gertrude took my gold watch from my vest pocket and laid it on the dressing table. How she removed my black dress coat, unbuttoned my vest and took it off. I remembered her undressing and standing before me, her thighs as white and hairless as eggs, her thick, curled and blond pubic hair nestled in her pubic crevice, her long blond hair falling to her waist, her cupola breasts nodding in the summer breezes, opening her thick arms, smiling and saying, "Gottlieb, come to me."

After the wedding, we moved to Heidelberg where I entered the university to study medicine. Gertrude worked in an American U.S.O. restaurant and gave birth to my children. First there were my three sons in 1953, 1955, and 1957; Ehrgott, Fürchtegott and Traugott. Then my daughter Maria in 1960. They all grew up healthy while I became a doctor and made my career. Gertrude worked on and became more and more depressed. When my daughter left home in 1980, Gertrude said to me over noodles and knockwurst, "That's it." That night, while I was working in an emergency clinic, she hanged herself in cur garage. She stood on a pile of my old medical textbocks, looped the rope over a joist, kicked the books out from under her and swung in the night breezes until I came home and cut her down.

It's my children I think about mostly now. All of them wanted to be writers because my father Lobgott Gerebernus Liebgott was a famous novelist. All of them failed and are now in St. Dympna's in Gheel. All four of them suffered from severe depression from an early age. Nothing seemed to help them, not religion, psychiatric counseling, parental love and patience, or reading and writing literature. It was almost as if it were genetic. Gertrude's mother and father were both Nazis, but everyone was during the Hitler years. My father and mother were some kind of socialists. But not seriously.

I consider myself a Christian Anarchist, but that doesn't stop me from doing my research and enjoying my stumbling into the literary world. I've never let my psychological condition distract me from my interests. My bad feelings and moods are not going to prevent me from learning to write good sentences and make good stories. I've never understood why my good humor didn't rub off onto my wife and my children.

One thing has come to me from all my disappointments and that is never to use them for story material. I have determined not to write about myself. I am not going to exploit the suffering of my family in order to make my literary career. It seems that all the contemporary fiction that I read is about suffering, about family turmoil, about divorces and betrayals, about deceit and lost affections, about a kind of bourgeois *Angst*, a kitchen *Sturm und Drang*, that seems to appeal to people who don't have the slightest idea what suffering is.

I have Vibini to write about. He's more interesting than I am, even to me. Whatever he is, he's a joy to behold, no matter how much he exasperates me. How can anyone be angry with a fifty-two year old man who listens to Mozart, smokes marijuana, solves petty crimes and marries an eighteen year old girl without thinking the least little bit about what might be ahead, without thinking once about how he might support her, without considering once my feelings in the matter? He's the most innocent fifty-two year old that I've ever met. I must make him known through my fiction.

I was depressed when I woke up this morning. I was still thinking of my own wedding until 9:00 A.M. when Saponata and her parents arrived for the wedding breakfast. Vibini had not told me they were coming to my house before going to the church. I heard the noise outside my bedroom and got up to see what was going on. Vibini introduced me to Panciuto and Squallida Santarellina. He slapped me on the back, she kissed my cheeks and Vibini beamed.

The breakfast was just dishes of grapefruit sections, buttered toast and coffee. It was the dressing of the bride and groom for the wedding that lifted my spirits. Vibini dressed first. He went into my bedroom and came out in his black beret, black cape, black shirt and trousers, black socks and black penny loafers, and gleaming white spats. With his beaked nose, his thin face, his sunken cheeks, he looked like a chic Savonarola. Elsewhere I've used "chic Savonarola" to describe Vibini. But I like the phrase so much I'm using it here again.

It was Saponata, who lifted up my heart. She was gone for at least thirty minutes. When she emerged in her bridal dress, I gasped. Her feet were bare. Her dress was a gauzy white and fell down around her ankles. The dress was covered with printed whole green plants with leaves and stems and with red shaped flowers that looked like carnations and daisies. The sleeves ballooned around the upper arms. Then the forearms were covered with a very thin lace down to and over the wrists. There was a wreath of small red and white flowers and green leaves around her pale neck. Flowers and green sprouts were woven into her pale blond hair that fell down the back of her neck and over her clean white collar. A knot of flowers rested on top of her head.

Her face seemed heavy with joy. The skin of her face was so pale it seemed almost transparent. Her cheeks were flushed. Her lips were pale red with no make-up. Her nose and light brown eyebrows thin. Her nostrils quivered with happiness. Her eyelids drooped with erotic anticipation. Her pale green eyes seemed gravid with immanent lust. I've used that phrase "gravid with immanent lust" before when describing Saponata, but I like it so much that I'm using it again. I like to quote myself when I've turned a good phrase. (See above.)

She clutched the skirt of her dress at her waist with her right hand and held up the bottom of her skirt as she walked into the room. Her left hand pressed against her stomach. With a nod of her head, she beckoned to Vibini. "Come on, Dally," she murmured. "It's time for our wedding." She extended her right elbow and Vibini laid his left hand lightly on her right forearm as they walked out the front door, followed by the laughing parents. I watched the black penny loafers and the glowing white spats of Vibini step over the threshold right next to the bare thin feet of Saponata Santarellina. I recently learned that "immaculate" means "unspotted." That's what Vibini's spats were and so was Saponata.

It's almost 11:00 A.M. Time for me to leave for the church to see Vibini and his blushing bride united in holy matrimony. I know that language is trite, but it's difficult to avoid clichés at times like this. I must learn how to avoid trite language at moments of high emotion. I was so taken by the dignity of Dallasandro Vibini and by the nubile beauty of Sudsy as they left my home that I almost wept. The great sadness of my life somehow was swept aside by the approaching nuptials. A marriage is a time of rejoicing. It is a time of happiness, no matter the prognosis. It is a time of happiness, at least for one day. Now it is time for me to go and be the best man that I can be. It is time for me to set aside my life and make sure that the coming marriage is successful.

I'll take a quick look in the mirror before I go. I'll make sure my big belly isn't sticking out through my white, starched shirt. I'll check the opening on my black trousers. I'll make sure my tie is tied right. I'll especially make sure my gold watch chain is hanging in the right arc. I'll check my black suit and the gloss on my black shoes. I'll rub any dust off my homburg. Forgive me. Forgive me, reader. I know what a cheap literary trick it is to have a first person narrator look into a mirror so that he can describe for the reader what he, the narrator, looks like. I will look into the mirror but I won't put it into my story. When I get better as a writer, I'll know how to describe the first person narrator without resorting to a mirror.

As they walked out of my house and headed toward the church, I wanted to say to the happy couple, "Blessings upon you and welcome to my house. With Vibini's great heart, my wisdom and the young woman's beauty, we can live together in peace and harmony. We will love each other in spite of all, and love should end in contentment and joy. Forgive me. Forgive me, Vibini, for whatever I might have said. It is all the foolishness of the day and of my old age. Let's be joyous and celebrate this wonderful event because there should be at least one happy day in every marriage."

Besides, I know that all this nonsense will make a great short story. If I can tell it right, this marriage may be the beginning of my literary career.

Amazing Grace

L AST NIGHT ABOUT 10:00 P.M. I was sitting at my computer. I was on the Internet to Monte Cassino and was deep into the *Annali Calabresi*. I had just read and recorded the sixth item in Salvatore's "Code of Conduct for the Italian Soldier in Wartime" when the phone rang. When I reached for the phone Dallasandro Vibini's new wife Saponata came up behind me and put her arms around my shoulders. I felt her breasts poke into my back and her breath against my neck and I said to myself, "To hell with the phone call." The man on the phone identified himself as Tomasso de Giovanni di Simone Guidi. He said his friends called him "Masaccio" and he'd called about a week ago and wanted to talk to the great Dallasandro Vibini. He needed someone to find out who was marrying his daughter. The name he gave was obviously false. I took his phone number and told him Vibini would call him in the morning. I didn't tell him that I was well acquainted with Masaccio.

When I hung up the phone, Saponata kissed me on the right side of my neck and I thought my old heart would snap. It had been a long time since a woman had shown me any tenderness. Not since my wife Gertrude hanged herself in our garage in Wuppertal, Germany, in 1980. Saponata's tears ran down under my collar, she sniffled in my right ear and I dared not move. I wanted that little sign of love to last as long as any little sign of love can. A label came to my mind, a label that I read somewhere. It was "sensual deprivation," and I knew that's what I had suffered since 1980. It frightened me to realize that Saponata's holding me might be the last time in my life that a woman would touch me. Her tears tickled my neck and she held on tight as she whispered in my right ear, "Gottlieb, will you come and pray with me?"

Vibini and Saponata got married on Saturday, June 20, 1998, and today is Friday, June 26, 1998, so they've been married some six days. I've got to get all this in my story so the reader will know exactly when all these events took place. On Wednesday, June 24, 1998, Vibini celebrated his fifty-third birthday. Saponata, who is eighteen, went out and bought him a birthday cake at the Virginia Bakery. Instead of fifty-three candles, she had the bakery put four candles on the cake and had them write on it "Happy Fourth Anniversary," because it was the fourth day of their marriage. It's only been a few days since all this began and already I'm having trouble keeping it all straight.

It was last night, about 10:00 P.M., Thursday, June 25, 1998, the fifth day of their marriage, that Saponata came up behind me and hugged me just as I was writing down more of the "Code of Conduct" that my Italian war hero Giovanni Battista Salvatore, whose biography I have decided to write, had written for the new Italian soldiers when at war. See *Annali Calabresi*, LIII, number 18, section 13. It was 10:05 P.M. when "Sudsy," as Vibini calls her, stopped my work. That might not be the exact time but it is close enough. I had just read and recorded the sixth item in the code, namely, "The Italian soldier does not burn, pillage, desecrate or destroy the enemy's places of worship or his holy shrines on Sundays," when Saponata came up behind me and put her arms around me. I reluctantly turned toward her and said, "Of course, Saponata. I'll be happy to pray with you."

All of this praying stuff started last Saturday when Vibini brought home his youthful bride. That morning I put on my white shirt, three-piece black suit, my black socks and my black shoes. I wore my black homburg. As usual I put my watch in my right vest pocket and let the gold chain hang across my fat belly. At exactly 10:55 A.M. I left my apartment on Vox Populi Street and headed for Saint Oholibamah's Chiliastic and Universalist Church of the Redeemer and All Saints of the Full Space-Time Continuum where I was to serve as best man for the wedding. Vibini, Sudsy and her parents Panciuto and Squallida Santarellina had left at, I think, 10:45.

It's just a couple of blocks from my apartment to the church and I arrived there at exactly 11:00 A.M. It made no difference when I got there because, as I realized later, there had been no rehearsal for the ceremony. When I walked into the church Father Thomas Takianopoulos, the defrocked Patriarch from the Eastern Orthodox Church, called "Thomas the Gymnast," was kneeling in front of Saponata and kissing and licking her bare feet. Saponata blushed and the gentle pink that flushed around under her white skin made her so lovely I felt like crying. Saponata stood and smiled in her wedding gown and held her bouquet of flowers that made her look exactly like Flora in the painting called "Primavera" by Alessandro di Mariano dei Filipepi, known to all as Sandro Botticelli. Beside her, Vibini dressed in his black beret, his black cape, his black shirt and black trousers, his black penny loafers and his brilliantly white spats. Such a tableau I would never see again, I knew.

Father Thomas' tears were tickling Saponata's toes and she began to laugh. Vibini whispered, "Liebgott, tell this idiot what to do." I said through the laughter, "Father Thomas, do you think it appropriate to kiss the toes of the bride before she has consummated her marriage?" I didn't have the slightest idea what to say or do. Father Thomas looked up at me and said, "Mind your own business, you fat son-of-a-bitch. I'll run this show." I helped him to his feet and he decided to get, as he said, "This show on the road." He led Vibini and Saponata to the front of the church. Saponata's parents and I followed. At the front Father Thomas turned, breathed out a cloud of Maker's Mark breath, looked at the empty church and said, "OK. Any objections?"

The phrase "robbing the cradle" kept running through my mind, but I said nothing. When no one demurred, Father Thomas the Gymnast took out a little black book he had concealed under his black robe. There were various colored ribbons marking certain parts of the text. Father Thomas rolled his eyes up so that his eyeballs seemed all white. He patted the unruly gray tonsure that surrounded his bald head. He grinned through his yellow teeth and his whiskey breath and said, "Listen, folks. I'm not sure what I'm doing here. But by God I'm going to get this affair done right. OK. Here we go. Mr. Dallasandro Vibini, you stand here to my left. That's the male side of the absolute, shithead empyrean. And keep your hands out of your pockets. You can play with yourself after the ceremony is over. No pocket pool is allowed at an Orthodox wedding. Miss Saponata Santarellina you stand to my right side. That's the female side of the deliquescent empyrean imperative. OK. Here we go. Oh, fat boy. You stand beside the male principle incarnate on my left and keep your bacteria-filled mouth shut. One squawk out of you and this ceremony is feloniously irreparable and fulgurous. Mr. and Mrs. Santarellina, hold hands and breathe deeply during the alexikakic gyrations of the iconolagnia. OK. Round and round we go and where we stop nobody knows."

Father Thomas the Gymnast Takianopoulos, defrocked Patriarch and all, raised his right hand and said, "Dearly beloved, etc. Let's cut the crap. Do you, Dallasandro Vibini take this lovely young eighteen year old piece of delicious virgin pussy for your wife, to be fingered, handled, licked, kissed and fucked until death do you part? If so, say 'You're god damned right.'" Vibini looked around to where I stood and said, "Liebgott, should I agree to all this crap?" I said, "Of course. You can't pass up this opportunity to create progeny and make yourself immortal in your descendants." Vibini then said, "Your fucking A." Father Thomas the Gymnast then turned to Saponata and said, "Saponata Santarellina, do you take this fifty-two year old piece of leftover shit to be your beloved husband, to honor, obey and do all manner of evil gyrations and bifurcations in your algolagniac fulminations and pharmakakic billywangs when the circle shall be unbroken by and by? If so, say, 'Fucking A.'" Sudsy turned to her mother and said, "Should I do this jelly-stomping razz-ma-tazz?" "Of course," her mother said. "Juice it up and learn to squeeze." Sudsy turned to Father Thomas the Gymnast and said, "Please. Lay it on. I'm ready for the tummy a-go-go." Father Thomas rolled his eyes up, spat on the floor, adjusted his underwear in his crotch and said, "Then, by the authority invested in me as the precursor of the inevitable follies of this undulating sphere we call the earth and by the dim stars that adumbrate the very pimples on our butts, I pronounce you man and wife and licensed to touch any sacred or profane part of the anatomies that you both now inhabit and shall share *in saecula saeculorum*. Vibini, you may now insert your tongue into your new wife's cephalic orifice and lick the plaque and leftover breakfast from her incisors. And Saponata, you may receive that tongue as a pregustation of all further insertions that may eventuate in the nocturnal repercussions of this light as a whiskey fart ceremony."

Saponata's parents and I broke into applause as Vibini leaned over, removed his black beret and handed it to me and kissed Saponata now Vibini on her pale pink lips. Father Thomas Takianopoulos said, "That's it and that's $75.00." I handed him the $75.00, which he stuck in the black book by a red ribbon. Saponata's parents said they had an engagement at the bowling alley and left. I said, "Let's repair to our domicile and celebrate this glorious nuptial." Saponata said, "I'm hungry." Vibini said, "I'm ready for Mozart's 'Coronation Mass' and some marijuana."

When we returned to my, now our, apartment, Sudsy looked around and said, "This place is a mess. I'm going to get this place straightened out." She started to walk into their bedroom, formerly my study, and change her clothes when I said, "Saponata, before removing your bridal gown, stop for a moment. Stop and let me look at you one more time." I can't tell you how lovely she looked. That pale, pinkish skin, the heavy green eyes, the thin blond hair wispy at the neck and around the ears, the flowered gown, the bare feet, the little bulge in her abdomen. I thought of the words "comely" and "fetching." She was all that and more. I told her to wait just a moment and I got out my Polaroid camera and took a quick shot of her. Then one of her and Vibini. The odor of lust was in the air, I thought. Then I realized that it was just that Vibini had lit up another of those little cigarettes. Sudsy changed into a pair of jeans and a white t-shirt and began scrubbing the kitchen floor, I turned on my computer and we settled down, I thought, into married life in our *ménage à trois*.

Wednesday, June 24, after our evening meal of pepperoni pizza, ordered in by me, cans of 7-Up and Vibini's birthday cake, I returned to my computer and clicked into the Internet. I found that passage where Salvatore had written down his new version of the "Code of Conduct for the Italian Soldier in Wartime." The first item on the list was, "The Italian soldier does not die for his country as long as Sicily is part of it." The second item was: "The Italian soldier never steals or plunders civilian goods from other Italian soldiers." Vibini had the "Gran Partita" blasting through our open windows. His aura permeated our rooms. Sudsy scrubbed the living room floor and I read number three: "The Italian soldier, if captured, must reveal only his name, rank, serial number, home address, the names of his father and mother, the size of his military unit, any plans for offense by the Italian army, his shoe size, his waist size, his favorite wine, his favorite food, his lipstick flavor, the last time he had pasta primavera, his weight, his height, the last time he went to confession, the last time he went to mass, the population of his hometown, the road system of his home area, the location of good water, where food is stored, the addresses of young women in his hometown, the best escape routes from the town and nothing else." Number four was, "The Italian soldier does not us dum-dum bullets against the enemy if a bottle of Grappa is at hand," and number five was, "The Italian soldier does not assault, torture, brutalize or rape the wives and daughters of the enemy over the age of eighty-five." I decided to wait until the next day to write down the rest of the items.

About 9:00 P.M. Vibini said he was going to go to bed. Saponata said she'd be there soon. When Vibini was gone, Saponata said, "Gottlieb, I wanted to talk to you alone." I turned off my computer and said, "What is it, my dear?" I didn't realize what was about to happen until she said, "Liebgott, who is Jesus?"

Is there an odor to innocence? I don't mean like the odor of Vibini's cigarettes. I mean a kind of non-odor. Maybe the complete absence of odor. That was what I experienced at Saponata's question. I thought I should breathe in deeply and sense the aura that way. I did. I breathed deeply and tried to sense the smell of the question. There must be something about it that gave off a scent, I thought. If I could smell that scent I could answer her question. It flashed through my mind that innocence is the absence of evil, so the scent of innocence must be the opposite also, the absence of stench. I thought that I perceived the scent of innocence in not perceiving any scent at all.

I was so taken aback that I spluttered something like, "Why, he's a character in the Bible. Don't you know who he is? Didn't you learn about him in your church?" She looked down at the clean floor and said, "I'd never been to a church until my marriage. My parents never went to church so I didn't either. I don't know anything about Christianity." Saponata seemed tired in her paleness. She seemed short of breath and she kept putting her right hand to her throat. Her left hand lay gently on her stomach.

I began the discussion by saying, "Why do you ask about Jesus if you're not interested nor have ever gone to a church?" "Oh, I'm interested. The reason I asked is that when I told Melissa Comb about my future husband's drug habit and what to do about it, she said, 'You should ask Jesus.' Melissa Comb works with me in the library. She's a good friend. We discuss our problems and she always says, 'Take it to the Lord in prayer.' Have you ever prayed, Gottlieb? Do you take things to the Lord in prayer? Can you teach me how to pray? I think I'll need it to save Dally from his drug habit. I want to keep him healthy so we can have a good marriage. Maybe I'm too young for all this, but I do love him, Gottlieb, even if he is way older than me."

Nothing in all my medical training prepared me for this kind of situation. Nothing in my marriage prepared me for this. I just assumed that young people got religious training and grew up and forgot about it and that was that. I said, "I'm not a theologian or a preacher. I'm not a priest. But I understand that anyone who wants to can pray to God. I think his blessings are available to everyone." Saponata looked into my eyes and said, "Would you tell me about religion and teach me how to pray?" I thought angrily, "Damn Vibini for doing this to me. I'm too old for all this. I'm sixty-eight years old. My wife committed suicide in 1980. My four children are in St. Dympna's in Gheel. My life has been a spiritual debacle. How can I make a spiritual life for a young woman who is innocent, beautiful, nubile, so gorgeous that I'm jealous of Vibini, who will this night or sometime soon corrupt this lovely young lady and turn her into just another piece of married meat?"

Then it came to me. It was like some kind of divine message. It was something I remembered that began, "Suffer the little children." I remembered my terrible marriage and my suffering after my wife's death and the institutionalizing of my children. It occurred to me that my soul was also at stake in this relationship. So I turned to Saponata, who sat with tears in those green eyes, those eyes that always seemed gravid with immanent lust, and said, "My dear, I will do my best. Let's begin with this. There is a book called the Bible. It is divided into two parts." When the time came for her to go to bed, Saponata said, "Gottlieb, will you tell me more tomorrow when I get home from work?" I said, "Yes, Sudsy. I will. There's a lot more."

Saponata went back to work yesterday morning and in the evening my instructing began again. Vibini lounged in his chair in their bedroom, smoked marijuana and listened to Mozart's "Great Mass in C," the "Vesperae Solemnes de Confessore" and the "Exsultate Jubilate" while I told Sudsy about the history of Israel, about the Jewish and then Christian notion of a Messiah. How the Christians believed in salvation, in being saved, in confession and penance, in prayer and divine guidance. How they believed that prayer changes things. That God listens to prayers and, if your heart is pure and your intentions just, He will answer them.

I told her about how Christians believe that Jesus of Nazareth was born of a virgin named Mary. How he was born in Bethlehem and how angels appeared to shepherds and told them to go and see the baby. How wise men came from the east after they saw a star that announced the birth of the Messiah. I told her how Jesus grew to manhood and then began teaching repentance, how he healed people and how he was crucified and arose from the dead. How people believe that the anointed one, the Christ, died for our sins. How he atoned for our sin. And how someday we will rise from the dead and be judged for what we've done on this earth. How if we believe in his message, our sins will be forgiven and we will live in heaven forevermore. I got in all the good stuff first. I told her what a great story it is. I didn't mention the idea of mysteries. I left the double-talk for later.

When I had finished my lesson, Saponata looked at me and said, "Do you believe? Do you believe in God and that Jesus is His son and that our sins can be forgiven?" I could hear Vibini playing Mozart's "Ave, Verum Corpus" in the next room. The irony of it all was so heavy I thought someone had laid out a mean script for my evening, a script to trap me in my own deviousness. I think Mozart's "Ave, Verum Corpus" is the greatest piece of music ever written but it was all out of place just then.

It occurred to me that there must have been some kind of a great plan whereby language was created so that we could deceive ourselves. We think language was created to answer to our needs, to communicate our human wants and wishes, our desires, our highest thoughts. Language, friends, is an instrument of deceit. Human kind created language to fit its corruption. Our language is made for lying, not truth. We might have created a language to answer to our needs but we have perverted it into a vehicle of deception. And why shouldn't language be deceitful? It comes from the heart of man.

When Saponata asked me if I believe, I lied. "Yes I do," I said. And for a moment I did because of the truth about lying and not lying. Because we can distinguish between truth and falsehood. How can you believe and how can you not believe? Only an omnipotent, omniscient God could put me in such a dilemma in order to test my spiritual mettle. If He created all things, He also gave me the slippery language that let me escape His trap. "Thank God," I thought, "that our language is implicitly dishonest."

So it was last night, Thursday, June 25, 1998, after the lesson in Christianity for Sudsy and just as I was about to close out my research for the evening and just as I answered the phone, Saponata came and put her arms around my shoulders. It was the first time a woman had touched me in eighteen years. She kissed my neck and said, "Gottlieb, will you come and pray with me?" Since there was no way of my weaseling out of it, I lied and said what I had to say, "Of course, Saponata. I'll be happy to pray with you. I'm not good at it. But I'll do what I can." I thought, "If God listens to everybody, which includes me, why doesn't He destroy us all right now and get it over with?"

She took my hand and led me into the bedroom where Vibini lay in a drug stupor and snored. We stood by the bed. Saponata wept. "Look," she said. "This is not what I want for my marriage. I'll do anything to save my husband. He's all I have." I thought, "What about me? I'm here. I'll help." When she knelt by the bed she pulled me down alongside her. She folded her hands, bowed her head, something I didn't teach her and said, "Oh God in heaven, forgive us our sins. Lead us in a right way. Forgive my husband and help me to be a good wife. Help him in his addiction to get out of it. Help me to help him. Amen." I assumed that Melissa Comb had been coaching her, but, whoever it was, Saponata was learning fast.

When she got up, I told her I needed some help too. She put her hand on my left elbow, grabbed my belt at the back and together we got me upright. It's not easy to lift three hundred pounds up from a kneeling position. I suppose that was the reason I quit going to church. Sudsy said, "Now it's time for me to go to bed. Please excuse me." I left the room.

As I prepared to go to bed myself, I sat for a while on the edge of my bed and tried to calculate or imagine what my life had come to. Living with a fifty-three year old man who is married to an eighteen year old woman. Me with no family. Me with an empty life. It suddenly occurred to me that what I had been missing all along about writing is that to be a good writer I must exercise endless forgiveness. It came to me that what we all need is forgiveness. Without forgiveness there is no life. Without forgiveness there is no love. Without forgiveness there is no point in living. Without forgiveness there is no narrative and the great writers are the writers who can forgive the most.

I decided that Sudsy's presence in Vibini's life was a wonderful development in the grand plot that I was recording. I felt as if some divine wisdom had sent her to help me in my belated literary career. What a wonderful addition she makes to the Vibini stories because she adds beauty, youth, innocence, even glory to our tawdry lives. I decided that when I finished my biography of the Italian war hero Giovanni Battista Salvatore I would dedicate the book to her.

I decided to forgive Saponata her ignorance. I decided that it is my duty to teach her. I decided that it is my duty to help her have a spiritual life, an intellectual life, a family life. I'll tell her about Botticelli, World War II, the horrors of suicide, the terrible disappointments in life, how forgiveness saves us from ourselves and how we have to forgive even ourselves. Otherwise there is darkness, neuroses, the dark night of the soul, suffering and suicide. Love and forgiveness are the only human traits that save us from ourselves. Love and forgiveness are the way God is present in our lives. Jesus taught that. I'll tell her he died for his teachings. I'll tell her that no one listened to him then and no one listens to him now and let her draw her own conclusions. When Saponata asks me, as she surely will, "Do you love and forgive Vibini?" I'll lie again and say, "Of course. I have no choice."

VIBINI IN THE UNDERWORLD

SOME JOKESTER has put up a sign at the head of our street. The sign is a three feet by three feet piece of white cardboard nailed to a wooden stake. On the sign in crooked black lettering is the message, "Abandon All Hope You Who Enter Here." The message from Dante's *Commedia* is indicative of what happens when you allow the citizens of Cincinnati to read great literature. The classics are for them just a source for graffiti. The cardboard sign stands right beside the official yellow metal sign that says "No Exit."

Our street is called Vox Populi Street. It runs straight east from Clifton Avenue between Glenmary and Woolper. It starts across the street from Father Schlag's church St. Eutychus of Troas, the church for which Dallasandro Vibini found the eponymous saint. You will be able to read about how Vibini discovered the saint for that church in my story "Vibini and the Virgin Tongue" (*North American Review*, September/October 1999, pp. 24-32).

Vox Populi Street is a *cul-de-sac*. I don't like to say that the street is a *cul-de-sac* because that label is usually mistranslated. *Cul-de-sac* doesn't mean "dead end" or "bottom of the sack." What the label means is the "ass end of the bag." It means the ass end of the sack because the French word "cul" is cognate with the Italian word "culo" as in Culofaccia, the nickname for Vibini's older brother. Culofaccia's name means "butt-faced" or "ass-faced."

Vox Populi Street might be called a *cul-de-sac* only if you realize that it is a mixed bag of people and that they represent the ass end of the city of Cincinnati. The street is inhabited, like all of Clifton, the area in which it exists, by the leftovers from the respectable parts of the city. If I ever get done with my series of stories about Vibini, I could call the book *The Vox Populi Street Stories*. It's better to think of the street as a kind of cecum, a blind gut, down at the end of the ascending colon where the vermiform appendix, a useless organ, grows and endangers the life of its host.

There are twelve houses on Vox Populi Street, six on the south side and six on the north side. Dallasandro Vibini, his new wife Saponata and I live on the first floor of the third house from Clifton on the south side of the street. Our address is 253 West Vox Populi Street, Cincinnati, Ohio, 45220. I don't know why our street is called "west" since there is no "east" Vox Populi. Our street just stops where the hill starts down to Vine Street, which is the dividing line for east and west in Cincinnati.

Since Vibini married Saponata Santarellina on Saturday, June 20, 1998, I've gotten to know who some of my neighbors are because Saponata, or Sudsy, as Vibini calls her, is gregarious. She's gotten to know most of the people on the street in just the seven weeks that she's lived here. I moved in here in 1980, when I first came to Cincinnati, but I've never met my neighbors, not even the people who live upstairs over my apartment. They have a side entrance so I never see them. My apartment opens onto the front porch and my former study, now Vibini's and Sudsy's bedroom, looks out over the street. When I get to know my upstairs neighbors, I'll include them in a story.

The one neighbor I do know about is Guido di Pietro. He lives next door on the west at 259 West Vox Populi Street. His house is two doors from Clifton Avenue. I know about him because Vibini solved his labor problems for him. Guido surreptitiously manufactures lipstick for the Italian army. He has his illegal factory in his basement and employs one employee, Emil Hasenpfeffer, who lives on the north side of the street at 250 West Vox Populi Street with his wife Isolde. Guido's business is illegal because our street is not zoned for industrial use, just for residences. You can read all about Guido and his labor problems in my story "Vibini in Labor," which was published in *First Intensity*, #10 (Winter, 1998), 95-100. You can get a copy by sending $9.00 to the editor Lee Chapman at PO Box 665, Lawrence, Kansas, 66044.

Across the street from us at 254 West Vox Populi Street is the married couple of Jeremy Scroggins and his wife Airball McGritts and their Schnauzer named Rhett Butler. Saponata tells me that Scroggins is a Southern poet, whatever that means. The wife is a novelist and has published a novel called *Puppy Love*. Saponata says that Airball was given that name by her father who played basketball for the University of Alabama but could never make his free throws. Whenever he went to the foul line, the fans chanted "airball, airball," and he would inevitably miss the shot. Airball doesn't like her name so she calls herself Ariel McPherson. I'll use them in a future story so I need not tell anything more about them here. I want you to know they are there and will appear later.

Saponata has also told me that Father Thomas Takianopoulos and his wife Leah have moved into the house at the end of the street on our side, number 231 West Vox Populi Street, because he wants to live close to his church Saint Oholibamah's Chiliastic and Universalist Church of the Redeemer and All Saints of the Full Space-Time Continuum. He is the defrocked priest who married Dallasandro Vibini and Saponata Santarellina. You can read all about that marriage in my story "Amazing Grace," if it's ever published. Across from Father Thomas, called "the Gymnast," at 232 West Vox Populi Street is the home of Sigismondo Pandolfo Salvatore, the oldest son of Giovanni Battista Salvatore, the Italian war hero whose biography I'm writing. I have yet to meet Sigismondo. That too will happen in a future story.

All of what I've told you to this point in this story is what is called setting. I've read that defining the setting is always a good way to start a story. You have to get a right narrative order, such as setting before dialogue or descriptions of characters before they appear in scenes, not after. As I work my way into my literary career, I'm learning the standard techniques and I'm finding out that they work. Great writers use the standard techniques for story telling and I'm trying to be like them. Moreover, I've read that the setting must be specific. It must give the reader the sense that the narrative is taking place in a real place at a real time. It's a way of masking the fiction. The details must be specific and correct so that the details do not unmask the fiction. The specific times of the narrative are about to be revealed.

I've also read that it's a good idea to define the point of view early in the story. And then never deviate from it. In my eleven previous stories about Vibini, I'm the point of view. And I'm the point of view in this story. I'm Gottlieb Liebgott, retired medical doctor. I came to the U.S. in 1980 when my wife Gertrude committed suicide in Wuppertal, Germany. My three sons and daughter had, by then, all been institutionalized in St.Dympna's in Gheel. They all wanted to be writers because my father Lobgott Gerebernus Liebgott was a famous German novelist. My mother Josephine Priedieu was a French whore whom my father met after the Battle of the Somme where he was wounded. My father always said, "Lobe den Herren, Gottlieb. It wasn't in the groin." Josephine nursed him back to health and after World War I ended he took her to Wuppertal and married her.

I was born in Wuppertal on January 9, 1930. I grew up there and, after World War II, I went to medical school in Heidelberg. I never expected that I would leave Germany because my medical career was rewarding. For some reason, my wife Gertrude decided to do herself in. On our twenty-ninth anniversary, June 24, 1980, she threw a rope over a beam in our garage, stood on a pile of my medical textbooks, tied the rope around her neck, kicked the books out from under herself and was swinging gently back and forth at 8:00 P.M. when I came home from my daily practice. Because she kicked the books into the dust of the garage and because she left her footprints on my copy of *Clinical Excision of Vital Organs* by Dr. Felix Hautmesser, I was unable to sell the books to a used book dealer.

Even without being able to sell my used medical books, I bought a flight ticket to Cleveland, Ohio, where, I was told, there was rampant disease and a serious shortage of doctors. That wasn't true, but I did learn about Cincinnati. I was told to go there because the citizens of Cincinnati love German doctors. They think because a doctor is German he is a good doctor and, besides, they said, there are lots of Nazis there who are generally called Republicans.

One of my fellow doctors took out a map of the state of Ohio and said, "Look how the state is like a large bathtub. Everything flows down to the southwest corner of the state and the city of Cincinnati is like the drain in the tub. All the dirt and junk of the state run down to that corner and out into the Ohio River. All the misfits and riffraff of the state end up there. It's a natural gravity flow." I went there and set up my practice.

I retired on January 3, 1995, and began my second career as a writer. I'm now sixty-eight years old and learning my trade very quickly. You'll see me often at the Clifton Branch of the Hamilton County Public Library. I'm five feet eight inches tall and I weigh over 300 pounds. White hair, thick metal-rimmed glasses, large nose. I look like Otto von Bismarck without the

Schnauzbart. I wear black suspenders and carry a gold watch. I often talk to one of the librarians. That's Saponata Vibini, eighteen year old wife of Dallasandro Vibini, who is fifty-three. She works there and checks out books for me: *The Sound and the Fury*, *The Great Gatsby*, *Collected Stories of Katherine Mansfield*, *Winesburg, Ohio*, *The Sun Also Rises*, *The Heart of the Matter*. The books all have a pink label on the spine, "Classics." She's the librarian who has thin, wispy blond hair, a pointed nose, soft pink lips, green eyes that seem gravid with immanent lust. She always wears a clean white blouse under a knee-length gray smock that covers her protruding stomach. When she smiles at you, you feel as if springtime has arrived and flowers are bursting into bloom in the air. When she points the little light gun at your library card and you hear the little bleep that records your book transaction you want to hug her and make her the mother of your children.

Now that you know the setting of the story and the point of view in the story, I can let you know exactly when the story begins. But that's a problem in narrative. How can you tell exactly when a story begins? All stories begin, I suppose, at the creation of the universe, or maybe even before, and they end whenever the universe ends. Stories are part of a continuum of events. So when I say this story begins on August 1, 1998, that's a narrative convenience. No one can chronicle everything that precedes and influences a narrative or everything that succeeds a story. There is no such thing as a series of discrete events. I've come to realize that our narrative devices are ways of deceiving the reader into thinking a story is a self-contained series of events with a beginning, a middle and an end and we all know that's why we call our narratives fiction.

My present narrative is called "Vibini in the Underworld." It's called that because in the story Vibini nearly gets himself killed. He escapes the danger because of the heroic actions of his young wife and because of my heroic silence. I've resolved that my stories should turn on the actions of and definitions of my characters, how they live and how they conduct themselves in a dizzy world. I don't mind telling you how the story is going to end. That's not what is important in narrative. I'll use some foreshadowing, but that's for the enjoyment of the literate reader who knows the ways of fiction.

All my narratives are told in retrospect. I realized early on that all narratives are about two things: they are about memory and the way in which the story is told, including the style that is used in the telling. That's why most stories are told in the past tense. The events are over. We pretend they are happening now in the historical present. Gatsby is dead when the novel begins. Raskolnikov is in Siberia when the novel begins. Lolita and Humbert Humbert are dead when the novel begins. Holden Caulfield is in a mental institution when the novel begins. Vibini is alive and well when this story begins. Despite the death threat, he survives. Don't worry about the ending when reading this story. Everything comes out OK.

I also don't mind telling you that I resolved at the beginning of my recording of the Vibini narratives that each narrative would begin with a phone call. I got the idea from the movies. When I was a youngster in Wuppertal, I went constantly to American movies. I soon realized that American movies could not have any action without telephone calls. A character hears a phone ring, he picks up the phone and talks, and the movie is underway. Often, I noted, when the action of the movie slowed down and there was a lull in the plot, a phone would ring and the plot would get back on track. And why shouldn't a story begin with a phone call? It's as good a device as the receipt of a letter, a book opening to the title page, pages of a calendar turning, a narrator telling preceding events, the finding of a dead body, a man about to jump off a cliff, a distraught woman hiring a private detective. A phone call jumps right into the middle of the action. A phone call is always *in medias res.*

Before I began this story, I asked Saponata where I should begin the story. She said, "Why, at the beginning." That's where I'm starting. It was Saturday morning, August 1, 1998, a hot and muggy day. Ninety degrees Fahrenheit and eighty percent humidity. At 9:32 A.M. the phone rang. I answered. It was Tomasso de Giovanni di Simone Guidi calling, he said, for the third time. He explained that his friends called him "Masaccio." He wanted to speak to the great detective Dallasandro Vibini. He had a job for Vibini. I called Vibini in from his bedroom, which used to be my study, and told him that he had a message. I held my hand over the mouthpiece of the phone and told Vibini that the caller was using a false name. I told Vibini that the caller was using the name of the Italian Renaissance painter Masaccio.

Vibini talked for fifteen minutes to the caller, said, "OK. I'll do it," and hung up. I said, "Vibini, what is it? It doesn't sound good. Why doesn't he use his own name?" Vibini stared at me strangely and said, "It's $10,000. This Masaccio is offering me $10,000 to find out the background of a young man who is going to marry his daughter." My disquiet was immediately dispelled when Vibini mentioned $10,000. Vibini's $100,000 in debt since he got taken on the Hemingway manuscripts. You can read about that episode in my story "Hemingway's Valise," if it ever gets published.

Vibini went into his bedroom and dressed for the hunt. Green beret, red cape, yellow trousers, blue shirt, purple spats. Saponata had not left for her job at the library and I heard her yelling at him to leave off the spats. When Vibini, who is six feet tall and weighs 150 pounds, emerged, he looked like a painted bunting, or, better, like Savonarola in a clown suit. He said, magisterially, as he is wont to do, "Liebgott, call me a cab." I said, "You're a cab." And they say we Germans have no sense of humor.

When the Quo Vadis Cab had taken Vibini off to his search and Saponata had gone to the library for her day's work, I had the whole day ahead of me. With unlimited joy I opened the windows and let out the smell of marijuana and turned on my computer to the Web site at Monte Cassino. Once into the *Annali Calabresi,* I began my surfing in the annals compiled by Fra Bartolomeo Masaccio and came upon one of the most amazing deposits I've found thus far (Volume CXIII, #46). I knew that my Italian war hero Giovanni Battista Salvatore ended his career in Falconara Marittima. When the Illyrian-Italian War (1945-1948) ended, Salvatore settled down and became a successful squid merchant. What I didn't know was that Falconara Marittima was but the remnant of a once great city.

Fra Bartolomeo Masaccio includes in his *Calabrian Annals* a document from 1529. He records that it was written by a Fra Griffolino D'Arezzo in the year 1529 when the forces of the Turkish Ottoman Empire under Suleiman the Magnificent had moved far into the Balkans and reached the Illyrian coast and were laying siege to Vienna and Bratislava. In that year the naval forces of the Ottoman Empire under the command of Suleiman's vassal Barbarossa entered the Adriatic Sea and threatened the fortress city of Calamar. I have recorded the whole document verbatim. (My translation.)

"I, Fra Griffolino D'Arezzo, give this record because I witnessed the end of the great fortress city Calamar. When the naval forces of the evil Turk under the command of the vassal Barbarossa entered our sacred Adriatic Sea in the year of our Lord 1529 and threatened the Marches of the Papal Power under the command of our Holy Father Clement VII, Sovereign of the State of Vatican City, Bishop of Rome, Vicar of Jesus Christ, Successor of St. Peter, Prince of the Apostles, Supreme Pontiff of the Universal Church, Patriarch of the West, Primate of Italy, Archbishop and Metropolitan of the Roman Province, the impregnable city of Calamar prepared itself for a defence against the ruthless infidels.

"When the forces of the Infidels conquered the Illyrian Republic in 1520 and established their power on the coast of the sea, the citizens of The Papal Marches under the command of Capitano Falconara di Capocchio Salvatore determined to fortify themselves against the certain danger of an invasion. To that end they commissioned the architect Catello di Rosso Gianfigliazzi to design for them a fortress city that could withstand the full power of the Turks. Said architect conceived for the citizens an island fortress such as could be breached by no known military force.

"The fortress city of Calamar was constructed in the tidal basin three hundred paces from the shoreline at high tide. The sea formed a moat about the city, even at low tide. The form of the city was a square, each side three hundred paces in length. The walls were thirty-three cubits in height and twelve cubits in thickness. The walls were painted a sepia color, the color of the dye derived from the squids of the sea. A tower arose above each corner over which flew the flag of Calamar. The four towers were named Matthew, Mark, Luke and John and atop each tower was a statue of the animal of the writer of the Gospel: a man for Matthew, a lion for Mark, an ox for Luke and an eagle for John. Twelve ravelins protruded from the towering walls. Three ravelins pointed east to the sea. Three ravelins pointed north to Venice. Three ravelins pointed south to the entrance to the sea. Three ravelins pointed to the shoreline of the Papal power."

Vibini called at 11:36 A.M. just as I wrote down the information about the ravelins to ask what MCMLXXIII meant. I said it meant 1973. I asked him why he needed to know that and he said that it was the year his quarry was born. He said he'd found a record of Paolo Vecchio da Polenta's birth. The record he found, he said, was in a copy of Dante's *Commedia*, a book which he found in the downtown public library. I said, "Vibini, that hardly passes for an official record." "Listen," Vibini said, "it's witnessed by four signatures, one of whom is a priest Father Gualdrada Guerra." I hung up the phone and went on with my writing.

"Each of the twelve ravelins extended from a gate in the wall. Each ravelin was connected to the wall by a bridge that could be opened or destroyed in case the ravelin were to fall to the enemy. The bridges to the gates served as wharves for bringing in supplies to the occupants of the city. The ravelins were named for the twelve disciples: Peter, James, John, Andrew, Philip, Bartholomew, Matthew, Thomas, James II, Thaddeus, Simon and Matthias.

"Each of the gates was constructed to look like a large jewel in the side of the wall. The three gates to the east were made to look like jasper, sapphire and chalcedony. The three gates to the north like emerald, sardonyx and sardius. The three gates to the west were of chrysolite, beryl and topaz. The three gates to the south were chrysoprase, jacinth and amethyst. In the center of each gate was a large shield made to look like a pearl that could be opened so the defenders could look out and the enemy could look in. Each gate was named after one of the twelve tribes of Israel: Reuben, Simeon, Levi, Judah, Zebulun, Issachar, Dan, Gad, Asher, Naphtali, Joseph and Benjamin."

Vibini called again at 2:15 P.M. He said, "Gottlieb, get my Italian dictionary and look up 'male acquistato.'" I got the dictionary and told him that it meant "ill-gotten." Vibini sighed and said, "I can see why the father of the would-be bride is concerned. Thanks. Oh, and Liebgott, do you happen to know anything about a tattoo of the number eighteen with an arrow through it from upper right to lower left?" The tattoo was familiar, but I couldn't recall where I'd heard of it so I said no and hung up.

The document by Fra Griffolino D'Arezzo, as transcribed by Fra Bartolomeo Masaccio in the *Annali Calabresi,* continues: "At each corner of the walls of the fortress city was a tower twenty-four cubits high with each tower surmounted by the flag of Calamar, namely, on a skyblue field a white unicorn rampant with a squid, its tentacles reaching downward, skewered on his horn. Under the rampant unicorn the motto of Calamar: 'Aut Lolligo, Aut Nihil.' At the center of the city was the Cathedral of St. Thomas Asdente, the shoemaker from Parma who foretold the coming of the evil Turks. The three spires of the cathedral, two at the west end and one over the chancel, rose above the walls and the towers. Each spire flew the city flag for all to see even far out to sea.

"It was in the evil year of 1529, the year predicted by St. Thomas Asdente, that the naval forces of the Turks under the command of Suleiman's vassal Barbarossa approached the fortified city of Calamar. As the Turkish forces approached, the ravelins were manned, the cannon prepared, the soldiers armed for repelling the invaders. The twelve gates to the city were closed and the bridges from the ravelins into the city were mined with explosives. The city prepared for a siege.

"As the forces of the Turks maneuvered into position for attacking Calamar, the citizens of the city gathered in the cathedral and sang the 'Vexilla regis prodeunt.' Candles and incense were lit. Bishop Giovanni di Buiamonte prayed at the high altar and said the mass in time of war. The prayers of the people fell on deaf ears. The candles and the incense sputtered and died away. Bishop Buiamonte forgot the ritual, began stuttering and fell in a faint. The paint fell from the face of the statue of St. Thomas Asdente. The city trembled and shook as the skies darkened and thunder and lightning rent the air. Massive tremors shook the city and, as the people prayed and sang, the city began to sink."

Just as I got to the sinking of the city, the telephone rang again. It was Vibini. I said, "What now, Vibini? I can't get any work done with you calling all the time." "Listen," he said, "write this down: JBW-582." I said, "What's that?" "It's a license plate number. Someone is following me. Two men driving a black Mercedes-Benz car. Four-door. Just keep a record of that car and keep that number in case I'm not home for dinner."

Vibini hung up and I went on with my recording. "The City of Calamar sank faster and faster. The Turkish ships put out to sea as fast as possible so they would not be drawn into the maelstrom. A huge wave rushed from the Illyrian coast, capsized the Turkish vessels and inundated the City of Calamar. The citizens and soldiers raced for the high places, tried to clamber up the walls, climbed to the roof of the cathedral, but to no avail. The city sank beneath the sea until even the highest spires on the cathedral were beneath the waters. Only twelve citizens survived. They reached the Italian shores by holding to pieces of wooden refuse.

"As the waters rushed in and covered the city, Capitano Falconara di Capocchio Salvatore climbed to the very pinnacle of the cathedral tower over the high altar, ripped down the royal flag of Calamar and leaped into the raging waters. There, by the grace of God, he fell next to the wooden statue of St. Thomas Asdente. Grabbing hold of the floating saint, Capitano Salvatore floated in to the beach, stepped ashore, lifted up the flag and cried out, 'Citizens of Calamar, once again God has saved us from our enemies. We have conquered the Turks. Our losses were great, but we have survived and we will, by the grace of God, rebuild our city on this shore. Our flag will once again fly over our sacred city. Let us sing a "Te Deum" for our salvation.' As the survivors sang the 'Te Deum,' Capitano Salvatore raised the flag over their heads and announced that their new city would henceforth be called 'Falconara Marittima' because it was born from the sea."

Fra Griffolino D'Arezzo's account, as transcribed by Fra Bartolomeo Masaccio concludes as follows: "The city of Calamar exists to this day in its underwater grave. When the tides run in and out, it is still possible to hear the muffled bells ringing in the spires of the sunken cathedral. If one lays his ear to the sands of the shoreline, one can hear the souls of the drowned citizens of Calamar talking and laughing in the submerged streets. One can still hear Bishop Giovanni di Buiamonte's uncompleted celebration of the mass bubbling up in the waves, his voice rising and falling with the tides. One can look down from above and see the houses, the streets, the cathedral just as it was in 1529 when the evil Turks came into the sacred Adriatic Sea. The squid fishermen of Falconara Marittima do not like the spires of the lost cathedral. Their nets snag on the high points. But they do not curse the troubles for the sunken city is now the home of swarms of squid and the new city has become rich on the new inhabitants of Calamar. Whenever the tide changes and the bells ring, the fishermen of Falconara Marittima know when to drop their nets because when the bells ring the squid swarm out of the sunken cathedral and the houses along the streets and out into the open sea. The fishermen have but to draw in their glutted nets."

I had just finished my transcription of the story of Calamar from the *Annali Calabresi* when Vibini's cab pulled up in front of the house and Saponata returned home from her job at the library. Both of them came in and said they were terribly hungry. I called Domino's Pizza and ordered a large pizza with sausage, onions, green peppers, pepperoni, black olives and mushrooms. While Vibini lit up his joint and Saponata set the table, I went into the vestibule and waited for the delivery of our supper.

While I was waiting I noticed a black car parked across the street from our house. Two men were sitting in the front seats. The car was parked so that it faced toward Clifton Avenue. Pretending that I was looking for the evening paper, I walked out onto the sidewalk and walked around. The license plate number was JBW-582. The car was a black four-door Mercedes-Benz.

I went back into our apartment where Vibini had locked himself in his and Saponata's room so that he could smoke a joint. Saponata was laying out plates and utensils for the meal. I said, "Saponata, do you know what a cliché is?" "Why, no." "You're about to learn. Look out the front door. There's a big, black Mercedes-Benz parked across the street. It has the same license plate as the one reported by Vibini to me this afternoon. Two men are sitting in it. One's fat and one's thin. They're both wearing black bowlers that are too small for their heads. They look like characters out of American gangster movies."

Saponata walked out into the vestibule. When she came back, she was completely pale. "What is it?" I asked. "You look ill." "Gottlieb," she whispered, "I know those two men. They're hit men. Their names are Rinier Corneto and Rinier Pazzo. Corneto is called 'the handyman' and Pazzo is called 'the spade.'"

"How do you know them? And what are hit men?"

"They've done work for my father. Hit men are professional killers. But why are they here on our street? What's Vibini doing?"

The answers to Saponata's questions came while we ate our pizza and drank our cans of warm 7-Up. She looked out from her pale face and said, "Dally, what did you do today?" Vibini, already loose with his dope, said, "Oh, I had a good day. You know that guy who called and offered me $10,000 to investigate the guy who is going to marry his daughter? Well, his name is not

'Masacchio' as you, Liebgott, rightly surmised. His real name is Mosca dei Lamberti. He's called 'the fly.' Anyway, he offered me $10,000 to find some dirt on this young guy who wants to marry his daughter. You see, the fly doesn't want his daughter to marry into that other family."

Saponata, who was getting more and more nervous, asked, "What is the girl's name?"

"Francesca. The fly says she's real beautiful. And she seems to be rich."

"She is beautiful and Mosca's family is very rich," Saponata whispered and then added, "What's the name of the young man who wants to marry her and who you're investigating?"

When Vibini said, "Ciacco Polenta," I thought Saponata was going to pass out. She put her right hand to her throat and her left hand on her stomach. "Saponata," I said, "Are you all right?" She whispered that she was and Vibini went on with his narrative. "So this morning I took the Quo Vadis cab to the public library downtown. I met the fly in the courtyard and we made our deal. I get $10,000 when I deliver to him a complete description of the young dope who wants to marry his daughter."

I could hardly hear Saponata when she whispered, "Are you sure the young man's name is Ciacco Polenta?" Vibini smiled and said, "I got it written down right here. Anyway, since I was at the library anyway, I searched the newspapers for anything on Polenta. Then I went to the police station at District Number One. When I left there and walked to the Historical Library in the Union

Terminal, that's when someone started following me. That's when I called you, Liebgott."

Saponata stammered quietly, "And what did you find out about him?"

"First of all, his real name is Paolo Vecchio da Polenta. He's called 'Ciacco,' which means 'the glutton.' He's been arrested six times for drunken driving. He's been charged with dealing in drugs. He's been sued four times for not paying child support. He's a high school dropout. And all this is just a beginning. Next Monday I plan to dig up a lot more. There's that thing about the tattoo on his butt, the number eighteen with an arrow through it. I have to find out what that's all about."

When we finished eating, Saponata said to Vibini, "You go on to bed, Dally. I'll be there soon."

When Vibini left the room, Saponata took me into the vestibule and said, "Liebgott, I need your help. Will you go to church with me tomorrow?"

"Which church?" I asked.

"Why the church of Father Thomas the Gymnast. You should enjoy it. He's preaching on the Apostle Paul tomorrow. You've told me about the Apostle Paul and now Father Thomas is going to tell us more. I saw him in the library and he especially invited me to come and hear the sermon this Sunday. He promised it would be educational. Did you know that Father Thomas is called 'Skialogos?' Besides, I need to talk to you alone. And please promise me that you won't tell any of this to Vibini." I agreed not to tell Vibini what Saponata had told me and I realized that our *ménage à trois* was about to become deceitful.

The next morning, Sunday, August 2, 1998, Saponata fixed her little I.G.A. breakfast, we ate, she dressed in her gray smock with her clean white blouse, I dressed in my black three-piece suit, gold chain and watch, and we walked over for the morning service at St. Oholibamah's. As I told you earlier, I don't care about surprises in narratives. I want the reader to know what is going to happen next. The only problem is that I don't think I can adequately describe what happened that morning at the church. I'll give it a try.

Saponata and I walked out of our *cul-de-sac*, Vox Populi Street, crossed Clifton and went along Resor to St. Oholibamah's Chiliastic and Universalist Church of the Redeemer and All Saints of the Full Space-Time Continuum. We entered to find Father Thomas, called "Skialogos," standing at the front of the sanctuary. He was dressed in a translucent and transparent pink robe. We could see his red boxer shorts under the robe. That's all he was wearing other than the robe whose long sleeves fell down around his wrists. He stood under a spotlight that was in the ceiling and the light coming down reflected off his bald head and outlined his berserk gray tonsure. The descending light refracted through his glasses and sent flashes of light out across the audience of eight people who were spread out through the twenty rows of ten chairs each. Sudsy and I sat down in the next-to-last row and near a window.

Father Thomas the Gymnast invited us to begin the worship service by singing "Eensie weensie spider went up the water spout." He showed us how to make the hand motions to indicate the spider climbing up the water spout, how the rain came down and washed the spider out, how the sun came out and dried away the rain and how eensie weensie spider went up the spout again. This was followed by a singing of "Three Blind Mice" and an invocation that began, "Lord, kick the shit out of our enemies and send us all a lot of money," or something like that. I have to reconstruct what happened in that vertiginous morning. "Vertiginous" is a new word I've just learned and I've been looking for a place to use it even if it doesn't fit.

After the invocation, Father Thomas, the defrocked Patriarch, ascended to the pulpit which was on the dais and illuminated by three spotlights. There he paused, looked out over the audience of ten, and said, "Dearly beloved, what the hell. It does my heart good to look down upon this mud puddle of sour faces and know that you have Jesus in your pissy-assed underwear. Today I'm going to talk about the origins of Christianity. You all know the story of how the Pharisee and persecutor of the early Christians, Saul of Tarsus, became the Paul of Christianity when he was struck blind on the road to Damascus. You all know how he recovered and how the newly named Paul became a great missionary and spread Christianity. It's that missionary work that gives him away. Hot dog, huh? I'm going to talk about the real Apostle Paul. Whoop-de-do, heigh-ho, feel my billywang and goose me if you don't give a shit about the miserable creep.

"The first thing you got to realize about the Apostle Paul is that you can tell he was chickenshit by where he didn't go. Look at the direction he went when he left the

Holy Land after he got knocked off his ass on the road to Damascus. Did you ever realize that he didn't head north? No sirree. If he had gone north he would have run into the Scythians. Just think for a moment, fellow believers, what would have happened to him if he'd have gone up there and told those savages about someone who was crucified and three days later arose from the dead and then ascended into heaven. They would have whipped him up on a cross of his own so fast that he wouldn't even have had time to yell, 'Let me explain.' Then they would have taken the corpse of that true believer and peeled the skin from his face and made it into a handkerchief, cut open the skull, scraped out his still twitching brain and used the skull for a beer mug. No sir, buster, chickenshit Paul was having none of that."

Saponata, who was sitting to my left, leaned over and whispered in my ear, "Gottlieb, can I trust you? I need your help and I need to have your silence. I have something very important to tell you, but you must promise me that you will never tell Dally, never, under any circumstances." I whispered back, "OK. I promise. What is it that is so important?"

"He didn't go east either. Had he gone east he would have run into the heathen Chinese. Can you imagine him walking into Peiping and standing on a street corner and crying out that he had good news? Can you imagine the heathen Chinese listening to him saying that the Messiah had come and all the world was going to be saved from itself? Can you imagine him telling them about shepherds who saw angels and kings who saw a star and came from the East to Bethlehem? Can you imagine him telling them about how this carpenter's son from Nazareth fed 5000 people on two fishes and five loaves of bread? The heathen Chinese would have sent his ashes back in a thimble before he could have cried out, 'It's just a joke.'"

Saponata whispered, "You know the young man who Dallasandro is investigating?" I whispered, "His name is Ciacco, I believe. But his real name is Paolo." "That's right," she whispered. "Gottlieb, I know him. I used to be a friend of his. I know the family." I whispered, "Is that why you were upset last night when Vibini was telling what he found out yesterday? I surmised you were hiding something. I noticed your reaction even if Vibini didn't." She whispered, "That's why I got you to go to church with me. I don't want Vibini to know any of this stuff."

"He didn't go south. No sir, you bet your sweet bippy. Had the Apostle Paul gone south he would have run into the Egyptians, who don't exactly like strangers, especially white folks from Tarsus. Can you imagine him going into Alexandria, the seat of all Western learning, and trying to tell those African intellectuals that their religion was all wrong and that he had the truth that would take away their ignorance and lead them into eternal life? Can you imagine him telling them about the son of a god who could still the winds, turn water into wine, cast out devils and put them into swine, heal blind people and raise his buddies from the dead? Those Egyptian priests would have mummified him faster than he could have said, 'I was just kidding.' So Old Paul didn't go north, he didn't go east and he didn't go south. So where did he go?"

Saponata pushed her lips right into my left ear and whispered, "Liebgott, listen carefully. Remember your promise not to tell any of this to Dally. I'm pregnant." I twitched a little and whispered back, "I had guessed as much. I first suspected it when I saw no evidence of your having periods. I couldn't figure out how I could miss it. Then I noticed the swelling. Vibini will be overjoyed to know he's going to be a father."

"He went west, of course. You all know that when he set out to convert people to Christianity he headed right toward those people he knew he could hornswoggle into believing what he was telling them. He went right at those people he knew would believe anything and would not ask any questions. He went right to those people he knew had more gods than they could count. He went right at those people who believed that gods could do anything and that they walked around on this earth. He went right at those European hillbillies who believed that the gods turned themselves into animals and fucked women. He went right at those southern European rednecks, those foot-stomping, lyre-picking, plectrum-plucking, hallelujah-hollering, wine-guzzling clodhoppers who believed that the gods turned people into flowers, trees, stars and rivers. He went right where he knew he could sell his snake oil and everyone would buy it and pay him for it because they believed that there were gods in everything and each god was ridiculous. He knew exactly where to go. He went right to the Greeks and the Italians."

Saponata leaned into my left ear. I could feel her hot breath. She whispered, "That's just it, Liebgott. He's not the father. I was already three months pregnant when we got married. Now I'm over four months along." I jerked away from her mouth. She held onto me and said aloud, "Please, Liebgott. I need your help." The thoughts that raced through my mind turned on deceit, duplicity, treachery, dishonesty and the guile of an eighteen year old girl. I'm not sure about the rest of what happened in St. Oholibamah's. The worst was yet to come.

"So there he was, the Apostle Paul, walking around Athens, telling those poor, benighted suckers that he had a message for them that would deliver them from hell. Telling them he had a message that would give them everlasting life. You know, it says something about your religion when those who believe it are the helpless and the gullible. It says something about your religion when the people who accept it are a bunch of illiterate foreigners along the shores of the Mediterranean. It says something about your religion when those who accept it are a bunch of southerners who have been washed over time and time again by foreign religions and accepted everyone that came along. It says something about your religion when those who accept it have believed every apostle from every religion that ever sprang up in the neighborhood. It says something about your religion when the only converts you can get are the clodhoppers of Europe. Paul knew what he was doing all right. He noticed their unknown god and he cashed in. He sold those Greeks his religion like it was a garage sale in Athens. He brought them salvation on the cheap."

Saponata began to cry. I got out my handkerchief and handed it to her so she could dry her tears. I think

Father Thomas saw it because when she dried her tears he began shouting. I guess he thought she was weeping because of his message in his sermon. Sudsy wiped her tears and leaned again into my left ear and said, "Liebgott, Ciacco is the father of my child."

"Then look what that hustler did. Not only did the Apostle Paul get those fish to believe his message, he got them to give him money so he could travel around and convert more people. They gave him money so he could live on Aegean welfare and spread his gospel. Look how he gouged the money out of them. He lived in their houses and took their cash. Telling them that if they didn't give him money they'd go to hell. The virtues and beliefs that Paul taught are just part of the cash flow. That's what's called 'sentimental fascism.' That's using a person's good characteristics, his loyalty, his sympathy, his honesty, his conscience, his decency, to manipulate him. Paul was a master at that, you got to hand it to him. That's how he spread his gospel without an army. That came later. The military force came later when Paul was getting cities named after him."

Saponata whispered, "Oh, Liebgott. What am I going to do? I need your help. Now they're threatening Dallasandro. I thought I'd gotten away from all that and that Vibini would be my salvation. That's why I married him. Tell me what to do." I said quietly to her, "Let me think about it. I might be able to help. You can count on me." I don't know why I said that because I was scared shitless. There's another word I learned recently. I sat and sweated as Saponata put her hand under my left arm and snuggled close. Her tears ran down my suspenders and dropped on my gold watch chain and then onto my belly where they soaked into my navel.

"Just look how Paul spiritually whipped those benighted Greeks and Italians. When they disagreed with his teachings, he kicked them out and told them they were going to hell. When they questioned his teachings, he bludgeoned them with his authority. When they started their own churches he called them heretics.

"He learned to use all the weapons of sentimental fascism to build his church. He learned how to manipulate the good characteristics of his congregations in order to whip them into line. He learned how to exploit their ignorance and their wonder in order to control the future of his church. Just look how he belittled women and got them to subject themselves to his overweening arrogance. He taught them humility in order to elevate himself. The Feminists ought to kick him out of the Bible because his teachings don't have anything to do with equal rights.

"Then he set himself up as a marriage counselor. Why is it, folks, that the people who pretend to know about marriage are always not married? Paul wasn't married but he was a Pharisee. He was trained in the Bible. Didn't he read the Old Testament? Didn't he read *The Book of Proverbs* and find out about quarrelsome wives? Didn't he know about bad marriages? Didn't he know that 'the contentions of a wife are a continual dropping?'

"All those dudes in the Bible who were married had troubles. Look at Jacob, for Christ's sake. No wonder God changed Jacob's name. He was probably a local joke because of the way Laban swindled him. His buddies probably snickered behind his back because Jacob got stuck with Leah when he thought he was getting Rachel. Look at all that swindling that went on. Not to mention the kids from the 'handmaidens.' Every time you see marital life in the Bible it's a mess."

Saponata snuggled closer and said, "Liebgott, let's go home. I want to see if Dallasandro is up yet. I want to see my husband."

"Then Paul put all his teachings in writing. His letters are now called 'Holy Scriptures.' That's how he got hold of the future and imposed himself on Christians for all time. The Christian Church was not built on the rock called St. Peter. It was built on the propaganda and the megalomania of the man we now call 'St. Paul.'

"And what of that future? Well hell, the Christians didn't learn from him. They tried for centuries to convert the Scythians, the Chinese and the Egyptians to their religion with absolutely no success. After millions of dollars in missionary salaries and millions of dollars in gifts to the heathens, all the Christians had to show for it was their livid butts after they were kicked out.

"What did the Christians do? They reached the final stage of Apostolic authority. First there was Paul and sentimental fascism, then there was Constantine and the political church and then the Christians spread their religion by force. The true Christian succession of authority fell down from the Apostle Paul to Rome and then to the gun.

"Paul set that pattern. When his message met resistance where the natives already had a perfectly good religion, it was the natives who got blinded and knocked off their asses by a gun and they didn't get back up unless, like Paul, they became Christians. You got to hand it to Paul; he spread Christianity without an army. That's difficult. The military force came later."

Saponata and I got up and walked out the door into the outer hall. As we left, I could hear Father Thomas, called "Skialogos," saying, "What Paul really accomplished was to give us a bunch of names for our cites: São Paulo, Santa Paula, Saint Paul." Saponata's tears glistened in the sunlight. I took out my backup hanky and wiped away her tears. She put her hand on my trembling left arm and I led her home.

On Monday, August 3, Saponata went to work in the library and Vibini drove off in a Quo Vadis cab to do his research and earn his $10,000. I watched out the front window as the black Mercedes-Benz followed the yellow Quo Vadis Cab out onto Clifton Avenue.

With my family gone, I decided to begin, finally, writing my biography of Giovanni Battista Salvatore, the Italian war hero. I dallied. I pretended to be thinking. I walked around the room. I put clean paper in my printer. I sat down at the keyboard. I blew my nose. I got up and went to the bathroom and took a piss. I opened a window to let out the marijuana smell. I told myself, "Stop the fooling around." I sat down and wrote, "The enemy's ships brooded offshore. The sun burned down on his exposed skin and onto the towering fortifications where the courageous Italian soldiers waited for the brutal, frontal assault of the Illyrian beasts. Capitano Salvatore knew that fate had dealt him a desperate hand

and he had to wager the future of the civilized world on his courage and that of his desperate soldiers. Capitano Salvatore looked into his thundering heart and said, 'Let them call my hand.'"

I read it over and decided to try again. I started over and wrote, "When the forces of the fascist powers withdrew from the Italian homeland and the powers of evil retreated north to the German hell, Capitano Salvatore stood defiantly on the fortifications of Brindisi and opposed the brutal onslaught of the Illyrian savages. He did not know that it was he beginning of his heroic defense of his beloved Italian homeland." I thought it not quite what I wanted.

I decided to give it one more try. "When the sun broke over the Adriatic coasts on that fateful day, June 6, 1945, and the overwhelming forces of the Illyrian devil queen, Queen Martha von Stoepf the First, gathered in the ominous dawn to destroy his beloved homeland, Capitano Giovanni Battista Salvatore marched boldly out upon the fortifications of Brindisi and called out to the bloodthirsty killers, 'Dov'è il gabinetto.'" When I re-read what I had just written, I decided to get some advice.

I packed up the three openings and walked over to the Clifton branch of the public library and showed them to Saponata. She looked them over and said, "Why don't you just begin at the beginning?" I thought, "Of course. Begin at the beginning." I walked back to Vox Populi Street, went back to my computer and wrote, "Giovanni Battista di Gesualdo da Castelluccio Inferiore Salvatore was born on March 21, 1925, in Castelluccio Inferiore. His father was Gesualdo Fuscaldo di Tomasso Salvatore.

His mother was Tinea Cruria Girandola. On the day of his birth he was baptised by Father Pietro Tagliacozzo Gleet and tattooed on his left butt with the number eighteen with an arrow pointing from upper right to lower left. The tattoo was to insure that if the child was stolen by Gypsies he could always be identified." The reader can find out more about all this in my story "Vibini and the Virgin Tongue" in the *North American Review*. I thought my opening sentence was excellent and I decided to keep it and go on from there.

When Vibini returned that evening and Laurel and Hardy were comfortably seated across the street from our house, I asked him what his day had been like. He said he'd gone to the dead files of *The Enquirer* and *The Post*. He said he'd gone to the Hamilton County courthouse and found the records of when the Polenta family came to the U.S. and when they were naturalized. He said that Ciacco, a.k.a., Paolo, Polenta had been involved in gang fights at Western Hills High School, had done time at Lebanon for stealing cars, was kicked out of Miami University at Oxford for refusing to join a fraternity, had joined the Unitarian Church at the age of six, was currently on probation for refusing to give money to the Republican Party.

When I reminded Vibini that Laurel and Hardy had been following him all day, he laughed and said, "Oh them. I talked to them today. They're great guys. Did you know they're being paid $100 per day each to follow me around? I told them I was doing research on politics and sports stadiums. They laughed and said, 'As long as that's all you're doing.' They made a joke about what size cement overshoes I wore. They even offered me a ride home. I said that the Quo Vadis Cab would pick me up at 5:00 P.M. at the library. I said, 'Why don't you come in and have a drink with me and Liebgott? Smoke a joint with me? Relax after a hard day in the front seat of a Mercedes-Benz?' They said they'd see me tomorrow morning. Are they still out there?"

Everything was quiet on Tuesday, August 4. Vibini left, Laurel and Hardy followed, Saponata went to work and I worked on my biography. I got on the Internet and discovered a Web site for underwater cities. The site had all kinds of stuff about Atlantis, of course, but the one that interested me was called "Vineta" and was presumably located in the Baltic Sea just off the north coast of Germany. I made my notes and decided to follow up on it.

On Wednesday evening, August 5, we had just finished our I.G.A. supper of "Del Monte Fresh Cut Peeled Tomato Wedges NET WT. 14 1/2 OZ. (411g)," "Freshlike Petite Sweet Peas," "Bumble Bee ALASKA SOCKEYE RED SALMON NET. WT. 7.5 OZ. (213g)," "Pepperidge Farm Mint Milano Distinctive Cookies" and a can each of "Pure Refreshment NO Calories* Sodium Mendota Springs Lemon 12 FL. OZ. Sparkling Water (355ML)" when the doorbell rang. I went to the door and opened it and there stood a man who introduced himself as Virgil Galeotto and said he had a customer out in his cab. I said, "Well, tell him to come on in." Virgil said, "He needs help getting out of the car."

I yelled to Vibini and we walked out to the Quo Vadis Cab, which was missing the front door on the rider's side. I said to Virgil, "Why is your front door missing? How can you carry passengers with a door off?" He said, "I had to take it off to get my passenger into the front seat. The door's in the trunk." Vibini looked into the cab and said, "Cristoforo, what are you doing out?" I looked more closely and I recognized Culofaccia although I'd only seen him once before when Vibini and I visited him at his apartment on Schadenfreude Street. The reader can read about that episode in my story called "The Hong Kong Umbrella," if it ever gets published. I knew it was Culofaccia because the obese man in the cab had "Mother Teresa" tattooed in skyblue ink across his forehead. Virgil gave us directions and the three of us managed to get Culofaccia out of the cab. When he walked up the steps to our porch, Culofaccia nearly passed out.

Once inside the house, Vibini introduced Saponata, his new wife, to Cristoforo. Cristoforo settled into our couch and Vibini began questioning why he had come out into the world because Culofaccia never leaves his apartment. He sits and watches TV all day. He is, he says, writing a history of "The Price is Right." Right off, however, he began telling Dallasandro to be careful. He said he'd received some phone calls from Bonturo Dati da Polenta telling him, Cristoforo, to speak to Dallasandro about his investigation of Bonturo's son Paolo sometimes called "Ciacco." He was telling. Vibini wasn't listening. He was sitting and humming "In diesen heil'gen Hallen." Saponata was turning pale again. Cristoforo kept on talking, "Bonturo says, 'Ciacco is a good boy. He needs a good wife, with some money. Francesca Lamberti has lots of money. Don't mess the marriage.'" Vibini wasn't listening. I said, "Vibini, Cristoforo has something to say to you. He says that the father of Ciacco says leave the marriage alone." Vibini said, "Bonturo has nothing to worry about. His son's scum. Besides, I need the $10,000."

Cristoforo, I could see, was becoming angry. "You don't see, Dallasandro. I'm bringing you a message from Bonturo. So anyway, listen to this story. Once there was a man named Cialtrone, who lost all his family and friends in a fire when his house burned to the ground. He needed a job. He discovered that his neighbor Guido Becchi had lost his best horse and that he wanted someone to find it. Cialtrone asked for the job. He found the horse, but instead of returning the horse to Guido Becchi he took the horse to a fair in Paccino and sold him for 1000 florins. Becchi found out about it. He called in his brother Malacoda and said, 'Get my money or my horse.' Malacoda went to Cialtrone and said, 'Guido wants his horse or the money.' Cialtrone said he had never found the horse. That night Cialtrone had his throat slit."

Vibini said, "So what? The story sounds like 5000 stories I've heard before. What's the point of the story?" Cristoforo struggled to his feet and said softly, "The point of the story is that it is a good idea to listen to the words of a brother." I said to Cristoforo, "A brother in need is a brother in deed." Cristoforo chuckled and said, "I didn't know you Germans had a sense of humor." We helped Cristoforo out to the waiting cab. The three of us managed to help him slide his huge bulk into the front seat of the cab. After he told the cabby to drive him home, Cristoforo leaned over and motioned Vibini to lean down into the cab. He did. I heard Cristoforo say, "Remember, Dallasandro, it is a good idea to listen to the words of a brother." As the cab departed, Saponata came up behind me and whispered, "Liebgott, I'm going to need your help again. Don't say anything."

On Thursday evening, when Vibini had retired into his marijuana sleep, Saponata told me to sit down and listen. She had something to say. "Listen, Liebgott, I need your help one more time. Again, you must not tell Vibini about this." I nodded. By then we were doing everything behind his back. Deceit had become a way of life for us two conspirators. "Tomorrow," she said, "I'm taking the day off from my job. I've got an important appointment and I want you to come along. We'll take the bus downtown. OK?" I agreed and the next morning at 11:00 A.M., Friday, August 7, we got on the bus at the corner of Clifton and Ludlow and went downtown to a restaurant called the "Gianni Schicchi." Saponata explained that the name of the restaurant was the name of an opera.

When we entered the Gianni Schicchi, there was a young man waiting to meet us. He was six feet tall, blond hair, brown eyes, thin, handsome, smiling, white teeth, thin nose. Saponata and he embraced briefly. She introduced me to Ciacco Polenta. We sat down. The waitress brought us coffee. Saponata looked Ciacco in the eyes and said, "Listen, sewer-face, I'm here to tell you to call off your two clowns that are tailing my husband." Ciacco looked bewildered. He said, "What husband? You mean you're married?" "That's right, asshole. And I want you to tell your fuck-face father that he'd better not hurt my husband or I'll blow your wedding with

205

Francesca clear to unholy hell." Ciacco looked bewildered, and I think he truly was. "I don't get it." Saponata hissed out, "Listen, you cocksucking son-of-a-bitch, you don't get it? Just turn around and bend over and you will. You know god-damned well what I'm talking about. I'm talking about your wedding to Francesca Lamberti." Ciacco frowned and said, "How did you know about that?" "A little bird told me. You mean you don't know that your asshole father has his goons threatening my husband?" Ciacco leaned over and said, "Who, for god's sake, is your husband? He's not that creep of a private investigator that Mosca Lamberti hired to get some dirt on me? That shithead creep is your husband?"

You've probably heard of a woman angered by insult, but I was proud of the way Saponata rose to the defense of her husband. "That shithead creep, as you call him, is twice the man that you are and that ain't saying nothing. We've been married now for seven weeks and he's taking care of me. That's more than you would fucking do, you scumbag asshole. He's a man. You're crap." Ciacco raised his right hand to hit her and I realized why I was brought along. Ciacco looked at me, lowered his hand and smiled. "So what's the deal?" he said. Saponata announced her terms: "Listen up, you scum. You tell your no-count father that if he harms Dallasandro Vibini, I'm going public with this." She stretched her smock tight over her stomach and patted her swelling womb. "I'll let everbody in this cocksucking town know how you raped me. I'll tell them how you and your fuckhead brothers Bocca and Focaccia ripped off my clothes and held me down while you dumped your scum into me. You know what will happen to you if my father finds out what happened? I'll tell them that you did it in my parents' bedroom. If they find that out, you won't be able to run far enough and fast enough to get away from the handyman and the spade. You won't just not get married. You won't ever have any kids when they get done with you, if you're still alive. I won't even bother to bring charges with the police. You won't be able to marry anyone for a long time. The only thing you'll ever marry is your hand. Unless you lose your hands along with your balls. I might even tell them about the tattoo just to make you look like the bastard you are."

Ciacco by then was turning some kind of funny white. His hands were shaking. Saponata stared right into his eyes. "OK," he said. "I get your point. But listen. I got to get something out of this too. What's that so-called husband of yours going to say to Mosca Lamberti? What if he says something that makes Lamberti call off my marriage to Francesca?" Saponata didn't miss a beat. That's a phrase I learned recently. She looked right at Ciacco and said, "I'll take care of that. I'll see to it that he says only good things about you. I'll write the report and substitute it for his report. That way you'll get married to that poor sap Francesca. Deal?" Ciacco smiled and said, "Saponata, you're great. OK. It's a deal. I should have married you." "Don't kid yourself," she snarled. "I wouldn't let some asshole creep like you touch me ever again. Now get the fuck out of here and go tell that scumbag of a father of yours to call off his torpedoes." Ciacco raised his right hand. I stood up and stepped between them.

We walked out the front door. Before leaving downtown Cincinnati, I went to the main library and found my stuff about the sunken city Vineta. Mainly I found a poem called "Vineta" by Wilhelm Müller and a poem by Heinrich Heine called "Seegespenst." I also got Günter Grass' novel *Die Rättin* where Vineta is used in the narrative. Grass makes Vineta a city of women, a women's republic. It is occupied by rats the way Calamar is occupied by squid. Vineta is a city of evil; Calamar is a city of love. Saponata and I took the number twenty-two bus to Clifton. That evening no one followed Vibini home.

On Saturday, Vibini took his report to Mosca dei Lamberti. I read it because Vibini wanted me to check it over for grammar. The report made Paolo Vecchio da Polenta, called "Ciacco," look like that favorite word of Saponata's, that is, "scum." How Saponata switched her report for Vibini's I don't know. I do know that Vibini got back from his meeting with Lamberti early enough that morning to still deposit $10,000 in the PNC Bank.

That Saturday evening, Saponata sat with Dallasandro Vibini and listened to Mozart's flute quartets. I turned off my computer so I could also listen. They sat on the couch together and held hands. I wish I did not have to say it, but it's true. Saponata wept quietly. Tears came from those wonderful green eyes that always seem gravid with immanent lust. They fell down over her lovely cheeks with their incipient freckles. Vibini stroked her wispy blond hair that was pulled back from her face and hooked behind her ears. I sat and thought about how terribly deprived my life was of any tenderness. I thought of that one day, my marriage day, when I had the only truly tender moment in my life. I recalled Gertrude's lovely hairless body, her open arms, my eagerness to enter her. I thought of Maria, my daughter, in her cell at St. Dympna's in Gheel. I thought of my three sons also there. I said a little prayer to myself that the moment of happiness that Vibini and Saponata were having would last all the days of their marriage and that the child would be whole, strong, happy and good. I asked for strength to keep my mouth shut.

The next morning, yesterday morning, Sunday, August 9, Saponata was up early. She knocked on my bedroom door and got me up too. I walked out in my red robe and my pink pajamas. Saponata had already laid out her I.G.A. breakfast for herself and me. Vibini was still snoring. I said, "What's up?" She said, smiling, "Get moving, Liebgott. You and I are going to church. You got thirty minutes to eat and get dressed and then we're off to hear Father Thomas, old Skialogos himself, preach on Cincinnati. I can't wait to hear what he's got to say about our lovely city."

I reluctantly accompanied Saponata over to Resor and St. Oholibamah's Chiliastic and Universalist Church of the Redeemer and All Saints of the Full Space-Time Continuum. This time I took along a notepad so I could write down what the Skialogos said. When we entered, Father Thomas the Gymnast was standing at the front of the church. He was dressed in a transparent and translucent royal blue robe. His blue bikini briefs were clearly visible through the thin cloth. The overhead light shined down on his bald head. His wild gray tonsure waved in the breezes from the air-conditioning. His dark eyes glittered behind his thick glasses and light flashed out from the thick lenses as the three spotlights reflected in them. He had a maniacal grin on his face. He looked surprised, like usual, but this time he seemed to be surprised by his own meanness. It was as if light had become evil and he was about to let his beams fall on the six other worshippers and us two.

The service began with us singing something called "This little light of mine, I'm going to let it shine." Again there were some finger movements as we sang. We all held up our right index fingers to indicate candles and sang a warning to others not to try to "poof" it out. We all went "poof" and then said that we'd hide it under a bushel, "no," as we covered the finger with the left hand and shook our heads "no." Then we all got out some ropes and everyone but me skipped rope to the verses: "Last night, the night before, twenty-four robbers knocked at my door. Asked them what they wanted and this is what they said, 'Dancer, dancer, do the splits. Dancer, dancer, do the kangaroo. Dancer, dancer, now skiddoo.'" Then everyone, except me, did ten deep knee bends and bent over and touched their toes ten times. "All right," father Thomas said, "now let's get down to business."

He opened the worship service with a prayer in which he asked God to punish the people who threw trash out of their cars. He asked God to clog up the dogs that shit along and on the sidewalks of Clifton. He asked God to break the hands of those who honked their car horns during his services. He asked God to shut off the electricity to nighttime football games. He asked God to make the Bengals lose all their football games for stealing tax pennies from the poor in order to enrich the rich. He asked God to punish northern Kentucky for stealing businesses from Cincinnati. The list went on. I ran out of space on a page so I quit recording the prayer.

Since I had remembered to bring along a notepad I was able to transcribe his sermon much more completely than I did the week before. Here's what I got put down: "Dearly beloved schmucks, dopes, creeps, etc. Fung gu." I hope I spelled "fung gu" correctly. "You're all from Cincinnati and that makes you creeps. You're all born into the flying hog shit of this town. You're all part of the virgin vulgarity of this city. You're all clean and pure in your stupidity. You're all part of the people who love to be despised, who love to be made contemptible, who love to be belittled and condemned because it proves something they've always known, namely, it proves they are the assholes everyone says they are.

"You know why? I want you to imagine with me this morning the state of Ohio. I want you to imagine that the state of Ohio is a man. Imagine the map of the state. Anthropomorphize it. Personify it. You'll note that if you think of Ohio as a man that Cleveland is his heart. Columbus is his navel. Dayton is his descending colon. Hamilton and Middletown are his sigmoid gut and Cincinnati is his anus. So this glorious Queen City, like the anus, is the place to which all the refuse of the state drains. I don't have to tell you what comes out of this city located at the end of that vile tube we call our bodies."

Saponata, who was sitting to my left, leaned over and whispered into my ear, "Dr. Liebgott, have you ever performed an abortion?" I whispered back, "Of course. Every doctor in this world has." She whispered, "Would you take my child?" I said aloud, "Absolutely not. You're too far along."

Father Thom leaned over the pulpit and said, "Cincinnati is a city where barbarism is never assailed by doubt. It's a city where hate is never ameliorated by mercy. A city where racism is never tempered by reason. Where poverty is never alleviated by compassion. Where suffering is never weakened by conscience. Where the Republicans are never guided by decency. Where the courts are never guided by justice. Where the citizens are never polluted by thought."

"Liebgott," Saponata whispered, "you're a wonderful man. I think I love you as much as Dally. I don't know what would have happened to me if I hadn't met you. Did you notice that I'm keeping my collars clean?" Saponata kissed me on the lobe of my left ear. I think the word to be used here is "melted." That's what happened to me. It was only the second kiss from a woman, both from Saponata, in I don't know how long and I blushed. Sixty-eight years old and I blushed because a young woman kissed the lobe on my left ear while the Skialogos vituperated. There's a word I've been looking for a chance to use. I also have to rewrite that last sentence.

Father Thomas the Gymnast blasted on. "I want you to remember what is wrong with this godforsaken city, because all of its sins are compounded by the fact that its citizens are fearful of, allergic to, resentful of, not titillated by and suspicious of irony. They have no sense of irony because irony requires thought, irony requires intelligence, irony requires education. Besides, you can't have a sense of irony in a city owned and operated by a banana company.

"Today I want you all to keep in mind as I speak that Cincinnati is a city of tasteless gourmets, pathetic chic and tacky swank. It is a city filled with shuffleboard intellectuals, foot fault minds and bogey intelligence. What I'm dealing with today is the tacky impudence of the mindless and the slipshod sophistication of this city. I'm talking about brain-dead politicians and half-wit artists. I'm talking about a city where the citizens don't vote because they can't read the ballots."

I'm pretty sure I got this part of Father Thom's sermon written down correctly. "My sermon today is called 'F-A-R-T-S.' That's 'F' for fearful. 'A' for allergic. 'R' for resentful. 'T' for titillated. And 'S' for suspicious. First there's the 'F' for fearful. In this benighted city, the citizens are fearful of feeling, fearful of giving, fearful of generosity, fearful of good deeds, fearful of kindness, fearful of decency and fearful of love."

Saponata took hold of my left arm, leaned over again and said, "Liebgott, have you ever delivered a baby into this world? Have you helped a mother give birth?" "Of course," I whispered, "I delivered all my own children. I've been present at the coming into this world of more than 500 children."

I felt pretty darned proud of myself as Father Thom hopped about the stage and cried out, "'A' is for allergic. Cincinnati is said to be a city where allergies thrive.

That's true. Cincinnati's citizens are allergic to just about everything. They are allergic to learning, to study, to knowledge. The citizens are allergic to wisdom. They are allergic to the very idea of using their brains for anything other than to calumniate minorities. They are allergic to using their sometime intelligence for trying to understand differences among people." I hope Father Thomas did use the word "calumniate" because that's another word I've been trying to find a use for.

Because I'm right-handed Saponata didn't interrupt my transcribing of the sermon when she leaned in again and whispered, "Dr. Liebgott, when the time comes will you deliver my baby? Will you help me bring my child into this shit-eating world?" "Of course," I said aloud, "I'll count it a privilege to preside over your becoming a mother. You can count on me being there. Only death could keep me away."

I turned from Saponata so I could get the "R" transcribed. "'R' is for resentful. The citizens of Cincinnati are resentful of any one who is extraordinary. They resent talent and accomplishment. They tear down and destroy anyone who rises above mediocrity. Their brutal censorship of the arts is ample evidence of their resentment. Whenever an artist comes from this city, the resentment of his or her genius sends that artist running from this city to a city where the resentment is at least not personal. That's why there are no great writers, singers, composers or painters living in this city."

I tried to think of a great writer, a great singer, a great composer or a great painter who lived in Cincinnati until Saponata interrupted my thoughts by whispering, "Liebgott, is birth a terrible painful thing? Does the mother suffer a lot when the child leaves the womb? Does the mother feel pain when the cord is cut?" "Dear lady," I whispered, "when the time comes I'll be there to tell you what's happening and I will help you bear the pain if there is any. I see you have a lot to learn about birthing. Let me be your teacher."

Just then Father Thom continued his teaching by shouting, "'T' is for titillated. Oh boy is this city titillated. It is titillated by tawdriness, by filth, by corruption, by dirt. This Queen City suffers from its massive titillation by the very contemplation of rot. Its titillation extends to the skin of the poor, the sores on the helpless, the cripples in the gutters, the mentally retarded in the dirty parks. It is titillated by the helpless patients in the hospices, by the gasping victims in the ambulances, by the rotting corpses in the morgues."

I turned from thoughts of rotting corpses in the morgues back to Saponata, who pulled at my left arm and said, "Liebgott, if I have a boy I will name him after you. How does that sound to you? Gottlieb Vibini." I couldn't answer. I could only pray, something I seem to be doing lately because I'm into deep shit emotionally. There's a phrase I never intended to use, but I hear it so often that it sounds natural and not offensive. So I prayed that the child would be a boy and that he would bear my name. Think of it; me, a doctor, and worried about progeny.

Father Thom seemed to be weakening as he wiped the sweat off his shiny bald head and began to conclude by saying, "And finally there is the 'S' for suspicious.

Here, in this rightly God-forsaken town, there is suspicion of anyone who tells these God-forsaken people what they are. They are suspicious of anyone who tells them the truth. They are suspicious of anything that might upset their complacency. They are suspicious of anything or anyone who might cause them a minor disruption in their indifference. They are so suspicious of anything strange that they are paranoid. And they embody their suspicions in their elected officials."

"Gottlieb," Saponata said, "let's go home. Dally should be up by now. I want to plant a big kiss on his lips, or his cheek if he has one of those little cigarettes in his mouth. Let's go out and get away from all this depression. You've made me feel so much better about my baby. Start behaving like a godfather and offer me your arm so I can walk home supported by a portly gentleman whose mind is filled with thought, knowledge and wisdom. Let's go out of here and let the people of Clifton see that there are at least two good people in this God-forsaken city."

Father Schlag was on the sidewalk in front of St. Eutychus of Troas. As we walked by he let out what I believe is called a "wolf whistle." He smiled at us and said, "Gottlieb, aren't you a bit old to be about to be a father? Be sure to bring the child over and I'll baptize it when it comes." "Like hell you will," I thought, and then said aloud to Father Schlag, "You see, you can teach an old dog new tricks." And they say we Germans have no sense of humor. I walked on in my dignity. It was a good feeling to have a handsome, young, pregnant lady holding on to my right arm. Saponata smiled up at me and said, "Next to Dally, I love you the most in this world. I know my child will have a good home with you and Dally to help me take care of him."

As we strolled along toward our apartment on Vox Populi Street, I began telling Saponata about my discovery of the history of the sunken city Calamar, which is just off the Italian coast by Falconara Marittima. I told her how the city was built and how it disappeared in what was probably an earthquake. I told her it sank below the waves just as the Turks were preparing to attack. I told her that Calamar is just as it was when it sank and that nowadays when young couples from Falconara Marittima get married they row out over the sunken city. They sit quietly and listen for the bells. If they hear the bells and look down and see the squid rushing from the cathedral and the houses, they know that they will have children and that their marriage will be a happy one. If they do not hear the bells, they weep.

"Did you know," I asked, "that there are a number of cities that are under the sea? We all know about Sodom and Gomorrah and that it sank out of sight because of its evil people. Everyone knows about Atlantis, but what they don't know is that Atlantis was founded by the god Poseidon, who married a beautiful, human woman named Cleito. Poseidon and Cleito became the parents of five pairs of twin sons. The island was divided up among the ten sons and the oldest son was made king. Atlantis prospered and became rich and powerful. But as the citizens of Atlantis grew rich and powerful they became arrogant and cruel. They forgot their divine origin. So Zeus, the main god of the Greeks, called together all the other gods in order to do something about it. The Greek philosopher Plato tells us all about Atlantis in the dialogue called the 'Critias,' because it is a character named Critias, who tells us about Atlantis. Critias doesn't finish the story, but we know that Atlantis sank into the Atlantic Ocean like the other cities that became fearful of generosity, allergic to intelligence, resentful of genius, titillated by suffering of the poor and helpless, and suspicious of anything new.

"The same thing happened to the city of Ys that sank just off the southern coast of Cape Finistère because of the evil of its citizens. The composer Debussy has written a beautiful piano piece about it, 'La cathédrale engloutie,' where the piano sounds the tolling of the bells in the sunken cathedral while the drowned Bretons chant the 'Dies Irae' in the depths of the Baie des Trépassés."

I figured I might as well give Saponata the whole tour of sunken cities so I continued. "Then there is the wonderful story of Vineta, a city that once existed off the northern coast of Germany. It was in the Middle Ages a very prosperous city. The citizens accumulated great wealth. But then they too became fearful of decency, allergic to wisdom, resentful of generosity, titillated by corruption and suspicious of truth. One night a storm came and Vineta suddenly disappeared beneath the waves where it remains at the bottom of the ocean, just like Calamar, intact to this day. Once a year, on the eve of May 1, Walpurgisnacht, the city rises at midnight for one hour. If sailors look down into the water and see Vineta, they are cursed and try desperately to sail down to its golden towers and its bells that ring as the tides of the ocean surge back and forth. The sailors will even risk wrecking their ships on the rocks in order to get to the city."

Saponata squeezed my right arm and said, "Oh Liebgott, you know such wonderful things. And I'm glad you tell them to me. I'd never before thought about what's under the seas. There must be all kinds of hidden things that we can't see, things hidden from our sight but still there."

I thought I'd bust my buttons, a phrase I heard in the library the other day, when she repeated, "You know such wonderful things." "Oh," I replied, "I wouldn't say that." Reader, I'm only reporting what was said.

This morning, Monday, August 10, 1998, Vibini and Saponata rose at 8:30 A.M. I was already up and had been for at least an hour. Saponata put out a Keller's I.G.A. breakfast for us: "The Original Thomas' English muffins" toasted, dishes of "Sunfresh chilled Grapefruit segments in Grapefruit Juice, Nt. wt. 26 oz. (1 lb. 10 oz) 737 g," a jar of "Polaner All Fruit seedless raspberry spreadable fruit sweetened only with fruit juice concentrates Net wt. 10 oz (283 g)," "IGA Assured Quality Since 1926 100% unsweetened Orange Juice from concentrates NET 46 FL OZ. 1 QT. 14 FL. OZ. 1.36 L" and "Taster's Choice, Original Blend, 100% Freeze Dried Coffee, Net Wt 2 oz. (57 g)." We sat down at the breakfast table. At each place there was a small dish of grapefruit segments, a small plate with the toasted muffin on it, a small glass of orange juice, a coffee cup, a knife, a spoon and a white paper napkin.

Before we began eating our breakfast, Saponata said, "Dally, what are your plans for the day?" Vibini said, "I'm going to the public library downtown. Bob is helping me in my project to listen to all the music that Mozart ever wrote." "Who's Bob?" I asked. "I don't know his last name. His name is Bob and he works in the music department." Saponata turned to me and said, "Liebgott, what are your plans for the day?" "I plan," I said, "to write our story. I plan to write down this latest episode in the Vibini chronicle. I want to get it down on paper while it's still fresh in my mind so that people can read about our adventure, if it ever gets published. When I finish that, I'm going to get going on my biography of the Italian war hero Giovanni Battista Salvatore. And what, Saponata, are your plans for the day?"

Saponata put her right hand to her throat, a gesture that indicates her shortness of breath, and said, "I plan to do my job at the library the best I can. Last week I was distracted. I didn't treat the customers the way I should. Today I'm going to be the best librarian that I can be. Today I'm going to be the best librarian in the whole public library system in Cincinnati."

I felt a paternal pride in Saponata's intentions. I wondered why my daughter couldn't have been like her. I am constantly amazed at what Saponata is, how she is learning so fast and how she seems more beautiful each day. How could she have come out of this God-forsaken city? I doubt Botticelli could paint her beauty now. I was even more amazed when she said, "Before we eat, let's say a little prayer to begin our new week."

Saponata bowed her head over the Sunfresh grapefruit segments, the glass of I.G.A. orange juice, the toasted Original Thomas' English muffin, the shining spoon and knife, the sparkling white napkin, the empty coffee cup, the jar of Polaner seedless raspberry spreadable fruit. She bowed her wispy blond hair, now tucked behind her ears and floating down the nape of her clean neck. She bowed her incipient freckles, her faintly pink lips. I noticed her eyelids lower quietly over her green eyes that seem gravid with immanent lust. I noticed her hands folded over her protruding womb. Vibini bowed his head. I bowed mine. And Saponata said quietly, "Come, Lord Jesus, be our guest and bless what you have shared with us. Amen."

PROLEGOMENA TO THE STUDY OF APOCALYPTIC HERMENEUTICS

TODAY IS TUESDAY, December 22, 1998, the first day of winter and it is cold and windy. This morning at 8:00 o'clock it was twelve degrees Fahrenheit and sunny. Now it's eighteen degrees Fahrenheit with high, thin clouds, but mostly sunny. The wind is from the west and northwest. It's afternoon and I'm free to start my newest story. Dallasandro Vibini has gone Christmas shopping in the shops along Ludlow Avenue and his pregnant wife Saponata is at her job as a librarian in the Clifton branch of the Hamilton County Public Library. Their absence is a blessing because I don't have to listen to Vibini's Mozart records and I don't have to work in a cloud of his marijuana smoke. Now I can get down on paper the events of yesterday afternoon while I can still remember them. My aging memory has become so fragile that I have to write down anything that I want to preserve.

Yesterday, Monday, December 21, the phone rang at 3:30 P.M. I answered it as I always do because neither Vibini nor Saponata will pick up the phone. The call was for me and it was Saponata calling from the library. She called, she said, to tell me that our friend Father Thomas Takianopoulos, who is called "The Gymnast" and "Skialogos," was there in the library and he had two friends that he wanted to introduce to me. Father Thomas, the defrocked Patriarch, officiated at the wedding of Vibini and Saponata and I was best man. Since the wedding, Saponata and I have attended two of his sermons at his church called Saint Oholibamah's Chiliastic and Universalist Church of the Redeemer and All Saints of the Full Space-Time Continuum, over on Resor Avenue.

I agreed to come to the library since it's only six blocks away so I put on my black fedora, my heavy black coat and walked out into the light rain that had just begun to fall. The temperature was sixty degrees Fahrenheit but the rain made it feel a lot colder. I walked out of Vox Populi Street, past the sign at the entrance to the street that says "Give Up All Hope You Who Enter Here" and the sign that says "No Exit" and onto Clifton Avenue. No one seems willing to take down that sign that quotes Dante, the sign some jokester put up months ago. I thought as I walked past the sign what a blessing it is to live on Vox Populi Street in Clifton, the last refuge of intelligence in this hate-filled city, a city where the people never let Christmas interfere with their narrow-mindedness.

I walked south on Clifton and crossed at Glenmary to the west side of Clifton Avenue. It was very dark for the afternoon. It was like nightfall. It was one of those days when you can't tell when day ends and night begins. I had the feeling I was walking under water or under some kind of shroud. These kinds of days happen often in Cincinnati and there was nothing unusual about the weather, unless it was the heavy warmth. It came to me as I walked that it felt like I was walking through the land of the dead. Everything was shrouded in mist and rain. Darkness dwelt on the face of Clifton. It all seemed a primal chaos encased in a dead light. The crowd of people seemed disembodied. They seemed to be only shadows, not real people, as they shuffled blindly through the drizzle. The Christmas lights overhead and from the shop windows glowed softly like the fires of a gentle Hell as they illuminated the paths of the tormented souls. I felt as if I had descended into the underworld, a feeling I had had many times before when walking around Cincinnati.

I walked south until I passed Clifton Florist and turned west onto Ludlow. Then past the Christmas tree sales, Ludlow News and Videos, Petersen's, Kilimanjaro: African Heritage, Catwalk Salon, Mediterranean Foods with Fresh European Bread, Fresh Pita Bread, Falafalas and Gyros, Hommus, Tabouli, Baba, Ghannouj. Then past the Thai Café with Royal Thai Cuisine, the Esquire Theater showing "Gods and Monsters," "Celebrity," "Elizabeth," "Touch of Evil," "Living Out Loud," "Under the Skin" and Saturday Night "Rocky Horror" with Gift Certificates Available. Then shaky puddin'; "a modern restaurant" and Tawana Imports where I crossed over Ludlow to the south side of the street to Michael's Little Ludlow Village, Bender Optical, College Cleaners, Dan's Clifton Barbers (closed Wed.), Ludlow Wines and Gifts, d. Raphael, Ladybug Fashions, Proud

Rooster Restaurant, New World Foodshop and turned into the Clifton Branch Library.

It was exactly 4:00 P.M. when I walked into the library. Saponata was behind the librarians' desk with Betsy and Melissa Comb. When Saponata saw me enter, she said something to Betsy and Melissa and they got out of her way so she could move her bloated body out from behind the desk. She got out and waddled over to me and said, "Come here, Liebgott. I want you to meet some of my best customers."

We moved over to the children's literature shelves and there stood Father Thomas Takianopoulos and two other men. I shook Father Thom's hand and he said, "Dr. Liebgott, I'd like you to meet Professor Peter Solomon Seiltanzer and Professor Aristarchus Skiamachos." I reached out and shook the hand first of Seiltanzer, who is about six feet tall, weighs about 170 pounds, has gray hair, wears glasses and hearing aids. He was wearing black penny loafers, blue jeans, a pale cream travel jacket with lots of pockets and a blue baseball cap with "Lions" written in script on the front of it. Seiltanzer shook my hand and said, "Folks call me 'Skyblue' and sometimes 'Skyblue the Badass.' And I'm a retired Assistant Professor of English, not a Professor, from the University of Cincinnati. They bought me out rather than promote me." I said, "You must be the one who put the pornography on the E-Mail in the Department of English at the University of Cincinnati. It was Dallasandro Vibini who solved the mystery. I wrote about all that in my story 'Vibini on the E-Mail,' which was published in *First Intensity* for Summer of 1997."

Skyblue flinched and said, "Was that who exposed my caper?"

I then reached over and shook the hand of Professor Skiamachos, who informed me that he taught Biblical History at Miami University in Oxford, Ohio. He too is tall. I'd say six feet and four inches. Heavy in the belly and gut, say 260 pounds. Reddish brown hair with a large face in a large head, a sure sign of a heavily developed brain. Blue business suit, black tie and a brown, wide-brimmed hat. He said he lived on Shekinah Avenue, just down Ludlow Avenue west of the Star Bank. He said his specialty was apocalyptic hermeneutics. He said, "People call me 'Ari the Hermeneutist.' You must be the guy who lives with Vibini. Tell him I want my copies of Bruce Rumbumsen's *Sleep and Its By-Products* and *The Gospel According to Oholibamah* back." I said I'd take care of it.

Saponata then said, "Liebgott, I've told them about you already. They know that you're a retired medical doctor. They know you live on Vox Populi Street and that Dally and I live with you." I said, "You gentlemen should also know that since I retired on January 3, 1995, I have taken up a new profession. I'm training myself to be a writer." Skyblue said, "Did you say you retired on January 3, 1995?" "That's right," I said. "Isn't that something," he said. "That's the same day I retired. How old are you, anyway?" "I'm sixty-eight and will be sixty-nine in January. I was born in Wuppertal, Germany, on January 9, 1930."

Skyblue slapped himself on his forehead with his right hand and said, "Isn't that something. That's the same day I was born in Newton, Kansas." Skyblue smiled and said, "Have you ever been married?" "Of course," I said. "I married Gertrude Schneespiel in 1951 and we had four children. Unfortunately, all four of them are now in St. Dympna's in Gheel. That's a mental institution in Belgium." "Well," Seiltanzer said, "co-incidences can only go so far. I've never been married and I have no children. My only living relative is my brother-in-law who was the town drunk in Newton, Kansas, but he's now in a nursing home that I pay for. At least he's there until they throw him out because while the patients are filling their throwaway diapers with piss and shit he's filling their hearts with Jesus."

Saponata broke in and said, "Listen, you fellows can't talk here. This is a library and you're disturbing the customers. Besides, the children can't get to the shelves here. Go someplace else." And we did. Father Thom suggested we go across the street to Uno's, the Original Chicago Pizzeria. We all agreed and we walked out of the library into the darkness and the rain.

Out on the sidewalk, I could see south down Ormond Avenue to the Urban Gypsy (closed), the branch post office where surly Bob growls at the customers next door to Marvin N. Kaplan, D.M.D., with his new black Corvette with the vanity plates that say, "104-MK."

We crossed Ormond and headed west. Father Thom and Skyblue walked together. Ari and I followed past the Roanoke Apartment Building, past the Hansa Guild and the CVS Pharmacy. We did not walk on up past the Columbia Savings, the PNC Bank and the Star Bank. Instead, we crossed over at Middleton Street to the north side of Ludlow and turned east away from Sitwell's Coffee House and Much More. Past Norka Futon, Burrito Joe's Restaurant and Bar, Zoco, Amol India with "Fine India Cuisine," Thatsa Wrapp: Feeding the Human Race, Ambar India Restaurant and past Ludlow Garage with Spiral Light, The Natural Shoe Store, KOWTOW's Goods for the Urban Soul, Bio Wheels, Paolo "A modern Jeweler" and Paolo Studio.

As we walked, Ari the Hermeneutist told me about his latest work. He said, "Dr. Liebgott, do you know that the words 'tavern' and 'tabernacle' come from the same root? They both come from the Latin word 'taberna,' a booth or a hut." I allowed as to how I wasn't aware of that. Then he said, "Do you read the Bible?" "Not recently," I said. "Well, in *The Book of Genesis,* Abraham directs his servant to find a wife for his son Isaac, and to bind the agreement Abraham tells the servant to put his hand under his, that is Abraham's, thigh. You know why?" "No, I don't," I said. Ari smiled and said, "It's so the servant can hold onto Abraham's balls. That's how we get our word 'testament.' It comes from 'testes.' So when you seal a deal you hold onto someone's nuts. That's how we get the Old Testament and the New Testament." I allowed as to how I didn't know that, but I said I'd be sure to tell Saponata about it because she loves wonderful information. When I tell her such things she thinks I'm terribly smart.

We walked into Uno's, the Original Chicago Pizzeria, and took a high table by the window so we could see out into the street. Ari and Father Thom sat on the high stools with their backs to the window. Skyblue and I sat facing the window. Father Thom wiped the rain off his bald head and I asked him if the rain was painful. I said, "Why don't you wear a hat?" He whispered, "When I was defrocked the Eastern Orthodox Church took the only hat I will ever wear. You know that I was a Patriarch and, as far as I'm concerned, I still am. The only hat I will ever wear is the crown of my office." The high stools were uncomfortable for me because of my fat butt. I felt like I was sitting on the point of a spear.

We ordered four bottles of Bud Light and, when the waitress set them on the table, I read the label which said, "Genuine Bud Light Beer 12 FL. OZ." We poured and sipped and Skyblue said, "I'm a writer too, you know." I looked over to him and watched him pull some white pages from inside his travel jacket. "I write essays. In fact, I've published a volume of them. The volume is called *Skyblue's Essays.*" Father Thom and Ari both snorted. At the time I didn't understand why because I had never before had to face the ego of a second-rate writer. I stared out the window into the darkness and the rain while Seiltanzer began reading his manuscript. It was called "Skyblue's Essay on Fairy Tales." To the best of my recollection it went something like this:

"There once was a king who had three sons. The king was very old and as the time of his death approached he became fearful as to who would be his successor. He called his three sons into his throne room and said, 'My time on this earth is nearly done. One of you will succeed me to this throne. In order that there be no question as to who is to be my successor, I have determined that my successor will be the one of you who in the next six months can commit the most dastardly, the most obnoxious, the most horrible, the most vicious, the most evil act or acts. Return to me in six months and report what you have done so that I can determine who is to succeed me and then I can die in peace.'

"The three sons left the throne room and returned six months later. The king summoned the oldest of the three into the throne room and said, 'What have you done in the past six months that would make you worthy to be the next king?'

"The oldest son said, 'I went into the slums and I stole money from the poor. I beat up thirty orphans and smashed forty-five beggars and took their hats and coats when it was freezing weather. I ran over twenty-six cats and forty-two dogs. I raised the rents on my properties 250 percent. I kicked and hospitalized fifty-two old ladies. I burned six soup kitchens. I bribed seven judges to settle law suits among my employees.'

"'Very good,' said the king. 'I'm proud of you.'

"The king called the second son into the throne room and said, 'What have you done in the past six months that would make you worthy to be the next ruler of this nation?'

"The second son said, 'I paid $120,000 in bribes to athletes to get them to come to your university. I got twenty-four young women pregnant and refused to pay for their hospital bills. I paid no income tax but I reported fifteen people who had cheated on their taxes. I stole 126 Bibles, 200 bottles of aspirin, 496 Snickers candy bars and forty boxes of wooden matches and sold all the stuff at football games. I let the air out of 126 tires. I set fire to four shelters for the homeless. I got the big industries to fire their poor people, 359 of them. I put acid in the public swimming pools. I forced ninety-three bicycle riders off the roads. I farted in thirty-eight elevators.'

"'Very good,' said the king.

"The king then called the youngest son into the throne room and said, What have you done that could possibly make you fit for ruling this nation?'"

While Skyblue read his essay on fairy tales, I looked out the window and watched the shadowy figures moving about the streets. I could see the faint bodies rushing down Ormond to Marvin N. Kaplan, D.M.D., to get their teeth cleaned and their cavities filled so they would have no plaque on their teeth or scum on their gums when the obolus was placed in their mouths so the bearer could pay Charon, the boatman at the River Styx. I saw the disembodied bodies hastening down Ormond to the post office so they could get from surly Bob the correct postage on their last letters that they would send out to the living relatives they were leaving behind. I saw the Clifton dead lining up at the public telephones on the corner by the library so they could make one last desperate phone call to the world they were soon to leave. I saw them dropping money into the phones and dialing frantically, hoping to get an answer that would lead them out of the mist of the dying afternoon. I watched them dial and smile at each other as they wished each other "Merry Christmas" in their Ludlow Avenue Hades. I wished them all a "Merry Christmas" and hoped that Santa Claus would bring them a life. I saw the Clifton spooks crowding into the New World

Foodshop in order to stock up on supplies before setting out on the long journey to eternity. I saw the Clifton dead crowding into the library, trying to find directions to their destination, searching on the shelves to find the dead words that showed a way out of the labyrinth of Clifton, searching through the dead words in dead books for something to illuminate their paths into oblivion. Disembodied heads floated past the window. The automobiles passed in silence, the drivers and passengers not seeing or maybe just ignoring the disappearing souls on the sidewalks.

While I watched the pedestrians, Skyblue went on reading: "The youngest son said, 'Well, father, I just sat and thought about it for five months and thirty days. I thought and thought about what might be the worst possible thing I could do and thus achieve your throne. Yesterday it came to me what I should do. I realized what the most despicable thing I could do was and I went out and joined the Republican Party.'

"The king leaped for joy from his throne and shouted out, 'You are the next king.'"

When Skyblue finished and put his manuscript away, Father Thom said, "Let's have another beer." The waitress came and we ordered four bottles of "Budweiser King of Beers Brewed by our original all natural process using the Choicest Hops, Rice and Best Barley Malt Anheuser-Busch, Inc., St. Louis, Mo.," and a basket of Papa Dante's Potato Chips. Outside in the darkening afternoon, the people of Clifton seemed to be gathering for one last reunion before heading off into the underworld. They shoved and pushed each other along on the sidewalks. In their silent gathering, they seemed to be wandering around in an urgency to get going into that last long night. The world darkened and the souls massed on the sidewalks. I wanted to go out and comfort them, but I had no idea what I could possible say to those mournful souls. I wanted to say "Sursum Corda," but that would be sarcastic to say that to the dead.

Skyblue turned to me and said, "How did you like my writing? Does it give you some kind of idea as to what good writing is? I'm a published writer. Maybe you can learn something from my skills."

I said, "I don't write fairy tales. I write narratives that center on the exploits of Dallasandro Vibini, who is a private detective and who solves petty crimes. So far I have twelve stories, but only three of them have been published."

"Listen," Skyblue said. "I taught creative writing at the University of Cincinnati for thirty-two years before I was asked to leave. No, told to leave. Have you learned how to control point of view? Have you learned how to manage detail and structure it? Have you learned how to arrange your character sets so the drama is implicit in character? Have you learned how to vary tone so your stories are not monotone? Have you learned how to punctuate? Have you learned how to pace your narratives so that the reader is carried through to the end? Have you learned how to use your setting for tonal control and for resonance? Well, what have you learned?"

I hesitated to speak with an expert, but I said, "I've learned that simple clear sentences are very important."

Skyblue the Badass jumped off his high stool, raised his arms over his head and shouted, "Hallelujah. Praise Jesus. Brother, you have seen the light. I taught creative writing for thirty-eight years and I swear that what I was mainly trying to do all that time was to get the students to write simple, clear sentences. I could never figure out why writing simple, declarative sentences was a mystery. What was so difficult about it? I finally came to believe that if we could teach people to write simple, clear sentences we could save the world. If we could teach them to write simple declarative sentences we would have the kingdom of God on earth. Jesus would come again and we would all live in eternal bliss. But no. Maybe God kicked Adam and Eve out of the Garden of Eden because they could only write confused, long, opaque sentences. I can see how it went. God said, 'Adam where are you?' And he answered, 'Considering the time of day and the fact that Eve has wandered off to the far side of this ridiculous garden and because there is a tree standing in my way when I want to go and look for her, and because you, whoever you are, are asking in a supercilious voice a question that I do not have to answer now or forever more, therefore, I say to you, shove off because my whereabouts is none of your god-damned business.' The response to Adam was brief: 'Get out and don't come back.'" I felt good that Skyblue confirmed what I had found out or thought out on my own. It all boded well for my literary career.

Father Thom intervened then and said, "You can't save souls by syntax. That's a ridiculous idea. If you want to know about salvation you should come to my church St. Oholibamah's Chiliastic and Universalist Church of the Redeemer and All Saints of the Full Space-Time Continuum." I said that I'd been there twice and I didn't see a whole lot of salvation going on. Father Thomas called "Skialogos" then talked about how we now live in "C.E." as opposed to "B.C.E." C.E., he said, stands for computer era and B.C.E. stands for before the computer era. Whereas once we marked all time as before and after the birth of our savior, now we mark all time according to a machine, the computer.

I see as I write this that I am piecing together the events of yesterday. I'm assembling a narrative from the bits and pieces of what I remember. That "bits and pieces" is redundant, but I'll use it anyway. My writing is thus like the Gospel writers who assembled their narratives from pericopes. Like me, they used bits and pieces for a holy purpose.

The conversation drifted back to writing. Ari said that Auerbach says that the Gospel writers were the first to use the simple style. They used it because they were writing for an illiterate audience. The style had to be clear and oral. It had to be capable of communicating with a general audience. Before the Gospel writers, only the educated elite was let in on the secrets of religion. Only readers could approach the mysteries. The Gospel writers said, "Here it is for all to see. Look, it's for you. You listeners and readers are the ones who must know in order to believe." So they were the first to take the written word to the people. To do that they had to write simply and clearly. The success of Christianity rested in that simple style. Where one style could fit all, everyone could know and believe and be saved. Heaven, he said, is peopled because of the simple declarative sentence.

Ari the Hermeneutist said, "Dr. Liebgott, if you want to be a fiction writer you have to know that all English and American Literature comes out of one book and that's *Pilgrim's Progress* by John Bunyan. There was nothing of importance before that and there has been nothing as important since. If you're going to be a writer, you have to know that book like the back of your heart."

I thought, "You mean the back of my old heart."

"Listen, Gottlieb. Old John Bunyan beat the modern writers to the punch all over the place. He understood the importance of a unity of point of view. He knew all fiction is a dream vision. He knew there is no such thing as verisimilitude and that the only reality of a narrative is the reality of the author's dream. He says that the dream must be made solid and the best way to do that is to give the narrative the shape of a journey. That journey he says may be geographical but in fiction it is always a journey of the soul. The setting becomes a *dramatis persona* as it reflects the spiritual state of the traveling protagonist. He figured out that a traveling protagonist passes through a constantly changing setting and thereby the narrative has a constantly changing tone. The context, the setting, of the hero's journey is a spiritual complex through which he must make his way to salvation in the denouement. It's a picaresque journey of the heart where the heart is orphaned, outcast and homeless and seeks to return to its proper body. It makes no difference if that journey is across space or across the soul. *Pilgrim's Progress* just happens to be over land. It could just as well be over the rainbow."

Outside in the enfolding darkness, I could see those pilgrims wandering along Ludlow Avenue. I thought, "Is this what Bunyan was talking about? Is one of those spooks out there a Christian pilgrim on his way to some better land? Did Bunyan see his fellow citizens wandering through the darkness of a winter afternoon and try to give them a direction? Did he try to make sense out of their being lost on this fading earth?"

Ari punched my shoulder to get my attention and continued. "That's why all English and American fiction is basically a spiritual allegory where the tone constantly changes because of the changing spiritual dilemmas which are reflected in the changing landscape, no matter what writers might think nowadays. All fiction is the journey of a symbolic hero through a spiritualized landscape."

I said that I had not thought of my fiction that way. I just wanted to tell a good story. I wanted to write something that would be interesting to any reader.

"Listen," Ari continued, "Bunyan was really smart. He realized that he had a good story, but he also realized that he didn't want to make it too didactic. He figured out how to infuse the point of view with the didactic intent. He realized that the moral imperatives implicit in narrative, the necessity of social transformation, can be made implicit in the point of view. With the focus through the mind of a single narrator and point of view, the moral comprehensiveness can be subsumed into an act of reception. The morality, the didacticism, are functions of the narrator's mind. His characters, for instance, are all named allegorically. Their names tell you what they are. Everyone does that now. Those names coalesce into a comprehensive vision of a whole society and are representative of the moral quality of that society. They form a paradigm of a moral state."

I wasn't too sure what a "paradigm of a moral state" is, but it sure sounded good. I could see how his students would be impressed by that kind of language. That was something they could write down in their notes.

Ari the Hermeneutist, called "Skiamachos," was just getting warmed up. "Where Bunyan was really smart was that he told the reader how his story would end. He told the reader not to worry about all the difficulties that Christian goes through. He'll be OK because he's a good man. He is a moral, decent person. His innocence and his piety protect him from all evil. That way the reader can concentrate on the human dimensions of the narrative, the way human character behaves when tempted. No reader has to worry about how the story is going to turn out. That's the wrong kind of tension. The real tension has to do with the perfecting of Christian's soul and his achieving of eternal salvation."

Father Thomas the Gymnast leaned over and said to me, "Remember that eternal salvation stuff. I'll give you the real scoop when Ari finishes."

Ari, called "Skiamachos," was not distracted. He went on, "What you've got to realize is that Bunyan's hero Christian journeys into the land of the dead. All fiction participates in or is a part of that journey. The important thing is that a divine protection saves him from all threats because he is innocent. He is saved because he is an exemplar of what is good in this world.

What writers do then, as a result of Bunyan's work, is to resurrect the dead. They give their blood to the dead souls and give them new life in narrative. We then remember them. The author gives up his life so that he might give new life to the dead so that the narrative might emerge that brings salvation to this world."

My mind drifted off to Cristoforos, vibini's brother. I couldn't figure out why he was always called "Culofaccia." Cristoforo is the bearer of Christ and Christ is the person who Saponata thinks can save Vibini from his dope. It was the word "Christ" that brought me back to Ari's lecture. "That's why all writers are Children of God. They are all Christians on a journey to the Celestial City. Every fiction is a *Pilgrim's Progress* and every writer is a Christian pilgrim. And that's why all writers must believe in the divine origins of their narratives or else they will each become a Man in an Iron Cage or perish in Doubting-Castle. So it was and so it ever shall be. John Bunyan set the pattern that has become imbued in our minds. No one can imagine our fiction without the nativity and formative presence of *Pilgrim's Progress*. It's always there on the back of one's heart."

I hope I've got this fragment of my story correct, or at least almost correct. I realized at the time Ari was speaking that I was listening to a canned lecture. I'm sure that's the kind of stuff he tells his students in Oxford, Ohio. I thanked him for telling me that stuff and we ordered four bottles of "Samuel Adams Brewer Patriot Boston Lager The Boston Beer Company."

Now as I sit and put these pieces together, as I assemble my narrative out of fragments, I realize that all that obsession of writers with resolution is silly. Resolution isn't important because no narrative is ever resolved or can be resolved. Because all narratives are endless, that makes the initiating of narratives far more important that the resolution of narratives. So I will regard this narrative as a preliminary attempt to tell the story and the fragments as incomplete and I will indicate that in my title. I will regard this narrative as the beginning of a narrative, which all stories are anyway, and I will not worry about an ending. What I've just realized must be the reason writers always feel their stories are unfinished.

Father Thomas the Gymnast, called "Skialogos," said, "Listen, Dr. Liebgott, what Bunyan was telling you is that to be a good writer you got to believe in the Messiah. You got to believe that mankind can be saved and you got to believe that he's worth saving. Writing fiction is an act of trying to save mankind from himself. That's why it's done. If the writer is not trying to save mankind from self-destruction, he has betrayed his art. Dr. Liebgott, if you insist on being a writer, come down on mankind in fire and brimstone and burn the crap out of his soul. Make him once again human.

"You probably realize that we live in a time of extraordinary and endemic literary mediocrity. Our literature lacks the first kind of intelligence and that is a moral vision of the world. What's wrong with modern fiction is that it has no moral infrastructure. Because it has no moral infrastructure it has no tone. It makes no judgements. It reduces the human endeavor to flatness, to meaninglessness. That's why it's all so dull. The writers are afraid to make judgements because they have no moral referent by which to make them. They have no conscience and no moral substance. Hemingway and his literary son Raymond Carver took salvation out of fiction. They took God and the Messiah out of narrative and made our world without a moral reference and hopeless. Now we have no moral infrastructure in our fiction and the moral base of our literature is dead. The result is that modern writers are emotional without spiritual substance and emotion without spiritual substance is sentimentality. Our writers write commonplace emotions supported by spiritual emptiness. They transform minor inspirations into dullness in their narratives. It's as if their spiritual selves have been shorted out by drugs or alcohol."

I remarked then that I had a great pity for the failings of our human kind. As a doctor, I pointed out, I've seen just about every form of degradation, failing, perversion, hate. How, I asked, do I do such a thing as saving mankind through fiction? I just want to tell a good story.

"And another thing," Skyblue said, "even with the moral question you got to be willing to cross the line."

I said, "What do you mean by that?"

Skyblue smiled and said, "You want to be a great writer? You got to be willing to cross the line that separates the mediocre from the great. That line is called 'safe.' And few writers are willing to cross it. It's usually referred to as 'risk.' Taking risks means knowing where the line is. You got to know all the fiction that precedes what you are writing. Then you have to go a step further and make narratives that have never been written before. Very few writers do that because in crossing the line you make yourself vulnerable to isolation and failure. Proust, Beckett, Faulkner, Katherine Mansfield, Flannery O'Connor, Melville, Kafka, Stanley Elkin, all crossed the line, took great risks and succeeded. We don't know how many writers crossed the line and failed because, of course, we don't read their failures.

"The 'safe' line in American Literature runs from Poe to Stephen Crane to Hemingway to Raymond Carver. They write a kind of prose that requires no intelligence to read it. You don't have to be sophisticated to read it. The Postmodernists took great risks and they were successful for a while. Postmodernist fiction requires the reader to think, to read carefully, to know literary history. It requires attention, thought and knowledge. It has a wide range of tone and includes humor, satire and irony. Postmodernism depends on a rich literary context, a context that is recalled constantly in the writing. The safe writers are humorless and can be read in a vacuum. You don't need to know your literary past in order to read them. For the safe writers, Postmodernism was an aberration.

"But just look at the reception for the fiction of Raymond Carver. The whole literary world breathed a sigh of relief when it appeared. He brought back conservatism to the literary world. He killed Postmodernism and once again our fiction became visceral. Thought and knowledge were cut out. His prose was to fiction what Ronald Reagan was to politics. Once again conservatism rose up against the smart alecs and everyone cheered. Once again the literary world was safe for mediocrity. That's why we got almost no humor anymore, or satire, or burlesque or parody. The death of Stanley Elkin may have been the death of American humor. The literary Republicans took over. They not only drew the line at safe; they built a wall that excludes anything new."

I didn't tell Ari, Skyblue and Father Thomas what I thought about our city. While they were speaking I did think about the mean, vicious men the Republicans elect to office, men who have the intellectual capacity of a clod. I didn't tell my friends how familiar the Cincinnati Republicans seem to me since I grew up in Nazi Germany. There the people elected the same kind of men, men who had what we now call "family values." They had nice families, stout wives, healthy, happy children, dogs, cats, flowers in the yard. And they hated the "others," as they called them. They hated the "not them," those who had different religions, who spoke different languages, who had different skin. The Republicans of Cincinnati all speak like the public officials of the Germany of my youth. They sound righteous, but they embody a massive hate. It often seems to me as if God had abandoned all hope here and said, "Let's see how low man can sink." I always pitied the poor souls who grew up in this slough of iniquity.

I told the waitress that I wanted a good German beer and she brought us four bottles of "America's First Reinheitsgebot Pure Beer Christian Moerlein Brewed in Accordance With the Bavarian Reinheitsgebot Purity Law of 1516 Select Lager." I knew it wasn't German beer but I was past caring. We touched glasses and started pouring it down.

I didn't tell my friends that in those Cincinnati Republicans I recognize again the death of compassion, the death of decency and love, the death of forgiveness, all that I saw as a child. In them I recognize the moral blindness of race hate. In them I see that Christianity is only a credential for election. Religion is, for them, a political necessity. They believe in God because it gets them votes. Christianity is for them a form of racial supremacy. I have always thought that we are lucky that there are only seven deadly sins. That way there is a limit to Republican corruption. Because of them it makes sense to say that Armageddon is now. The great battle of light and dark is going on right this minute.

It is at this moment that I realize why I have such a great tolerance, patience and love for Saponata. Not only is she hugely pregnant. Not only is she uneducated. What makes her so pitiable is that she was born and grew up in Cincinnati. You have to feel sorry for anyone who suffers such a fate. That's a horrible fate that I wouldn't wish on anyone. She grew up in this dead city. That's why she has no sense of humor. That's why learning was never important to her. It's the Germany of my youth all over again.

Father Thomas said, after my question about saving mankind, "Do you know what 'Apokatastasis' means?" "No," I said. He smirked and said, "It means the doctrine of universal salvation. Contrary to most belief, the Apostle Paul didn't believe in original sin and universal damnation. Original sin was something the commentators cooked up. The idea of eternal damnation was never God's intention. A merciful God would never let people suffer forever. All that suffering might be attractive to someone who wants to write a long poem, but the punishment was not what God intended. Eventually everyone will be saved. There is universal salvation. *Deus vult*.

"Here's how it goes. Since we are commanded by Jesus Christ to forgive our enemies, then surely God the Father will forgive His enemies. I mean the disobedient, the sinners. If God does not forgive His enemies, then Jesus Christ deceived us. If God has no forgiveness, how then can we? That Christ might have deceived us is an intolerable idea. Then Christianity is in vain."

"You mean," I said, "that we are not going to be punished for our sins?"

"Not forever. Hell is just the ultimate 'sentimental fascism.' That's what Skyblue calls the ploy. The idea of hell is a mechanism to frighten people into belief. It's used to manipulate the gullible into joining and supporting churches and paying the salaries of priests and pastors. My church, St. Oholibamah's Chiliastic and Universalist Church of the Redeemer and All Saints of the Full Space-Time Continuum, believes that everyone will ascend to heaven after death and that everyone will have a joyful reunion with the heavenly father. We preach joy, not fear."

At that point, I remember, I said, "Hold on a minute. I have to go to the bathroom."

When I returned, Skyblue looked at me and said, "You know what Erasmus of Rotterdam said, don't you?" "No," I said. "What did Erasmus of Rotterdam say?" "He said, 'You can shake it, you can hit it, you can slap it on the wall, but you have to put it in your pants to make the last drop fall.'" I said, "Ist das auf Ihrem Mist gewachsen?" I don't know why I said that. I guess it's just my German sense of humor.

Father Thomas, called "Skialogos," went on with his half-wit theology. "In *The Gospel of Thomas* the writer says that Jesus said, 'What you await has come, but you do not know it.' That's the writer I was named after, Didymus Judas Thomas, the one who poked his finger into Christ's wound. He's the one we still call 'doubting Thomas.' Doubt is OK, but there is no doubt that what the writer said is true; 'Cleave a piece of wood, I am there. Raise up a stone, and you will find me there.' He writes, 'His disciples said to him: On what day will the kingdom come? Jesus said: It will not come while people watch for it; they will not say: Look, here it is, or: Look, there it is: but the kingdom of the father is spread out over the earth, and men do not see it.'"

While Father Thom was talking, I looked at my watch. It was 5:55 P.M. and I realized that Saponata would be laying out our little Keller's I.G.A. supper. I began to worry about being late, but then I thought about how much she and Vibini are indebted to me and I decided to miss supper and ordered another round of German beers: "Beer Brewed under License and Authority of Lowenbrau Munich Löwenbräu Special Lowenbrau Established 1383 Munich Germany."

Father Thom didn't stop: "What this all means is that 'Apocalypse Now' is redundant because it is going on right now. The Apocalypse began at the moment when Jesus was strung up on the Cross. It began with the death of God's son and has gone on ever since. We have always assumed that revelation and its aftermath was a one-time event. Not so. God's events never end. It's like God's grace. It comes down perpetually. It started with creation and never ends. It falls on us corrupt humans continually and without end. Just think, Armageddon may last thousands of years or more. We always thought it would be instantaneous. We thought it would happen in the twinkling of an eye, come like a thief in the night, come with the sound of a trumpet. All this is true because in God's mind all time is but the twinkling of an eye, his trumpets are always sounding and his thieves are continually and forever entering our houses during the night. We are in the midst of Armageddon right now. The great battle of light and darkness is going on right now. The Second Coming is happening right now except we can't see it. We are sitting in the midst of the ending of the world because the world is always ending. It has never ceased ending since the day it was created. That's why we are in the midst of Armageddon as we slowly and inexorably destroy our planet.

"That's why our prophecies are always wrong. Our prophecies are irrelevant because they are all too late. The events we foretell are already over because they are from the beginning, in the beginning, of the beginning and ongoing forever. Our attempts to set specific times for spiritual events are always wrong because we assume they will happen in the future when, in fact, they are happening right now. The end times were in the beginning. All of our prophecies are 'vaticinia ex eventu,' prophecies after the fact. We prophesy what is already over.

"That's why in my church, Saint Oholibamah's Chiliastic and Universalist Church of the Redeemer and All Saints of the Full Space-Time Continuum, we believe and preach that the Crucifixion of our Lord and Savior Jesus Christ goes on forever. It goes on every minute of every day. We crucify the Messiah, who would save us from our sins, every minute of our existence. Only the eternal and divine mercy of God prevents our immediate destruction. The Christ of our redemption suffers on the Cross every moment of our lives and we put him there moment by moment and day by day and year by year. The Crucifixion, like our guilt, is unending because we humans have no mercy one for another, have no compassion one for another, have no love one for another. We crucify Christ every time we go into a voting booth and vote for a Republican. We crucify Christ every time we buy a ticket to a Bengals football game. We crucify Christ every time we go to a Reds baseball game. We crucify Christ every time we pay for a subscription to *The Cincinnati Enquirer* or *The Cincinnati Post*. We crucify Christ every time we watch the cross-town shootout between Xavier and the University of Cincinnati. We crucify Christ every time we buy Papa Dante's Potato Chips. We crucify Christ every time we drive to a mall and walk into the corruption of business. We crucify Christ every time we buy Chiquita Bananas or an Ohio lottery ticket."

I looked out the front window of Uno's, the Original Chicago Pizzeria, and into the light rain coming down like gentle blessings from God, like a small grace for the moment. I looked out into the descending darkness and thought of Saponata in the library with Betsy and Melissa Comb, the three wise women who point the little light gun at the numbers on the books, watch it plink and register the book. I could imagine Saponata behind the counter with her bloated belly, standing palefaced by her pals and gamely carrying on her duties as the best librarian possible, given the circumstances, with Betsy and Melissa giving her aid and comfort and with gentle smiles giving her extra room to move about until she could go home and fix supper for me and Vibini. I could imagine Sudsy putting her left hand on her monstrous belly and her open right hand around her larynx as she fought for breath. I could imagine the fetus bouncing around as *The Sinking of the Odradek Stadium, Camden's Eyes, The Eight Corners of the World, Our Asian Journey, All Fall Down, Edwin Mullhouse* and *Failure to Zig-Zag* passed across the desk and into the hands of the Clifton dead. I must admit that I hoped that Father Thomas was right about that constant flood of grace. I didn't relish the thought of my neighbors burning in hell. I remembered that I read somewhere that "A day that ends in disaster can't be all bad." I knew I was heading for that disaster because I wasn't respecting Saponata's consideration for me.

Father Thom went on outside my diversion: "In our religion all time is but a moment in the mind of God. In our religion, every day is Good Friday. And in our religion everyday is Easter. Because if Christ is crucified every day, he also arises every day and brings light and salvation to this world. The marking of time into before and after Christ is meaningless because the events that mark the division never end. They have been there for all time and will continue to be there for all time. The Passion happens while you eat your breakfast. It happens while you drive your car. It happens while we sit here and drink beer. Right now Christ is suffering and dying. The Passion is right now. Right now he is rising from the dead. Right now the stone is rolling away and he is walking out of his tomb. The Parousia is going on right now. Right now God's eternal grace is raining down on us because God is love and light and goodness. He is right here in Uno's, the Original Chicago Pizzeria."

At 6:45 P.M. I said, "I'm tired of sitting here. Let's leave." It was agreed that we should go since we'd been drinking since 4:30. We managed to get down off the high stools and get our coats on. I paid our bill of $64.95; the other three each left a tip of $1.00. They protested my generosity, but I explained to them that we Germans had a great sense of humor—I think I meant "honor"—when it came to paying for beer. I went back to the bathroom and when I returned Skyblue said, "If you shake it more than three times you're masturbating," and we walked out the front door into the heavy rain and into the complete darkness. We headed east past Golden Lions, Byrd/Braman: Vintage Furnishings, New World Bookshop and Graeter's. We crossed over Telford to the Tawana corner where I could see down Telford to Toko Baru, More Than Boxes and More Than Boxes Gift Shop.

We started to say good-by when Aristarchus the Hermeneutist said, "Let's stop for one more at Arlin's Bar and Garden." I agreed to go along since I was already in trouble with Saponata anyway. So we crossed over to the south side of Ludlow to the Clifton Town

Meeting office, Ludlow Shoe Repair, Pangaea Trading Company, China Kitchen, Keller's I.G.A., Semesters, (Retail Office Space Available), Chiropractor and into Arlin's Bar and Garden. We walked into the back of the bar and sat down at a table. This time Ari and Skyblue sat on a church bench against the wall. Father Thom and I sat on chairs facing the wall.

Aristarchus Skiamachos said he wanted something Irish so we ordered four bottles of "Imported from Ireland Harp Lager Brewed in Ireland for Guinness by Harp Brewery, Dundalk 12 FL. Oz. Brewed in Dundalk, Co. Louth." We had no sooner got our beers than Skyblue said, "So, Dr. Liebgott, you want to be a writer. You know what you must do first of all if you want to be a writer? Get out of Cincinnati. This city is illiterate and hates writers. The people who run the arts in this city are a bunch of nitwits. You can see that in the way the Republicans are trying to destroy the public schools. They know that if the public schools succeed in educating their students there won't be any Republicans in office. No one will vote for them. They want public funding for privileged education where they can brainwash the rich kids. They know those rich kids can't and don't think. If you want to be a writer, get out of Cincinnati and don't come back. So, anyway, what's this book you're working on?"

When I told them that I was writing the biography of an Italian war hero, all three started laughing and I didn't understand why. "Look," I said, "we Germans have a good sense of humor. I don't understand why you're laughing. What's so funny?" "Oh, nothing," said

Skyblue. "It's just that there are jokes about Italian war heroes." "What jokes?" I asked. "You can tell me." "Who," Ari said, "is this Italian war hero?" "His name is Giovanni Battista Salvatore, like the guy in *Nostromo*. But this Gian' Battista is a squid fisherman and lives in a town called Falconara Marittima on the coast of the Adriatic Sea. I have discovered recently that his oldest son Sigismondo Pandolfo di Giovanni da Falconara Marittima Salvatore lives right on my street, right on Vox Populi Street just at the end across from you, Father Thom." "That's right," said Father Thom, "but Siggy told me that his father is just a squid fisherman. He certainly doesn't sound like a war hero." I replied that my research told me differently, that I was getting all my information off the Internet from the Monte Cassino Web site.

Ari looked at me strangely and said, "You're getting your information from the Benedictines at Monte Cassino?" "Yes," I said, "it's all in the *Annali Calabresi,* all written by Bartolemeo Masaccio, who was present during the Illyrian-Italian War in 1945 to 1948. He's the writer who recorded the attacks by the Illyrian army under the leadership of Queen Martha von Stoepf the First. It was Salvatore who led the Italian troops to victory for which he received the Victor Emmanuel III Royal Order of the Tin Star with Garlic cluster and the Royal Order of the Yellow Heart for his wounds. It's all in the *Annali Calabresi.*"

Aristarchus Skiamachos said, "Have you ever studied the Benedictines? Do you know anything about them? You know, don't you, that they have a great sense of humor, that they sit up there in Monte Cassino and have nothing else to do but load up the Internet? Their motto is 'Laborare est orare,' but it just as well be 'Scribere est orare' or 'Ridere est orare.' They're great jokesters and they're famous for forging documents. Monte Cassino was bombed into rubble in World War II by the Allies and since then they've been rewriting their library." I looked at him, squarely, and said, "You mean all those volumes I've been seeing on the Internet were written by the monks at Monte Cassino? You mean the *Annali Calabresi* are forgeries? I don't believe a word you're saying. I can't believe a word you're saying." "OK," Ari said, "don't. But just remember that those monks got nothing else to do." Father Thom added, "Siggy told me that his father supplies the Friday squid to the monks at Monte Cassino. That's his main business. You think that just because something is written that it's true? History is fiction you know. History is the journalism of necromancy. It's about as reliable as reading Cincinnati newspapers." I could only meekly reply, "I trust the written text. That's all I got. Besides, I'm just trying to tell a good story in a clear, concise style."

"How is it," Skyblue asked, "that no one else knows about these things you're writing about? How is it no one else knows about the Illyrian-Italian War? How is it no one else knows about Queen Martha von Stoepf the First except you? How is it no one else knows about Giovanni Battista Salvatore, the war hero? Haven't you ever asked yourself how it is that only you have read the *Annali Calabresi?* Haven't you ever questioned your sources? Have you seen the original manuscripts?"

"Only on the computer screen," I replied. Skyblue giggled and said, "And you accepted its validity? You realize how easy it would be to fake documents on a computer network? You don't look at bindings, you don't look at watermarks, you don't look at gathering signatures. You have no physical evidence that the manuscripts exist. No one does on a computer. How do you suppose the *Annali Calabresi* got to Monte Cassino? How did they get there and who put them there? Can anyone else get to the Web site? You better get someone on the scene. You'd better get someone to go there and take a look. Send this petty crime detective what's his name Dallasandro Vibini. Have him look at the documents if you don't want to go there."

"But all the volumes," I said. "Right," Ari said. "They got nothing else to do. Just suppose the Benedictine monks were writing all that stuff just to hoax you." "But," I said, "there's so much and besides there's the hero himself." Ari sneered, "A squid fisherman from Falconara Marittima is a war hero? Remember their great sense of humor." "I hope so," I said. "Because they live an austere but rich life. They deserve a sense of humor. It must keep them entertained. They need entertainment just like the rest of us." "That's it," Ari remarked casually. "They need entertainment. How do they get it?" In spite of my cheerfulness, I felt a terrible abyss opening at my feet. What if it was all a Benedictine joke? What if what they said is true and the Benedictines have been putting me on? They say we Germans have no sense of humor and they may be right.

I checked my watch and it was 7:30, time for me to get home for supper. I whispered, "Forgive me, Saponata. Forgive me for coming in late." I could hear that it was raining hard again. Father Thomas Takianopoulos, called "The Gymnast" and "Skialogos," called the barmaid over and ordered four double shots of Maker's Mark Bourbon with one ice cube in each glass. We sipped and Father Thom said, "You see. Something good can come out of Kentucky other than an empty bus."

To change the subject, now that I was completely depressed, I said to Ari, "What kind of book are you writing?"

Ari cleared his throat and announced to all the room, "I'm writing a heavy volume called *Prolegomena to the Study of Apocalyptic Hermeneutics*. It will be a study of the way in which the Apocalypse is happening right now. In my book I will prove that syntax is eschatological, that the teleological imperative of our thought is exercised in our acts of writing. I will prove that the Parousia happens whenever we write proper syntax. As long as our syntax is clear God appears on this earth. The Eschaton happens because of bad grammar. Armageddon is fought out in our punctuation. I will prove that the mark of the beast is the dash. I will prove that the dash is sloppy punctuation and therefore the sign of the Second Coming because the dash is used as a universal punctuation mark and is therefore the work of the Beast from the Sea of the People. That's why our popular writers never learn to write a simple, clear sentence. They thrive on confusion. They are paid millions of dollars to deceive their readers because they are in the army of evil. Nowadays confusion is confused with profundity. That works with a mindless audience, like here in Cincinnati. I will prove that if you write nonsense you will be paid big bucks. But woe to the thoughtful. Woe to the intelligent. Woe to the writer of excellent prose. You make sense and you will be run out of town. You make sense and you'll be lucky to survive the night. You tell the truth and your life is in jeopardy. I will prove that the will of God rides in a perfect sentence, that God reveals himself in clear syntax. I will show that all style tends to the condition of Apocalypse."

I said, "That's all very interesting. But I just want to write interesting stories."

"What's interesting?" Father Thom popped in. "We preach in our church that art is a hard and gemlike flimflam. We preach and believe that God plants his footsteps in our prose and rides upon the syntax. We preach that sinners plunged beneath good prose lose all their guilty stains. We preach that perfect prose, how sweet the sound, can save a wretch like me. That's why we say that the resolution of a narrative should be an Eschaton. Each short story should recapitulate man's salvation, that is recapitulate the Passion. A short story should reveal the divine plan in history to save the soul of man. We say that this little sentence of mine I'm going to let it shine. We say Jesus wants me for my syntax to shine for him each day. We say don't you try to poof it out. I'm going to let it shine. We say Jesus bids us shine with a clear, pure prose. Well he sees and knows it if our prose is dim. He looks down from heaven, sees us write, you with your crude dashes and I with perfect grammar.

"Aristarchus is right. Sin and bad writing have everything in the world to do with each other. The Paraclete is in our care with which we record anything. All our prose should be a doxology, a song of praise to God because that's how the Apokatastasis can be made true. We can have universal salvation if we can but teach people to write simple, clear sentences. Lead me, Lord. Lead me in thy righteousness. Teach me to write a God-damned good sentence."

I intervened and said, "You know, I grew up in Nazi Germany. I was first one of the Pimpfe and then I was a member of the Hitlerjugend. We all read *Mein Kampf*. I know what bad prose is. I know about the falsity of historical documents. I know about the small print in the historical records. I lived in the Third Reich and I never knew why it was called that. What were the first two Reichs? Why would it last 1000 years? You know, that Italian war hero. I was planning to publish some trading cards. You know, like the ones for baseball players. Saponata said she'd help me put them together and we'd make some extra money for her new baby."

Ari, Skyblue and Father Thom laughed. I said, "What's so funny? We have a new baby coming and we have to support it. None of you has any children. Don't laugh. We Germans don't laugh at the miracle of birth. We see new birth as God's divine will."

Father Thom went on. "You know the cross of Jesus goes forward all the time. I told you the Messiah is being born every minute of our lives. The Passion is going on at all times. Salvation comes down on us like a soft rain. We but have to recognize it. That's why prophecy is nonsense. There is no future salvation. There is no future punishment. God and his son Jesus go forward. 'Vexilla regis produerunt.' The end times were in the beginning. The Apocalypse and Armageddon are going on right now.

"If you don't believe that God works for our salvation overtime, just look at our nuclear submarines. Those submarines carry enough explosive force in their bellies to destroy the world ten times over. But God has used them for his divine purpose. Those submarines might carry death in their bellies but they carry the Cross of Christ on their backs. There it is for all to see. Put there by God to tell us of His eternal presence and His eternal grace. Put there by God on a nuclear submarine. Jesus is always coming again and receiving us. We have but to knock. Instead, we build our Cross on the superstructure of a weapon of war. We carry the central Christian symbol to the world above twenty-four missiles that can annihilate the earth. Those submarines are the new St. Christophers who bear our Savior across the waters and into all the world. Christ the conquer of the world. Wherever those submarines go they carry the Cross of Jesus and spread the Gospel, the good news of salvation. They may be named 'Nevada,' 'Cincinnati' or 'Thresher,' but each one should be called 'Theotokos,' Bearer of God. Even when they go underwater for seventy days they are doing the work of the Lord. God works in a mysterious way His wonders to perform. He puts His behemoth of death into the sea and rides upon its steel. All around the world, it carries its Christian message along with its cargo of megatons of death. Even in our attempts to eradicate ourselves from the surface of the earth, God gives us a sign that He is present and that we must look to the cruciform tower on the sub and not to its satanic missiles. He sends His word even unto the depths of the seas. God would have it no other way."

I said, "I have discovered that to be a good writer you must be able to forgive man for his shortcomings. The greatest writers are those who can forgive the most."

Ari said, "You wouldn't say that if you tried to teach at Miami University in Oxford. That place is a white man's refuge from thought and conscience. It's a fraternity and sorority dunghill in the country. That's the new whore of Babylon. There they are up there spending tax payers' dollars to enhance the privileges of the rich. It's a rich man's playground pretending to be an educational institution. I think that if I could teach those students to punctuate carefully and precisely it would be like baptizing them in the Jordan River. If I could teach them to organize paragraphs it would be inviting them to the Last Supper. If I could teach them the beauty of denotation it would be like showing them the glory of the Resurrection. If I could teach them to write simple, clear sentences it would be like pointing them to the first steps on the path of righteousness. If I could teach them to understand point of view I would put them on the path to salvation."

Skyblue said, "They're all Republicans. What do you expect? I'm writing an essay about that so-called university. They need some reality adjustment."

I looked at my watch and said, "Friends, it's 8:30 P.M. I have to go home. It's been very enlightening to talk to you and I am most pleased to have met you. We should keep in touch, especially about our publications. But now I have to get home. Saponata will be worried about my not showing up. She has become concerned about my health." We emptied our whiskeys and got up to leave.

After I paid the bill of $32.50 and put down a $5.00 tip, I mentioned how hard it was raining. "We need umbrellas," Ari said. "Let's ask the barmaid if she has some we can borrow." She had two under the bar. One was an ordinary black umbrella. The other one was a kind of beach umbrella with alternating black and red panels and a shaft with a well rubbed wooden handle. "I know that umbrella," I said. "It's the Hong Kong umbrella that was involved in the second petty crime that I saw Vibini solve. You can read about that event in my story 'The Hong Kong Umbrella,' if it ever gets published."

It was 8:45 P.M. when we walked out of Arlin's Bar and Garden. The rain came down in torrents. The streets were empty. The shops were empty. The Christmas lights and the lights from the shops glittered on the wet sidewalks like the fires of a wet Hell. The Clifton dead had all gone off into the darkness of oblivion. Even the store clerks seemed to have left their businesses.

We were all loaded with beer and junk food, but we still made a joyful quartet. Ari took the black umbrella and Skyblue took the Hong Kong umbrella. I said Father Thom and I had just a short way to go so we could do without one. We stopped at the corner of Ludlow and Clifton, by the firehouse, and said good-by in spite of the fierce, cold rain. We shook hands and headed each in his own direction. Skyblue south up Clifton towards Riddle Road, Aristarchus Skiamachos westward towards Shekinah Avenue, and Father Thomas the Gymnast and myself north across Ludlow, past Clifton Florist and towards Vox Populi Street. We crossed over at Glenmary to the east side of Clifton Avenue and walked to and into the entrance to our street.

When Father Thomas and I reached my apartment, he invited me to his house where, he said, his wife Leah, whose name means "wild cow," would make us a cup of coffee and he'd show me the first draft of his new book entitled *Via Crucis: A History of Execution in the Holy Land*. I explained that I was too tired to examine more writing that evening and Father Thom said he understood. The rain ran off his bald head and down over his thick glasses. The rain ran into his gray-white tonsure and onto his shoulders. I said, "Isn't the rain awfully cold on your bald head?" He gave me one of his habitual surprised looks and allowed as to how uncomfortable it was and thanked me for my sympathy. So we shook hands and he walked on down towards his house at 231 West Vox Populi, the last house on our side of the street.

Before leaving, Father Thomas, a.k.a., "Skialogos," said, "Someone should record this first meeting of the Gang of Four. It's not quite a cabal, but it is a fierce quartet of protest. We could call our group 'Cincinnatians Recognizing Apocalyptic Parousia.'"

"I'll write it down," I said. And so I have. These fragments made into narrative. The writer's burden to record, to remember, to preserve for posterity, this moment, a moment in time for all time.

As I turned in the rain to walk up to our apartment, it was exactly 8:56 P.M., the Winter solstice, and for some reason I remembered Father Thomas called "Skialogos" saying, "Don't you know that the Messiah comes to us everyday, every hour, every minute, every second? He is walking amongst us right now. We don't recognize him because we don't want to recognize him. We don't see him because we don't want to see him. We don't speak to him because we are afraid to look him in the face and say, 'Forgive us. Forgive us for what we've done to our world.'"

And I remembered Aristarchus Skiamachos saying, "Apocalypse is the paradigm of our existence. We are born into an Apocalyptic scenario. That's why we are obsessed with violence. That's why we kill each other. We are in a scenario that we can't or won't change because we lack the imagination to do it. That's why we invent cold wars and massive engines of destruction. Jesus tried to change the scenario, tried to end the cycles of revenge and violence, but failed. Apocalypse is a self-fulfilling prophecy. We say there will be war and, by God, there is."

Before entering the vestibule, I carefully shook the water off my hat and my coat. I went in and hung them carefully on the hall tree. I didn't want to offend Saponata, who keeps everything neat. I didn't want to carry water into our apartment and onto her clean floors. She becomes very upset if we dirty up what she now calls "her" apartment.

I entered my, now our, apartment and walked into a cloud of marijuana smoke and Gundula Janowitz singing at full volume Mozart's "Ah, lo previdi!" I've heard Vibini's records so many times that I know them all now by heart. And I walked into the bloated Saponata with her hands on her hips, her jaw thrust forward and her tongue already rattling out, "Where have you been? Don't you know that I put on your supper at exactly 6:00 P.M. every evening?" I said meekly, "I was out drinking with my new pals. I didn't think you'd mind since you introduced me to Skylue and Aristarchus. It won't happen again. I'm sorry." "Well," she said, "just get in here and eat your supper so I can clean up the mess and get some rest."

Saponata had laid out my little Keller's *I.G.A.* supper. She turned on the burner under the hot water kettle and sat down opposite to where I usually sit. I excused myself and went into the bathroom. I think I excreted five or six gallons of beer. There seemed to be no end of urine in my bladder. I remembered Skyblue saying that the Pythagoreans said, "Never piss in the direction of the sun." I realized that was not likely in Cincinnati, not in this land of the dead. When I finally finished, I washed my hands and went and sat down to eat.

Saponata got up and poured the hot water for my "Please tear here. Bigelow I Love Lemon Herb Tea, A special blend for lemon lovers. No caffeine. One tea bag." She sat back down opposite me and said, "Where have you been all this time? You been drinking for five hours? How can you do that and lose weight?" That's her newest thing. I'm supposed to lose weight. I said, "It was just four hours" as I cut off a slice of "Amish Country Old Fashioned Amish Swiss Cheese. The Natural Cheese People. A natural semi-soft cheese made from pasteurized milk, cheese cultures, enzymes and no salt. Amish Country Cheese. Linwood, MI 48634. Real. The cheese worth having a party for! NET WT. 8 oz. 227 grams." "Look," she said, "you can't get in the habit of associating with those crazy people. They'll ruin your mind." I picked up two "Fruit Stand Freshness And Flavor. Perfect For Snacking And Baking. SUN-MAID CALIFORNIA SUN-DRIED APRICOTS. NET WT 6 OZ. (170 g)" and put them in my mouth. They were refreshing. Truly delicious. Saponata said, "You're too old for carousing around with Clifton crazies. Besides, I need you here." While I chewed on my dried apricots, I asked Saponata if she knew what "apocalyptic hermeneutics" might be. She got up angrily from the table. "Hurry up and finish," she said. "I need to clean up."

"Saponata, my dear," I said, "did you know that the word 'testament' comes from the word 'testes?' Did you know that when Abraham wanted a wife for his son Isaac he sent a servant out to get one but before the servant left Abraham had him hold onto his, that is Abraham's, balls? And that's why we have the Old Testament and the New Testament?" "Listen," she said, "Doctor Gottlieb Otto Liebgott, don't try that 'Saponata, my dear' stuff on me. It won't work. And don't tell me that screwball, silly-ass information that you drag home from the library. I don't want to hear it. Just leave it in the library where it belongs. I don't care if it is free information. And don't put it in your writing."

What I said was wrong, and I knew it. I said to myself, "Forgive me, Saponata. Forgive me. I just thought it was a good story."

I sat and chewed the delicious fruit and wondered what the day will be like when the Messiah arrives. What kind of day will it be when he comes? What will he look like? What kind of person will he be? What hour, what day of the week and what will the date be when he arrives? How should we address him? Will we recognize him when he arrives? What language will he speak? What signs will be manifested and where that the Messiah has come? Will we ridicule him and crucify him when he comes? Will our chronic low-grade stupidity again make us miss our chance for salvation? Will the Republicans impeach him? Will they greet him with their usual dirty tricks? Will they withdraw all tax support for his mission? Will the people in Western Hills vote him out of office? Will our salvation be postponed because it conflicts with a Bengals football game? Will Covington outbid the city of Cincinnati for Second Coming rights? Will the governor of Ohio execute a criminal to celebrate the end of the world? Will the Republican governor, an equal opportunity employer, give us all concealed weapons so we can participate in Armageddon?

After I finished eating, I brushed my teeth and went into the little room that is now my bedroom at the back of our apartment. It's the only room left for me because Vibini and Saponata have taken all the rest of the space. I closed the window to the back porch because it was getting colder fast. The rain had stopped. I took off my suit and hung it up carefully so Saponata wouldn't get on me about it. I then hooked the hanger on the rope that runs across the southeast corner of my room, a rope that is now my clothes closet. I took off my shirt and my shoes and wet socks. I sat down in my boxer shorts on the edge of my narrow cot, Vibini's old bed. I stared at the blank computer screen. Until there was a knock upon the door.

I got up and went to the door. It was Saponata. She said, through the crack between the door and the door frame, "Doctor Gottlieb Otto Liebgott, my baby is kicking without stopping. I can't stop him. Is that bad? Should we do something?" I said, "Don't worry, Saponata. He wants out. He wants to be released from his bondage. He wants to come out so he can save this terrible world from destruction. He wants to be born so he can save us from ourselves."

IN EXCELSIS DEO

HAVING BEEN A MEDICAL doctor for thirty-eight years and having retired on January 3, 1995, at the age of sixty-five, I decided to start a new profession. I decided to become a writer of fiction. Since retiring, I have worked hard at learning my new trade. What I didn't realize when I decided to become a writer is that being a writer is a lot like being a doctor. When a patient is ill, the doctor must take care of him. The doctor can't say, "See me next week" or "Go away and come back when you are well." Likewise, when you are a writer and a story is at hand you must write it then and there. You can't say, "I'll write it when I get around to it. Come back later when I feel like writing." If that situation is what is meant by inspiration, then inspiration is like a disease. You have to deal with it immediately. You can't just wait until it goes away. In short, I've discovered that there is in writing an artistic imperative just as there is a Hippocratic imperative in medicine. Since stories are as ubiquitous and omnipresent as illness, the writer like the doctor is always "on call."

Just last Tuesday, December 22, 1998, I completed a story called "Prolegomena to the Study of Apocalyptic

Hermeneutics." I had to write it that afternoon while the events of the previous day, December 21, 1998, the shortest day of the year, were still fresh in my mind. It was a story that had to be written, so I, the writer, had no choice and had to take care of it. The artistic imperative left me no choice.

Today is Friday, December 25, 1998, Christmas Day, and once again I must attend to a story even though I've hardly recovered from doing the last one. Once again I have no choice because last night Saponata, the eighteen year old wife of Dallasandro Vibini, who is fifty-four, gave birth to a seven pounds and twelve ounces baby boy whose name is Amadeo di Dallasandro da Clifton Vibini. And even though I haven't recovered from last night and even though I've had no sleep for twenty-four hours, I must write the story because last night I reverted to my medical practice, became a doctor again, and delivered the baby.

Right now it is afternoon. The phone was ringing but I refused to answer it. I've turned off the sound and I will not respond to the callers. Saponata and Amadeo are asleep in their, formerly my, bedroom. Both are exhausted from the birthing. The baby is making strong efforts to nurse. He's hardly stopped since I first put him to her breast. Vibini is asleep on my cot, formerly his cot, in the tiny back bedroom of my, now our, apartment at 253 West Vox Populi Street. Saponata and Vibini and now the baby have pushed me and my computer back into the tiny back bedroom and have taken over my apartment even though I pay all the bills. They have taken over the big front bedroom, the parlor, the dining area, the kitchen and the bathroom. All I have in my room is my one-man cot, my computer, a small table, my printer and a rope across one corner of the room, which serves as a clothes closet. My clothes all hang on the rope and there is a window to the back porch. Now, to top it off, I can't even lie down and rest because Vibini has my cot so I might as well write this story. So here it is. It is called "In Excelsis Deo." I have to answer to the artistic imperative no matter where I am and no matter how tired I am. Doctors on call could at least stay home and rest after treating a patient. Writers on call have to stay where they are and get the story written.

Saponata was pregnant: to begin with. She was so pregnant she gave new dimensions of meaning to "gravid" and "heavy with child." Saponata is normally five feet and four inches tall. She normally weighs about 120 pounds. But her womb was so large that it was all she was. She looked like a huge skin balloon with attached legs, arms and head. Her lovely blond hair, her Botticelli face, her almost transparent pinkish skin, her incipient freckles, her soft green eyes gravid with immanent lust, all were subverted to the service of the huge fetus that knocked about in her swollen belly. When she walked, her legs splayed out to get around the inflated abdomen. Her arms and shoulders leaned backwards because she couldn't lean forwards. Even her chin was lifted and her head tilted backwards to counterbalance the awful weight of her frantic child. He wanted out, no question about that. Even if it was Christmas Eve.

On Wednesday, December 23, I spent all day getting ready for a home delivery. Because all the deliveries I had done before had been in hospitals, I walked over to Good Samaritan Hospital and talked to my former colleague Dr. Nabal Almah. I told him I was going to do a home delivery for the first time and he helped me get together the material I needed. He lent me a forceps, a fetal stethoscope, a portable sphygmomanometer, a surgical scissors for an episiotomy and to cut the cord, anaesthesia for the episiotomy, umbilical clamps, a suturing kit, a bulb syringe and a DeLee Mucus Trap to clear the eyes, nose and throat, a scale to weigh the baby. He gave me sterile syringes and drugs for controlling hemorrhage and Betadine for disinfecting. He got for me a surgical mask and gown, head and shoe covers in sterile wrap. He gave me a hospital gown for the mother. He gave me some surgical soap, the silver nitrate pearls, oxytocin and a phone number in case of complications. We arranged to have an ambulance available if needed. I purchased 4x4 sterile pads and twenty pairs of long cuffed sterile latex gloves.

As I left with my two bags of stuff, Dr. Almah said, "Who's assisting?" I said, "I'm doing it myself." He smiled and said, "Not a good idea. You need psychological and physical support for the mother. When you delivered babies in a hospital you had nurses present to support the mother. Don't try to go it alone." I stopped at Keller's I.G.A. and got a double paper grocery bag to use as a waste receptacle.

Then I called a Quo Vadis Cab and drove out to Forest Park to Babies "R" Us, "The Baby Superstore," and purchased a little stocking cap to keep the newborn's head warm, a little blue body suit that zipped shut to cover the whole body of the baby and a small crib to keep the baby in by the bed. I got some small diapers and some cotton swabs to clean the child. I also purchased washcloths, baby blankets, towels and some olive oil, all the stuff that Vibini hadn't even thought about.

When I got back to my house on Vox Populi Street, I set up the front bedroom, formerly my bedroom and my study, to be ready for the delivery. I borrowed a small table from Guido di Pietro and set it alongside the big bed so that it was slightly lower than the main bed. That way I could lay the newborn child on it and the blood would flow down the umbilicus to the baby. I put a large table near the bed to put my equipment on. I covered both tables with clean white sheets, laid out the equipment and I thought I was ready.

That evening, I prepped Saponata. I explained everything that I could. I told her what to expect and that we couldn't know when it would all happen. I explained the contractions and the passage of the child. I coached her on how to breathe during the contractions. I told her that I had everything ready for a home delivery and had even made arrangements to take her right over to Good Sam if necessary. I told her that each delivery is different, but I would tell her what was going on. She listened and smiled and said she was ready. She said she didn't want to go to the hospital for the delivery and that she would do it herself. Her attitude was perfect. She wanted the child and she listened carefully to my instructions. I listened to the child's heart and it was just fine. I took her blood pressure and listened to her heart. Never had I experienced such a perfect prepartum prognosis. It was surprising to me how easily I fell back into my role as a doctor.

When Saponata asked what Vibini would do, I said, "It's best to make this delivery a partnership between you and me. He will just be in the way. You need to trust me and do what I tell you." She smiled and said, "Gottlieb Otto Liebgott, I trust you more than anyone else in this world. I don't know what my life would have been like without you. I love you very much." I blushed and said, "Saponata, there is nothing in this world that is more loveable than a woman about to give birth. I love you very much too and I will make everything as good as possible. Now rest. You'll need it when labor begins." I couldn't tell her that a doctor who loves his patients is in trouble. Before I left the room, Saponata said, "Gottlieb, will you pray with me?" I said, "Of course," and Saponata said a little prayer for the health and safety of her child while I thought about the role of prayer in delivery. "Not a bad idea," I thought. "Prayer gets the expectant mother ready for suffering. It's all very Christian."

Yesterday morning while Vibini was still asleep and Saponata had gone, against my wishes, to her job at the library, I checked the arrangement of everything in the bedroom. I was ready in case Saponata came home in labor. I was ready because I thought the delivery would be soon.

When Saponata did come home yesterday at 4:00 P.M. from her job as a librarian at the Clifton Branch of the Hamilton County Public Library, it was because the library had closed early because it was Christmas Eve. I don't know how she could even walk because she was so large. She waddled home to Vox Populi Street and managed to get up the front steps and into the house. Her feet swollen, her knees and ankles bloated with water, her face pale, her right hand at her throat as she caught her breath. When she came in she said, "Dr. Gottlieb Otto Liebgott, why doesn't he come?" I said, "Saponata, we can't change nature. He'll come at his own good time. No one knows for sure what causes labor to begin. In fact, some people think that it is the unborn child who determines when it starts. But, Saponata, whenever it is, I'm ready. I have everything I need. Everything is ready and sterilized for whenever the child leaps in the womb and enters this world. Eat your supper and get some rest. You'll need all the rest you can get."

Saponata went into her and Vibini's bedroom and all was quiet for about an hour. At a little after 5:00 I heard her yell, "Liebgott, get your fat ass in here. Something's happening." I rushed into the room. "What is it?" I asked. "Look," she said. She lifted up her skirt and I looked. There it was, the "bloody show," the blood colored mucus that signals the onset of true labor. I told her to take off all her clothes while I went for some warm water. When I came back, I washed her vaginal area with surgical soap and told her to put on the hospital gown I had for her. Before she lay back down, I told her to stand still while I felt the fetus to see what position it was in. It used to be called the "Leopold Maneuver," where the fetus is felt in four different ways to determine its position in the womb. I said to her, "Vertex presentation. Head down. Face towards the umbilicus." "Is that good?" she said and I assured her that that was the perfect position for birth.

She lay back down until 6:15 when she again called me into the room. I said, "What is it?" and she said, "I felt pain." "Where is the pain?" "It's a low back pain and it sort of comes around here to the front." I said, "What's the pain like?" and she said it was kind of like menstrual cramps. "That's a contraction," I said. "From now on they will get more intense and more frequent and last longer." I sent her to the bathroom and told her to empty her bladder and her gut as much as she could. When she returned, I told her to lie still so I could start monitoring her contractions and the fetal heartbeat. I explained that the contractions didn't necessarily mean that birth was imminent and that it might be some time before the baby would come.

At 7:00 P.M. I arranged Saponata on the bed. I piled pillows against the headboard of the bed which was pushed against the front wall of the room. I had her lean against the pillows so that she sat at about a forty-five degree angle from the bed itself. That was the position that I wanted her in when the time for the delivery might come. I asked her if she was comfortable and she said that the pillows gave her back good support. From where I sat beside the bed, I could see out the front window onto the front porch and into the front yard. With the curtain open I could look out over Vox Populi Street. That seeing out was important because I was looking for Vibini, who had disappeared about 6:00. I needed him to supply me with warm water when I needed it, just like in the movies. I remembered how, in the movies, the anxious husband was always told to heat water when a baby was on the way.

After I had finished arranging Saponata into a delivery position, I heard a rustling from the front yard. Because it was dark, I could not see what was causing the noise. It wasn't the noise of passing traffic. It sounded like running water or the whirring of wings. I went out onto the porch to see what was the matter and turned on the porch light. What I saw was Vibini talking to some of our neighbors. They were standing on the sidewalk in front of the house and on the sidewalk up to the front porch.

Vibini, who stood by the steps to the porch and under the porch light, was dressed in his black beret, black cape, black shirt, black tie, black trousers, black penny loafers and white spats. He looked like a chic Savonarola. He was talking to Jeremy Scroggins. They were talking about a poem Vibini was writing for the evening. Jeremy was showing Vibini the poems he had written for the event. I heard Vibini say, "But when will I get a chance to read my poem?"

"What's going on out here?" I asked Guido di Pietro, who was standing with his wife Pallottola. Both of them were wearing heavy coats and red stocking caps. It was about thirty degrees outside. The day had been cool with some high, thin clouds, but no wind. It was crisp and dry and mostly sunny all day. All told, it was a fine day for December, but in the evening it was getting uncomfortably cold. Guido called up to me, "Vibini has invited us all over. We're getting ready for a Vox Populi Street party to celebrate Christmas and the birth of the new baby." It was then I noticed that both of them were holding lawn chairs and that they had a sign on their front porch that said, "Men." Across the street, on the house of Jeremy Scroggins and Airball McGritts there was a large sign that said, "Women."

As my eyes became adjusted to the darkness, I saw that Sigismondo Pandolfo Salvatore and his wife Beatrice were already there. He was dressed in a green, white and red striped jacket. He was wearing a broad-brimmed brown hat that was decorated with a brush and two long feathers. He was carrying a skyblue flag and on it was a white unicorn rampant with a squid skewered on its horn. Beatrice was stunning in a white leather coat with a white fur collar and a white fur hat. They too carried lawn chairs. I saw others coming along the street and up the sidewalk, all dressed for the cold and carrying lawn chairs and candles: Father Gottlob Schlag, Emil Hasenpfeffer and his wife Isolde, Barry and Tallulah Vermis, Don Robin Pugh, Peter Solomon Seiltanzer, Sharon Holiday Inn Towel, Aristarchus Skiamachos, Father Thomas and Leah Takianopoulos, Panciuto and Squallida Santarellina, Melissa Comb, Airball McGritts and Jeremy Scroggins. The whole populace of Vox Populi Street and friends were gathering for the Christmas revels.

Jeremy Scroggins came into the yard carrying the sign that was once at the entrance to Vox Populi Street. But he had altered the sign to read, "Give Up All Dope You Who Enter Here." I asked him what was going on and he said, "We have read your stories in *First Intensity* and in *North American Review* and we are come to be a part of them. When it comes time for you to write the story of this night we want to be part of it. We want our names inscribed as witnesses to the birth." I replied solemnly, "Tonight I'm a doctor, not a writer." "Oh, that's OK," he said. "We understand that. But tomorrow you will be a writer again and then you will write the story of this night and we want to be in it. We have come to fulfill your plot. We have gathered to fill out your narrative. You need us to give substance to what you write. We are here to be your details. We are here to mask your fiction."

When I went back into the bedroom, Saponata asked what was going on. I said, "The neighbors are gathering for a Christmas party. They want to celebrate the birth of the child as it happens. They want to be in on the first level of the narrative. They've brought candles and chairs and have dressed for the outdoor cold. They're here to see Christmas and the new baby into this world."

At 8:00 o'clock I went out onto the porch to get some air. I was already getting cramped from sitting and waiting for the babe to decide to exit his womb. The contractions were coming at fifteen minute intervals. Saponata was inhaling in rhythm with the onset of the pain and exhaling as it passed. I got her up and walked her to the bathroom so she could urinate. I gave her some orange juice and got her back in bed. I checked her blood pressure and her pulse and listened to the baby's heartbeat. When I went out onto the porch I saw that there was a black four-door Mercedes-Benz parked across the street. The license plate was JBW-582. Two men dressed in black bowlers, black dress coats, black shirts, black ties, black trousers, black shoes and white spats were unloading cases of beer and wine from the trunk of the car. While they carried them up onto the lawn and began opening them for the Vox Populi crowd, I noticed that a young man was sitting in the back seat of the car. It was, I'm sure, Ciacco Polenta, and the two men were Rinier Corneto and Rinier Pazzo.

While the beer and wine were being passed around, Jeremy Scroggins, who had taken over the celebration, yelled at Pallottola di Pietro, Isolde Hasenpfeffer, Tallulah Vermis and Sharon Holiday Inn Towel to get the candles lit. I only then noticed in the darkness that the sidewalk to the porch was lined with brown paper bags. And as the women lit the candles in the bags I realized that there was sand in the bottoms of the bags and that's why they stood there while the candles sputtered into life. The women then lit candles in dishes and candle holders on the porch railings and at various places around the yard. I must admit that it was a wonderfully Christmas sight, especially for an old German like me. It reminded me of how we had real candles on our Christmas trees in Wuppertal. It recalled for me how when he was just three years old our second son Fürchtegott Franz Gottlieb, born on Halloween, 1955, tried to set our house on fire by pushing the candles on the tree into the branches. He got some third degree burns, but he survived to be committed to St. Dympna's on New Year's Eve, 1975.

When the candles were all lit and everyone had a drink, Jeremy Scroggins stood on the porch steps and called out, "Let's start the party. Let's have my poems that I've written for tonight." Father Gottlob Schlag stepped to the first step of the stairs to the porch and read, "The voices from on high/ Sing a Vox Populi doxology." "More passion," Jeremy yelled. "More passion. Do justice to my poems. Next." Guido di Pietro limped forward, stepped on the first step and read, "While the aging father/ stands in silence,/ Angels on the wing/ sing our deliverance." Then Emil Hasenpfeffer came up and read, "Let's welcome to life/ this holy child/ With verses/ rich and mild." Tallulah Vermis read, "His star has risen/ in the east/ To stand above/ Vox Populi Street." Peter Solomon Seiltanzer cleared his throat and declaimed, "The year has turned/ to give us light./ The savior will be born/ this night." Sharon Holiday Inn Towel, "The wise men now/ have left their homes./ Look! From the east/ the light comes." Beatrice Salvatore, stunningly beautiful in her white coat and white fur hat, "For unto us/ a child is given./ Let's raise our voices/ in thanks to heaven." Aristarchus Skiamachos spoke from the lower sidewalk, "We bring our gifts/ both rich and odd/ To this new baby/ loved of God." Finally, I hoped because I was getting very cold, Father Thomas Takianopoulos called out, "The child of God/ is now our burden,/ His holiness/ our guerdon." "That was great," Scroggins called out. "You all did great by my poems. I'm proud of every one of you. Now someone get me a beer and let's get this party rolling." As I walked back into the vestibule, I heard the first beer bottle smash on the sidewalk.

I sat down beside the bed and asked Saponata how she felt. She said the contractions were starting up again. I said, "I'll time them," and thought back to my first

Christmas with Gertrude. It was wintertime. It was Heidelberg in a time when Germany was still in rubble. We had been married on June 24, 1951, in Wuppertal and that fall I began my medical studies. Getrude had a job at the U.S.O. where she worked behind what they called a "soda fountain." She dipped ice cream and made malted milks and milk shakes for the U.S. soldiers who flirted with her and left tips in military scrip for her. We could buy American goods at their PX with that scrip and that made life a lot easier for us.

On that first Christmas Eve in 1951, I was on duty in the hospital as an orderly, a job that we first year medical students had to do. At midnight, I left the hospital. The church bells were ringing to signal the midnight hour and the beginning of Christmas day. I had purchased a small Christmas tree that day and I took it along to surprise Gertrude and have her help me decorate it for the Christmas season. I also had for her presents of some wool stockings and a bottle of Mosel wine called Elendthaler Erlöungsuhr, Spätlese.

When I entered our apartment on Sankt Sebastian Strasse, Gertrude was sitting on the floor in a corner of our room that served as dining room, kitchen and living room. That room plus a bath and a bedroom was the whole apartment. I said, "Gertrude, come. Help me decorate our tree. It's Christmas." She had her head down between her knees and she did not look up. I said, "Gertrude, come. Let's begin the celebration." She looked up and I was, for the first time, frightened. I hardly recognized her face it was so distorted. I said, "Gertrude, are you ill?" "Yes," she said, "I'm sick of serving those rotten American soldiers. They make me sick. First, they come over here and destroy our cities, destroy our nation, kill our soldiers. Then they think we have to serve them like peasants. We are the German people. We could have ruled for a thousand years and taught those beasts some civilization. At least I don't have to wait on the filthy British swine."

I said, "Gertrude, think what you are saying. We Germans invaded those other countries. We attacked them. We started the war. We lost and we committed horrible crimes against the Slavs, the Gypsies and the Jews. We must now undo the wrong and get on with our lives. Now is the time, especially at Christmas, for forgiveness." Gertrude jumped up and rushed up to me and screamed in my face, "Have you forgotten that my father and my mother were burned to ashes in the Hamburg firestorm? Have you forgotten that my three brothers, Ehrgott, Fürchtegott and Traugott, all fell at Stalingrad? Have you forgotten that I survived only because I happened to be in the Allgäu when the bombers destroyed Hamburg? Have you forgotten the promises of a great future that we learned when we were in the Hitlerjugend? Have you forgotten all that?"

"Gertrude," I said calmly, "have you forgotten that my father Lobgott Gerebernus Liebgott was arrested and executed by the Nazis in 1934 because he made fun of them? My father, the most powerful novelist in Germany, the essence of the German soul, author of six novels and many short stories, was garroted in Spandau prison by the brown shirts because he said that Hitler was a clown and that he would destroy Germany."

"Your father," she said, "was a traitor to what our nation stood for. It was people like him that made us lose the war. My brothers were honorable and brave. They volunteered and they marched against the Bolshevist menace. They laid down their lives for our German soil, not cowards like your father. Your father who married that mongrel French whore did not care for his own country. When we have our sons, we will name them after my brothers who were great heroes. We will name them Ehrgott, Fürchtegott and Traugott. Agreed?"

I agreed. And when our three sons were born in 1953, 1955 and 1957, we named them after her three brothers who died for the fatherland. I did not remind Gertrude that it was that "mongrel French whore," Josephine Priedieu, who saved my father's life after he was so badly wounded in the Battle of the Somme in World War I, for which he received the Iron Cross.

More than the inculcated hate and the visionary deceit of the Hitlerjugend, more than the race hate and the suffering of German soldiers, more than the firestorms and the death and the surrender at Stalingrad, what I remember most from that evening was that after Gertrude got out of me the agreement to name our sons after her dead brothers she suddenly became very quiet, put her arms around my neck, kissed me on the neck and said, "Gottlieb, will you come and pray with me?" In Heidelberg. In wintertime. Amongst the rubble.

Soon after 9:00 P.M. the singing began. By then the party was getting going real good. The contractions were coming about every ten minutes. I could hear the beer cans and the beer bottles banging against my porch and rolling into the street. I heard Scroggins yell, "Let's have some Christmas music," and Melissa Comb started the first verse of "Silent Night." The singing sounded like a bunch of drunks, because that's what they were by then. I didn't know that Vibini was already passing out marijuana joints to everyone. I opened the window a little so Saponata could hear the singing, but when the hopped-up neighbors launched into "White Christmas" she told me to close the window. She didn't want to hear that noise during her contractions.

I closed the window and remembered the first Christmas when Gertrude and I had our complete family. It was 1960. Christmas Eve, a Saturday. Our daughter Maria Anna Constanze had just been born that year on March 2. Our sons were seven, five and three. I had hired a photographer to come in and take a family photo. He arrived at 9:00 P.M. and tried to get us arranged for a shot. My oldest son Ehrgott kept hitting Fürchtegott and Traugott on the head with a toy hammer. The younger sons were bleeding from the forehead when the picture was taken. Gertrude refused to smile. She hid her face in her long, blond hair. I alone stood up and smiled, knowing that my wife was not psychologically well. Our daughter vomited her supper on the rug. The sons refused to speak to each other. It was our last family photo ever taken. It's the only photo of my family that I still have.

When the photographer left, I tried to teach my sons how to sing "Stille Nacht, Heilige Nacht." They laughed and spit on the floor. I forced them to sit on the couch with me and I told them about the holiness of the evening. I explained to them what Christmas is all about. They sucked on their thumbs, punched each other, pulled hair, tried to stick pencils in each other's eyes. Gertrude said, "They will make good soldiers. When we reunite Germany into one great nation and again make Europe ours, once again the spirit of my brothers will walk in this land and we will be the great nation that we once were when all the world trembled before us. This time we will make Russia into rubble. Germany will rise heroically from all our rubble and we will rebuild and make Europe our own. Our boys wouldn't behave like this if we still had the Hitlerjugend. They would learn discipline and obedience."

When the children were asleep, Gertrude and I sat among the broken toy trains, the decapitated puppets, the airplanes without wings, the toy cars without wheels and drank a toast to the future of our children. We had a bottle of Elendthaler Erlösungsuhr, Spätlese, that I had saved for that night and we clinked our glasses. Gertrude downed her glass in one gulp and said, "Gottlieb, will you come and pray with me?"

At 10:00 P.M. when Saponata's contractions were seven minutes apart, the lawn party was rowdy. I opened the front window a little so Saponata could get a little fresh air and hear some of what was going on outside. She tried to turn her head around to look out, but I told her to stay where she was. I promised to tell her what was going on, if not this evening I would do it later in my story. I said I'd go out and see what was happening.

When I went out on the porch to check on the party, Aristarchus Skiamachos and Panciuto Santarellina were arguing about the Christmas star. Panciuto was pointing to a bright object above the moon in the southwest. I looked up and could see that the moon was almost a half-moon and was waxing. There was indeed a bright star above the moon, but I explained to Panciuto that it was Jupiter and was not, in fact, a star. I also pointed out a dim Saturn farther east from Jupiter. "See," Arie the Hermeneutist cried out, "I told you the star had to be in the east because it says in the Bible, 'We have seen his star in the east, and are come to worship him.' And there it is." He pointed to the southeast where Sirius stood about forty-five degrees above the horizon. "That," he said triumphantly, "is the Christmas star. And later tonight it will come and stand over the place where the child is born. It will show all the world where this place is." Panciuto admitted that he was no astronomer because you can't see stars in a bowling alley. "Now you know," Ari said complacently. And he was right, to some extent. Before the night was over, Sirius and Canis Major would come to stand over the place where the child was born. The brightest star in the heavens would shine in the clear night over the house where the new child lay. The brightest star in the heavens would come to announce to all the world the beginning of a new life.

Just as I turned to go back into the house, the side door of our house opened and three dark strangers emerged. I had never seen them before. I decided they were the people who lived upstairs. Their appearance momentarily surprised the celebrants. Everyone stopped to stare. All three strangers were tall and were dressed in black fur hats like the Russians wear and ankle-length black capes like monks and black boots made of rope. I could not see their faces clearly. Each man had a long gray beard.

The first one who descended the side steps said, "Do not be afraid. We have come to worship. We appear at the births of extraordinary children. We have waited here for twenty years because of a prophecy by our master Zoroaster, the living star, in our holy text *The Apocalypse of Ahura-Mazda*, which his disciples have studied for 500 years in Mesopotamia. Tonight we saw the long promised star in the southeast and we must make ourselves known. My name is Eutychus of Troas and my companions are Oholibamah of Decapolis and Thomas Asdente of Calamar. We have brought gifts from *The Book of the Cave of the Treasures* for the child. I have brought him an icon of St. Theotokos, the bearer of God, who is the patron saint of all those who would be the Messiah."

The dark stranger called Oholibamah of Decapolis stepped down and said, "Zoroaster, the living star, predicted that in the end of the twentieth century a child would be born who would save the world. We have searched long and wide to find that child. We have waited here for him to appear. I have brought him from *The Book of the Cave of the Treasures* a vellum palimpsest that contains the sayings of Seth and his descendants who are astronomers." When Oholibamah of Decapolis moved closed to me, I saw that he had no left arm.

The third dark stranger called Thomas Asdente of Calamar spoke from the top of the stairs to the side porch. "We have undergone many disappointments. We have tarried in more than forty cities in more than forty countries for the child we were told would come to our salvation. Each child whose birth we witnessed turned out to be a false savior, even though he, as predicted, was born into a city filled with corruption and hate. Each child we saw into this world turned into a criminal. The saviors we found are now all in prison. We have suffered great disappointment until we came to this city, a city rife with deceit and immorality. I have brought, once again, for our hope never fades, from *The Book of the Cave of the Treasures, The Enchiridion of Nebo*, who is the god of writing and knows all things."

Jeremy Scroggins stepped forward and said, "Well, friends, welcome. Come and join the party. It sounds to me like you all need a beer. We got some Harp Lager here that should hit the spot." The three strangers consulted among themselves and Eutychus of Troas announced that they would take a beer called "Harp Lager" because it was harps that the angels played on when they came to the shepherds on that first Christmas. "Don Robin Pugh," Jeremy yelled, "pop the brothers here a Harp Lager and let's get on with the revels."

A strange murmur ran amongst the celebrants as the strangers took their first sips. Someone whispered, "Gifts? No one thought of gifts. We'd better find some right away." As I walked into the house, the revelers dispersed, scurrying to their houses and to their cars to find something to give to the child when he was born. The silence last only about ten minutes before everyone was back and I heard them carrying their gifts into our parlor and putting them on the table where my computer used to stand.

As I sat back down beside the bed and timed Saponata's contractions, which were coming now irregularly but about every six minutes, I began to think about how I would write my story about the birth of the child. I thought about it because of my troubles with the language when I try to write a story. I've realized many times already this early in my writing career that language distorts meaning and makes liars of us all. No matter what I write, I never get it quite right. I can never say exactly what I want to say. Part of that is this illiterate city that I live in. It's difficult to care about exact meaning in a city that is a moral and cultural slum. It's difficult to care about precise articulation in a city where the arts and the government are controlled by half-wits. But I know I can't blame others for my problems in writing.

It came to me that it is strange that medical doctors are such jerks when it comes to their incomes and what they charge their patients when doctors live in a magical world of words. Just look at the words associated with birth: anterior, posterior, cervix, uterus, episiotomy, diagonal conjugate, peridural puncture, paracervical block, "Iowa trumpet," subarachnoid, ectopic, parturient, nullipara, primipara, multipara, adolescent primigravida, perineum, introitus, modified Ritgen maneuver, post-partum, Brandt-Andrews maneuver, Lamaze and Leboyer methods, psychoprophylaxis, bonded family unit, silver nitrate.

All of which proves that no matter the glory of our words the words don't necessarily civilize us. The words may sound wonderful, but they don't create virtue in the user of those words. It is, as I've discovered since becoming a writer, that language is an instrument of deceit. Language emerged to hide our corruption, not perfect our virtue. Maybe that's why silence is so often associated with wisdom and saintliness.

Language, the ability that presumably separates us from the rest of the animals, a development that presumably makes us the greatest achievement of evolution, something that puts us next to God, is but a means of deception. Instead of drawing us humans closer into a more coherent and a more benevolent society, it separates us into hate groups and mutual hostility. The most forceful and most effective language we have is the language of bigotry. When we try to speak about virtue, we lapse into incoherence and babble. Is that the origin of the story of the Tower of Babel? Maybe the Pentecostals are right. To get back to God and save our souls we have to speak in tongues. We have to speak in a language that only God can understand.

But then, I thought, no matter the problems of language and no matter the oppressive world of Cincinnati, I would have to write the story. I knew, as I've always known, the birth of a child is the greatest narrative there is. Not dying. Writers are obsessed with the ends of things. They are obsessed with death. They think a narrative ends when someone dies. One of the sure signs of a bad writer is that his stories end with the death of one or more of the characters.

Maybe so. But for me it's the initiating of narratives that's important. Initiating stories is what writers do.

Not resolutions. Anyone can end a story. It takes skill to begin them. Beginning stories is what makes writers important, just as the beginning of new life is what makes humankind important. It's easy to die. That's why, like birth, it's the beginnings of stories that are most difficult.

Birth is the beginning of a story that lasts a long time and has no ending. To begin life, that's the great wonder, not to end it. To begin a narrative, that's the great wonder, not the ending. The great wonder of life, like fiction, is the beginning, not the ending. The birth of a child is the greatest story there is. All the rest of the stories are just addenda.

While Saponata's contractions increased to every five minutes and I listened to the fetal heartbeat, my mind wandered to my last Christmas with my family in Wuppertal. I didn't know, of course, that it was my last Christmas there but it was. It was again December 24, 1979, a Monday. My three sons were already in St. Dympna's in Gheel. So there was just me, Gertrude and our daughter Maria, now nineteen years old. Maria Anna Constanze would join her brothers in Gheel on Wednesday, June 25, 1980, the day after Gertrude committed suicide by hanging herself in our garage on Werther Strasse in Wuppertal. Maria was trying to be a writer, like her brothers, all of whom failed miserably. They finally wanted to be like their grandfather Lobgott Gerebernus Liebgott, a famous novelist who was strangled by the Nazis in 1934 for ridiculing Hitler. My next Christmas, unbeknownst to me that night, would be in Cincinnati, Ohio, in the U.S.A.

That last Christmas Eve in Wuppertal was completely without forgiveness. Gertrude sat on the floor in the corner of the room. Her head was down between her knees. She rocked and moaned throughout the whole evening. I said at midnight, "Come, Gertrude. Open your present. It will delight you." I had purchased her a lovely red shawl. It was wrapped in silver paper and underneath the Christmas tree I had set up and decorated with electric lights. No more candles for our family. I missed the real candles, but in our family they were too dangerous. Gertrude refused to move.

I went and knocked on Maria Anna Constanze's bedroom door and said, "Maria, come out now. It's midnight. Come and listen to the bells of Wuppertal bring in the Christmas day. There is a present for you under the tree. I've turned on the Christmas lights. Come and see." Something smashed against the other side of the door. I heard Maria screaming, "Go to hell, you filthy doctor. Go back to the hospital and play with the women's genitals. Go back to the hospital and give them the present of death for this Christmas." I had purchased Maria a new Olympia typewriter, the best available, for her writing. I said, "I have a new typewriter for you." Again she screamed, "Go away. Go back to the hospital and cut out the women's ovaries and their wombs. Kill their newborn children. Make them suffer for being women."

When I returned to the front room where Gertrude was, she had pulled all the lights off the tree and was throwing the tree out the window. I grabbed the gifts and let her throw out the tree. I said to her the only thing that would calm her down, "Gertrude, will you come and pray with me?" That was, unbeknownst to me, the last words I would ever say to her.

Also unbeknownst to me was the fact that my Christmas in 1980 would be a lonely one, but the first one in my life when all was peaceful, or so I thought. Gertrude's death ended a life of moroseness, hate, depression, a life of psychological illness without let up. Maria would follow my sons and all would be in order in my life, or so I thought. I would go to the U.S.A. and I would begin my medical career all over again. I would practice medicine and not have to live in the terrible and frightening world of my wife and children, I thought.

I remembered, last night as I sat by the bed in the front bedroom of my apartment and waited for Saponata to give birth to her child, how on my first Christmas Eve in Cincinnati I made a mistake. It was a Wednesday, maybe about 8:00 P.M. I was alone so I decided to go out and have a Christmas drink. I left my apartment on Vox Populi Street and walked over to a bar called "The College Inn." It was the only business open along Ludlow Avenue. I ordered a glass of Mosel wine. I asked for Elendthaler Erlösungsuhr, Spätlese. The bartender said, "We got white and red. What you want?" I said, "I'll have the white."

The bartender set the glass of white wine in front of me and I paid him the price of $1.50. I sipped the wine and it was awful. The man next to me elbowed me on the right arm and said, "Merry Christmas," and held up his glass to touch glasses. I clinked his glass lightly and sipped my wine again. It was still awful. The man said,

"We Germans know how to celebrate Christmas." I didn't tell him that I had just moved to Cincinnati from Germany. Maybe my accent gave me away. The man said, "The young people in this town don't have no discipline. They don't respect their elders. You probably noticed how stupid the young people are nowadays. They don't know art and culture. Just look at them. Wearing beads and long hair. They look like Bolsheviks or Gypsies. It's the Jews who sell them all that stuff. It's the Jews and the Communist Liberals who are ruining this nation. Those people don't love this country. They're the ones who hand out our tax dollars to the Black people of this city. All those Black people want is to get on welfare and live off the fat of the land. You should see them drive up in their Cadillacs to collect their welfare checks. What they need is some good old German discipline. It's too bad Hitler didn't succeed. He had a lot of good ideas. He just went too far."

I finished my glass of lousy white wine, set the glass down and said, "Remember, sir. 'Arbeit Macht Frei,' 'Kraft Durch Freude' and 'Wir werden London ausradieren.'" I walked out and went back to my apartment on Vox Populi Street. It was my first realization that I had settled in a city that is a moral and cultural slum.

By 11:00 P.M. the contractions were coming every five minutes and increasing in intensity and length and I realized I was going to need help. I realized that Dr. Almah was right, the birthing mother would need support. I helped Saponata to the bathroom so she could urinate and defecate and again I gave her some orange juice. Then I went out onto the porch and called in

Squallida Santarellina and Pallottola di Pietro and I said to both of them, "Saponata is about to give birth. I need help. I need someone to give her support and comfort while the child comes. You both have children, don't you?" "My God," Pallottola said, "I got eight" and Squallida laughed out, "I got four. I know what to do." I said to both of them, "Come in and scrub. I need you to help the young mother." They both marched into the vestibule, took off their coats and headed right into the bathroom to wash up with the surgical soap I gave them. They came out ready for the delivery.

While the two women began to touch and stroke Saponata, I went into the tiny back bedroom, took off my suit and put on the sterile surgical gown, head cover and shoe covers. I washed my hands with the surgical soap, put on my surgeon's mask and went back into the front bedroom. Saponata was babbling. She said, "You know everything, Gottlieb. I have to trust you." And I said, holding her hand, "I am a doctor. I know patient confidentiality. It's part of my professional integrity." As she rolled about in her contractions, she said, "Keep the marijuana away from my baby. I don't want him to breathe it." I said, "I'll see to it." She mumbled, "You're my best friend, Gottlieb. You're my best friend."

Squallida held Saponata's hand, stroked her back and murmured into Saponata's ear, "Dear daughter, your mother is here." I told the ladies to rub Saponata's lower back with olive oil. They did and Pallottola began to sing softly in Italian. When she paused, I said, "Pallottola, what is it you're singing?" She looked at me calmly and said, "It's an old song from the Abruzzi. We women always sang it to the mother as her child came into this world. We sang it to make the passage easier for the mother. It's a song about the earth, how we take our life and our strength from the earth. From earth all life comes and finally it all goes back to where it came from." I said, "Did the song always work when the labor became difficult?" The old lady looked at me with contempt and whispered, "If it is sung with adoration and praise for all life, it never fails."

When I saw that the two ladies had taken up their roles as assistants to the laboring young woman, I realized how much birthing is a female affair. I never felt that when I was delivering babies in a hospital. I felt, for a moment, as if I were an intruder and that I should leave and let the women do what they knew best how to do. Like Pallottola's song. It never occurred to me that one might sing a baby into this world. Of course, song and birth go together, like narratives and birth. Mozart must have known that. I realized that I was just there to help and that I was not essential. Somehow or other birthing goes on and life is renewed and extended from generation to generation, and we doctors might think we're big shots but, in the final analysis, we're just in the way. We don't have a clue into the great mystery of giving new life to this God-forsaken world.

While Squallida and Pallottola took Saponata to the bathroom and walked her around the room a little, I remembered the night Gertrude delivered our first child Ehrgott Karl Wolfgang. Gertrude said to me, "Gottlieb, I hope it's a son. We need men for the new Germany that will arise out of this rubble." I told her that it would certainly be a son because she was carrying the baby so high. She said, "I let you defile my body so that our great dream of the German state can still be fulfilled. Someday we will be strong again, we will reunite from the Rhine to the Weichsel and our sons will stand in the forces of resurgence. Remember the days when we stood in our ranks as Hitlerjugend and we were taught to dream great dreams about the fatherland? They can still come true."

When our just-born first son Ehrgott Karl Wolfgang was in my gloved hands, I almost strangled him. I almost took his life because I wanted no more of all that German nonsense. Instead of ending his life then and there, I thought, "My son might be what my father was. A great novelist. He might restore the greatness of German Literature that was debauched by Hitler. I will see to it that he is not a Nazi bigot." So I let him live. I realized as I watched Saponata that I hadn't heard anything from Ehrgott since Christmas Eve, 1973, when he was committed to St. Dympna's. I don't even know if he is still alive. If he is still alive, he and my other sons Fürchtegott and Traugott and my daughter Maria are probably this Christmas still in St. Dympna's and sucking their thumbs and trying to poke out each others' eyes.

A little later, about 11:15, Saponata said, "Liebgott, will you pray with us? Melissa told me to pray when the time came for me to deliver." I said, "Of course, Saponata. Now's a good time for God's help." I held her hands in mine while she mumbled something like, "Lord, hear my cry. In my agony and my distress, stand beside me and give me strength. Lord, lead me in thy righteousness. Make thy way plain before my face." Then she added, "Now you, Liebgott." "Now me, what?" I said. "You pray, too. We both need help." While my two assistants bowed their heads and crossed themselves, I whispered into her right ear, so no one on the porch would hear, a prayer from Vibini: "O Isis und Osiris, schenket der Weissheit Geist dem neuen Paar. Die Ihr den Schritt der Wand'rer lenket, stärkt mit Geduld sie in Gefahr." Then for Saponata, "Bless this marriage. Bring this child to his place in this world. May he be whole and healthy. May he be an eternal blessing to this world." Saponata smiled and whispered, "You didn't say 'Amen.'" "Amen," I said. "Amen." Then I said a prayer to myself in which I prayed for the soul of the young man who was going to be born into Clifton, the last refuge of intelligence in this Republican city. I prayed for his soul in a nation busy lynching its own President, a city whose main industry is the destruction of American democracy, a city where poverty is a crime.

"Now, Saponata," I continued, "it's time for me to feel the progress of the baby. I need to put my fingers inside your body as I explained to you last night." "I'm ready," she said. "I'm used to having someone poke around in there. Vibini's been poking around down there for over a year." I put on my sterile latex gloves and inserted my index and middle fingers of my right hand into Saponata's vagina. I felt the cervix and it was very soft and dilated. The cervix was smooth against the fetus' skull. I changed gloves, throwing the first pair into the Keller's I.G.A. paper grocery bag. I checked the fetal heartbeat and it was at 130 beats per minute. I inserted my right index finger into her anus and felt the head, which was low in the perineum. The child was ready to emerge. I said, "Saponata, it won't be long now. The perineum has effaced and dilitation of the cervix is complete." She said, "What the hell does that mean?" and I said, "It means breathe deeply as the contraction begins and get ready to push."

While I changed gloves again, Saponata burbled between contractions, "Is it a good day for my baby to be born? Will it be a boy?" I said, "Saponata, any day is a good day for a child to be born. But, as the nursery rhyme says, Thursday's child is full of grace. And the child will be a boy because you're carrying him so high. That's a sure sign that the child is a boy. Just think, Skyblue and I were both born on a Thursday in January of 1930. Even more important, Jesus was born on a Thursday evening. You can't do much better than that."

While I checked the fetal heartbeat again, Saponata said, "Did Mary feel great pain when her child was born? Did she have contractions like mine? Did she have a 'bloody show' before she began to suffer in order to have her baby?" I said, "God plays no favorites when it comes to birth. It's the one democratic institution throughout the world. Mary probably suffered more than any other woman ever has because she gave birth to the savior of the world. Even if a merry host of angels on the wing sang him into this world, even if shepherds came to worship and wise men came with precious gifts, Mary suffered for all mothers for all time in order to bear the Messiah. In any case, your body releases endorphins that make the pain bearable." Squallida and Pallottola murmured, "Amen," as Saponata doubled over in a severe contraction. For a moment, it crossed my mind that that was a good idea to put into one of my stories. I felt a bit of pride that I had thought it up and the bit about Jesus being born on a Thursday and the switching of the Tuesday rhyme to Thursday. So it was phony. So what? It would make a good story.

I felt the baby move and the two old mothers felt it also, I'm sure. They both began murmuring and stroking Saponata's back and stomach. I told them to support Saponata's lower back. I said, "Saponata, raise your knees and spread them apart. The child is about to emerge. Don't push too hard. Just let it come." As I spoke, the perineum gave way without tearing. No episiotomy necessary. I pulled the labia aside. I heard the heavy breathing of Saponata and her whimpering moans. I quickly swabbed up the bits of feces and the spurts of urine and the dripping amniotic fluid. While the ladies held tightly to Saponata's hands, pushed up on her lower back and stroked her body, I said, "One last push, Sudsy. One last push." The head crowned. The scalp was nice and pink and it had thin blond hair on it. When the eyes appeared they opened just briefly and closed in the light. The eyes were a soft green like Saponata's. It would be her child.

As the head of the child crowned and emerged and as I held it and watched the anterior shoulder appear, I thought, "I can kill this child. I can end his life now so that he will not have to suffer or live in this God-forsaken world. I could do him a favor by blessing him with death before he has to face a horrible life. I could obliterate his already bad luck of being born into this moral and cultural slum called Cincinnati. I could erase the horribly bad break he is getting from the beginning of his life by being born here."

But then it occurred to me that each child that is born into this world might be the Messiah. Each new child might be the savior of this world. It was worth the risk, so I turned the body ninety degrees and caught the child as it came free from the mother's body, lifted him gently in my hands and realized again how irrelevant I was in the whole birthing. I was just there as a technician and who was I to make decisions about life and death.

While Paollottola smiled and said, "See, I told you the song works," I laid the newborn child onto the low table beside the bed so that the blood could drain through the pulsing umbilicus into the body. I covered his eyes and adjusted my lamp so that the child would stay warm under its glow. I pushed back Saponata's gown and laid the child on her stomach and covered the child with a blanket to keep him warm. Saponata lay and looked at me, her wispy blond hair stuck to her forehead with sweat, her green eyes emptied of pain, regret, lust, all emotion. She stared at me as if I were the cause of all her suffering. I said, "Hold the child and rub his back gently." She looked down at her new child and said, "It's a boy, isn't it?" And I said through my surgeon's mask that the child was a fine boy and she smiled and said, "Tell Dally he's now a father and that he can't smoke dope around the child." I said, "What about the Mozart?" and she said, "I want the boy to grow up listening so that he will know that not everyone on this earth is scum."

Pallottola and Squallida wiped the sweat from Saponata's forehead and made her comfortable and gave her some juice. I tucked the blanket close around her and went to work. I had to work fast. I turned the baby's head towards me and suctioned the excess mucus and amniotic fluid from the baby's eyes, nose and throat. Then, because the umbilicus was through pulsing and the baby was breathing evenly, I clamped the umbilicus by the navel and cut the afterbirth loose. I covered the cut with a sterile gauze pad and taped it down. I cleaned the baby's body gently with sterile wipes. I put the pearls of silver nitrate into his eyes. I put a little diaper on the baby to catch the meconium plug, even though he lay on Saponata's abdomen. Only when I lifted him from Saponata's body did he start to cry and twitch. I wrapped the baby in clean cloths and laid him back beside his mother. I reached under the cover to check the afterbirth and it had already separated. Then I sponged off Saponata and covered her and the baby with a blanket. I quickly cleaned up the gauze pads, the mucus trap and the afterbirth and dropped them into the paper bag from Keller's I.G.A. When I looked at my watch, I was surprised that all that activity had happened in just six minutes since the head first crowned. I was proud of my competence. I had forgotten how good I was as a doctor. For a moment I felt a kind of nostalgia for medical practice which has satisfactions no writer of fiction can ever know.

After the ladies dressed the new baby in his skyblue birth suit and put on his little white stocking cap, I swaddled the babe in a white blanket and asked

Saponata if I could borrow the baby for a moment. She nodded and I said, "Don't go away." And they say we Germans have no sense of humor.

While the two old ladies stroked and kissed Saponata and washed her lower body, I took the by now twitching and squalling child and went out into the parlor. There, on the table where my computer used to stand, was a pile of gifts from the citizens and friends of Vox Populi Street. Because I had written all the stories about Vibini's famous cases, I thought I knew exactly where each of the gifts came from. Where once I had sat and tracked the exploits of the Italian war hero Giovanni Battista Salvatore in the *Annali Calabresi*, there was an old and dried-out aspergillum from Father Gottlob Schlag. There was an umbrella with alternating red and black panels, probably sent by Cristoforo since he would not come out of his apartment on Schadenfreude Street for the birth of anyone. There was a tube of oregano lipstick from Guido di Pietro and his wife Pallottola. There was a stuffed animal, a tiny orangutan, from Al and Max via Emil Hasenpfeffer and his wife Isolde. There was a box of chocolates shaped like female breasts from Barry Vermis and his wife Tallulah. From Don Robin Pugh, a six-pack of Harp Lager, and from Peter Solomon Seiltanzer a copy of *Skyblue's Essays*. There was a copy of *The Sacred Buck* from Sharon Holiday Inn Towel and a jar of smoked squid from Sigismondo Pandolfo Salvatore and his wife Beatrice. A copy of *The Gospel According to Oholibamah* from Aristarchus Skiamachos, and a silver framed icon of St. Pruritis the Kynosargite from Father Thomas Takianopoulos and his wife Leah. Panciuto and

Squallida Santarellina gave a used, left-handed bowling ball and Melissa Comb, a Gideon Bible. Airball McGritts brought her novel *Puppy Love,* and her husband Jeremy Scroggins his book of poems *After Appomattox: A Southern Tragedy.* Ciacco Polenta left a condom with a Bible verse printed on the packet: "Suffer the little children to come unto me." The three mysterious strangers had left their gifts: an icon of St. Theotokos, a palimpsest of the sayings of Seth and his descendants, and *The Enchiridion of Nebo.*

I carried the baby boy out onto the front porch, stood by the top of the stairs from the sidewalk to the porch, lifted him high over my head and cried out, "For unto us a child is born. Unto us a son is given. And his name shall be called Amadeo di Dallasandro da Clifton Vibini. Lobe den Herren and buon Natale!" And they say we Germans have no sense of humor. My announcement was met with a loud cheer as the citizens of Vox Populi Street with one voice celebrated the birth of the babe.

As I lowered the babe and held him against my left shoulder, the black Mercedes-Benz across the street drove off, and Jeremy Scroggins, who had become the master of the revels, leaped to the top step of the stairs to the porch and yelled, "We have poems to greet the child. Let's hear the poems for the new kid." Melissa Comb stepped onto the lowest step of the stairs to the porch and read, "For unto us/ a son is born./ Let's celebrate/ this happy morn." Airball McGritts came next and recited, "Love flows through darkness/ into light./ Amadeo has turned the night/ round right." Next came Eutychus of Troas, who recited, "When the newborn babe/ opened his eyes/ He saw first/ a face just and wise." Next, Oholibamah of Decapolis stepped forward, held the poem in his right hand, and read, "The skilled physician/ met labor's demands/ When the babe's soft head/ crowned in his hands." Thomas Asdente of Calamar followed with, "The skilled physician/ said 'Get a life,'/ And cut the cord/ with his knife." Jeremy Scroggins, the poet himself and master of revels, jumped to the top step and cried out, "The midnight hour/ now has come./ Let us all speak,/ not stand here dumb."

Vibini stepped forward and read his poem; "Now that I'm a father/ my life is filled with hope./ I'll not give up Mozart/ but I will give up dope." Around the yard, the marijuana joints lit up like fireflies on a summer's evening as the revelers all took a drag and Don Robin Pugh cried out, "No. No. Life's not worth living if you give up marijuana." I thought the laughter that followed Vibini's poem and the outburst of inhalation that followed that and the ribald celebration of drugs were not humorous. We Germans don't find narcotics funny, even though we invented most of them.

Jeremy Scroggins followed that with, "People of Vox Populi Street, let's hear it for our new child." He raised his arms into the air and conducted the people as they chanted together, "Amadeo, Amadeo, he's our man. If he can't do it, nobody can." "That's good," Jeremy yelled, "but we can do better." And he led them again in a cheer; "Two bits, four bits, six bits a dollar, all for Amadeo stand up and holler." The shouts and cheers of joy ascended into the cold empyrean where, I'm sure, the merry host of angels on the wing joined in, but in a more sedate manner. The child twitched and began to cry when the cheering began, so I said to the revelers, "Go home and rest. Just keep all these things and ponder them in your hearts. Now let's have a silent night." I asked Scroggins if I could have a copy of the poems so I could include them in my story, and he handed me a copy.

I carried the babe back into the parlor, added the poems to the gifts on the table, and almost tripped over Vibini, who was kneeling on the floor. "Vibini," I said, "what are you doing now?" "Look," he said, "I'm writing 'It's a boy' on the cigarette papers that I'll give to them as they head home." I looked and saw the bag of marijuana that he was dipping from and making the cigarettes. He was, in fact, writing on each paper and then rolling it into a marijuana joint. As I walked away, he said over his shoulder, "I can't afford cigars."

I carried the babe back into the bedroom and and told Squallida and Pallottola that they could leave now and they did. When they were gone, there was silence in the night as the neighbors turned and headed to their homes, leaving behind the yard covered with beer cans, wine bottles, marijuana stubs and the candles still burning in the paper bags. I thought, "Yes, we're all for Amadeo. He is our man. He can do it. We'll all stand up and holler for him because he might grow up and solve the first and worst of all petty crimes, the creation of mankind."

In the room, once my study and now the bedroom and nursery of Saponata and the child Amadeo, I put the child down beside the exhausted mother and put his mouth to her left breast. I showed Saponata how to help the child find the nipple and listened to Vibini knocking about in the parlor and the kitchen. I heard him stumble into the little bedroom at the back of the apartment, the bedroom that is all that remains of my apartment for me. I heard him collapse onto my cot and I knew there was no place for me to sleep that night.

I went to the front window and looked out over the trash-filled yard and the still-sputtering candles in the paper bags. I realized that it was Christmas Day and that a spirit of holiness had descended on Vox Populi Street. Across the street, the Christmas lights on the house of Jeremy Scroggins and Airball McGritts burned and twinkled brightly. I could see that all along the street the colored lights were on for the beginning of Christmas.

As the trash faded away into the darkness and the candles sputtered out, I closed the curtains on the window and wondered how I could tell the story of this night. But, then, I knew how I would do it. I felt a confidence that I was ready to write it the way it should be written. I knew I had nothing to dread. The story would tell itself. When the time came, I had but to write it down. A birth narrative, I realized, is so full of mystery and wonder that it need be only recorded for what it is.

I turned back to Saponata, who lay in a stupor while the child breathed fast and nursed hesitantly. Her lovely, soft blond hair was pasted to her head by the sweat from her labor. I pulled the cover over her and the nursing child, drew up my chair and sat by the bed. I said, "Saponata, well done. Now I need to get some results for the records." I measured the child's heart rate and it was

120. His respiratory rate was excellent and he cried when I pulled him away from the nipple. His muscle tone was excellent as he squirmed and flexed his limbs. He coughed when I put a catheter into his nostril. And his color was completely pink. His APGAR rating was ten. I weighed him and he weighed seven pounds and twelve ounces. I measured him and he was twenty inches long. I put the child back to Saponata's breast and said, "Rest now. I will keep watch through the dark hours as I did many times when I was a doctor and a father. All will be OK. I'll be here in case you need me. I'm used to that. I'm accustomed to going without sleep when necessary."

As Saponata closed her lovely green eyes and sighed into a deep sleep and Amadeo closed his eyes and turned his head away from her breast, I took off my surgical gown and mask, my latex gloves, the foot coverings, the surgeon's cap. I went out into the hall where I found a bottle of Mosel wine, Elendthaler Erlösungsuhr, Spätlese. I opened the bottle and went into our kitchen. I found a glass and poured myself a nice full drink. It occurred to me that Bunyan would be pleased with the name of the wine. I returned to the bedroom and sat down beside the bed and said to myself as I lifted the glass, "Saponata and Amadeo, may your lives be as blessed as any life can be on this earth. Good luck, my dearest ones. You're going to need it in this God-forsaken city."

As I sipped the wine, I remembered the night when I delivered my first son Ehrgott Karl Wolfgang on Walpurgisnacht, April 30, 1953. I remembered how, after the delivery, Gertrude held him while I kept watch through the long hours of darkness. I remembered, as if it had happened just minutes before, how Gertrude held the whimpering, gasping child and sang to him in German: "Hush, poopsie, and sleep./ Beat the little rooster dead./ He doesn't lay eggs/ And he eats all my bread./ We'll pluck his feathers/ And make for my poopsie/ A soft, little bed."

This book was designed and computer typeset in 10 pt. Palatino with Dom Casual titles by Rosmarie Waldrop. Printed on 55 lb. Writers' Natural (an acid-free paper), smyth-sewn and glued into paper covers by McNaughton & Gunn in Saline, Michigan. The cover is by Keith Waldrop. There are 1000 copies, of which 50 are numbered and signed by the author.

BURNING DECK FICTION SERIES:

1. Tom Ahern, *The Capture of Trieste*
2. Jaimy Gordon, *Circumspections from an Equestrian Statue*
3. Lissa McLaughlin, *Seeing the Multitudes Delayed*
4. Harry Mathews, *Country Cooking and Other Stories* [o.p.]
5. Dallas Wiebe, *The Transparent Eye-Ball & Other Stories* [o.p.]
6. Robert Coover, *In Bed One Night & Other Brief Encounters* [o.p.]
7. John Hawkes, *Innocence in extremis*
8. Barbara Einzig, *Life Moves Outside*
9. Lissa McLaughlin, *Troubled by His Complexion*
10. Dallas Wiebe, *Going to the Mountain*
11. Walter Abish, *99: The New Meaning*
12.. Elizabeth MacKiernan, *Ancestors Maybe*
13. Dallas Wiebe, *Skyblue's Essays*
14. Paul Auster, *Why Write?* [o.p.]
15. Alison Bundy, *DunceCap*
16. Jane Unrue, *The House*
17. Robert Coover, *The Grand Hotels (of Joseph Cornell)*
18. Dallas Wiebe, *The Vox Populi Street Stories*

In Translation:

Marcel Cohen, *The Peacock Emperor Moth* [trans. from the French by Cid Corman]

Pascal Quignard, *On Wooden Tablets: Apronenia Avitia* [trans. from the French by Bruce X]

Ilma Rakusa, *Steppe* [trans. from the German by Solveig Emerson]

Ludwig Harig, *The Trip to Bordeaux* [trans. from the German by Susan Bernofsky]